Lady's Rock

SUE LAWRENCE

CONTRABAND

Published by Contraband,
an imprint of Saraband,
3 Clairmont Gardens
Glasgow, G3 7LW
www.saraband.net

ISBN: 9781915089922
eISBN: 9781916812055
Audiobook ISBN: 9781916812000

1 2 3 4 5 6 7 8 9

For Faith,
with love

Glenara

O, heard ye yon pibroch sound sad in the gale,
Where a band cometh slowly with weeping and wail?
'Tis the chief of Glenara laments for his dear;
And her sire and her people are called to her bier.

Glenara came first, with the mourners and shroud;
Her kinsmen they followed, but mourned not aloud;
Their plaids all their bosoms were folded around;
They marched all in silence, they looked on the ground.

In silence they reached, over mountain and moor,
To a heath where the oak-tree grew lonely and hoar;
"Now here let us place the grey stone of her cairn;
Why speak ye no word?" said Glenara the stern.

"And tell me, I charge ye, ye clan of my spouse,
Why fold ye your mantles, why cloud ye your brows?"
So spake the rude chieftain; no answer is made.
But each mantle, unfolding, a dagger displayed.

"I dreamt of my lady, I dreamt of her shroud,"
Cried a voice from the kinsmen, all wrathful and loud;
"And empty that shroud and that coffin did seem;
Glenara! Glenara! now read me my dream!"

O, pale grew the cheek of that chieftain, I ween,
When the shroud was unclosed and no lady was seen;
When a voice from the kinsmen spoke louder in scorn,
'Twas the youth who had loved the fair Ellen of Lorn,

"I dreamt of my lady, I dreamt of her grief,
I dreamt that her lord was a barbarous chief;
On a rock of the ocean fair Ellen did seem;
Glenara! Glenara! now read me my dream!"

In dust low the traitor has knelt to the ground,
And the desert revealed where his lady was found;
From a rock of the ocean that beauty is borne;
Now joy to the house of fair Ellen of Lorn.

Thomas Campbell (1777–1844)

Foreword

Scotland was a dangerous place in the early sixteenth century. It wasn't just that everyday occurrences such as childbirth or the common cold were likely to kill you; treacherous battles and feuds persisted over the centuries.

Scottish clans fought constantly. When a truce was proposed, intermarriage was the most common form of reconciliation. A sister or daughter of the clan chief would be married off to the brother or son – or indeed the chief himself – of the enemy clan. The girl (invariably young, perhaps just twelve years old) could only hope that once she was settled into her new role as wife, her new husband would not start fighting her clan again. She was of course also expected to produce heirs for her new husband, to cement the newly created bond.

In the fourteenth century, in Argyll and on the islands of the west coast of Scotland, two clans had emerged as the most powerful: the Macdonalds and the Campbells. The former became the Lords of the Isles, whose influence extended at its peak from the northernmost Hebridean island of Lewis, south through all the islands and as far as the north-eastern tip of Ireland, and east into the Highlands. The Lords of the Isles were based on Islay – geographically central in sailing terms for access to the islands, Ireland, and the Scottish mainland.

As a general principle, the Macdonalds of Islay did not support the kings of Scotland, whereas the Campbells of Argyll did. Indeed, Colin, chief of the Campbell clan, was made Earl of Argyll by King James II circa 1458 to provide a stronger royal presence in the west of Scotland.

In the middle of the disputes between these two clans was the Maclean clan, vassals of the Lords of the Isles between the 1360s and 1493, when King James IV forfeited the Lordship. This loyalty was initiated when Lachlan Lubanach Maclean married John of Islay's daughter Mary circa 1367 and was given extensive lands on the Isle of Mull, including Duart Castle. And so the bond was forged between the Macdonalds of the Isles and the Macleans of Duart.

At the battle of Flodden in 1513, the Duart Macleans and the Argyll Campbells both played prominent roles. Each lost their clan chief in battle as they fought together with King James IV, who was also killed. This hitherto unlikely bond between the Macleans and Campbells, brought about in part by the loss of their chiefs, continued, culminating in a marriage contract being drawn up between the two noble families – the Macleans based on Mull and the Campbells at Inveraray, near the head of Loch Fyne on the mainland.

This is the story of how that union played out, at a time when brides were mere pawns in the grand schemes men devised to shore up their power and maintain peace. Sometimes, depending on circumstances and on the resolve of the bride or groom, things did not go to plan...

Prologue

The tide was coming in fast. She scrambled up the slippery rocks as the water lapped over her feet. She had reached the top of the jagged, rocky outcrop in the middle of a tempestuous sea; she had nowhere else to go.

The icy water was soon up to her ankles and all she could do was stretch her head high, imploring the heavens to save her. A grey and white sea bird with red legs soared overhead and she sighed, envying the bird for its freedom to fly. She hoicked up her skirts as the waves splashed onto her legs. Through tear-filled eyes she looked around, panting for breath as panic set in.

Suddenly she saw something on the horizon. She wiped the tears on her sleeve and stared towards the east, where a pale sun had begun to emerge. She was sure she could see something. Was it a boat or was she hallucinating? Her arms reached high and she waved her hands with wide, frantic gestures. Her long red hair flew in the wind like the fluttering sails of a shipwreck.

Part 1

Chapter 1

1517
Catherine

The first sight I had of my new home did not please me. Of course, I was used to living in a castle by the sea; that was where I was brought up. But this looked to me to be actually in the water. We had just crossed the Firth of Lorne by boat, but even now, on dry land, on the island, we did not seem able to escape the sea.

"Catherine, we are nearly there," my new husband shouted above the wind. "Isn't Duart Castle glorious?"

I sighed as I steered my horse towards the bleak stone edifice perched high above the water. "I just need to be inside, out of the storm, Lachlan," I yelled as my steed sped up over the shingle beach and up the cliff towards the entrance. I did not listen for a reply, for the only thing I heard was the wind howling and the waves crashing on the rocks below. I shivered as the cold and wet continued to seep through my clothes; I swear my bones had turned to ice. When we'd departed from Inveraray, the sun had been high in the sky and there was not a cloud to be seen. But as soon as we'd left the shore and set sail for Mull, the heavens had opened and we'd become drenched. And now the miserable dark clouds and damp chill reflected my mood. Lachlan, on the contrary, seemed to become more and more animated and happy as the rains lashed; or perhaps it was just because we were about to arrive at his castle.

Once we were inside the courtyard, a groom rushed to help me down from my horse and I shook myself to remove some of the surface water, but I was soaked to the skin. Waiting for my husband to lead me up the steps into the castle, I watched him dismount, clap his horse's flank then chat to the grooms, laughing and joking, as if there was all the time in the world. The rain continued relentlessly; it was heavier than I had ever seen. I looked around and saw only men and only grey. I wished once more that Mama had allowed me to bring one of my sisters with me, if only for the first few weeks. Grandmother would have permitted that – she always knew what was good for me. But Mama insisted a bride should take time to get to know her new husband. The very thought of this filled me with dread: from the first time we met – just two days ago, the night before the wedding ceremony – I felt there was little I wanted to discover about him.

"Catherine, come inside, my dear," Lachlan shouted, striding towards me, hand outstretched. His pockmarked nose dripped with rain and his swarthy cheeks were spattered in grime, but I forced a smile, as Mama had insisted, and extended my hand to this man to whom I must devote the rest of my life. I was numb because of the cold and this numbness also made me somehow inured to my fate.

He led me up the narrow, winding steps, telling me the Great Hall was at the top and this was where a roaring fire would warm us up. But as he heaved open a heavy wooden door at the top and ushered me in, I felt no warmth nor saw any light – only a dark and dingy room. The cold dampness was so dispiriting, I almost burst into tears. He looked around and bellowed at a servant, "Why is the fire not lit? Fetch the candles, light the fire! I told you we'd be arriving today!"

A boy wearing filthy clothes ran towards the vast fireplace and began to lay the wood, while an older man hobbled towards us. "Sorry, your Lordship, you said you would be arriving tomorrow."

"For God's sake, does no one listen to my instructions?" Lachlan shouted at the two servants who were both busying themselves at the fire. Another boy was hovering beside them, rubbing his hands together, trying to get warm; the older man sent him for more wood.

I was frozen and wet, and I could feel tears prick my eyes; the room felt somehow colder than it had been outside. I took a deep breath and attempted to lift my mood.

"Is there at least a smaller fire that could be lit in my chamber so I can change out of my wet clothes?"

He nodded and yelled at a girl who had slunk into the hall from a door at the other side. She scampered over to us and he instructed her to take me upstairs to my bedchamber.

"I'll have your luggage sent up, Catherine. Then we shall meet later, at supper."

But I was not listening, for I was looking around the room, brighter now that candles had been lit. Compared to Inveraray Castle, it was drab and plain. Yes, there were family portraits and suits of armour, shields and swords hanging on the walls, but in contrast to the elegance and comfort of home, it seemed unbearably bleak.

"I know it's not quite as splendid as Inveraray, but you can spruce it up," Lachlan said, watching me gaze around the room. "Ever since Mother died, it's lacked a woman's touch." He smiled, but I saw only his blackened, crooked teeth, not any sign of affection.

Dear God, what had I let myself in for? Why had I been selected as the pawn in this arranged marriage, which was, after all, a diplomatic union between the Campbells and the Macleans, a token of peace? Though I wouldn't wish this on any of them, part of me wondered why one of my seven sisters hadn't been chosen in my place. As the girl led the way across the cold stone floor to the stairs, I tried to erase from my head the picture of my cousin Archibald's beautiful, unblemished face and his thick blond hair. I paused and turned from the first stone step to see my husband grab a goblet from a salver and tip his head back to swallow the contents in one gulp. As I watched, I remembered the elegant way Archibald held a glass between his finger and thumb and sipped like a true gentleman. And I had to stop myself sobbing out loud at the realisation that yesterday, in my family's chapel, God's will had been done. This was my life, forever.

Chapter 2

1517
Catherine

I warmed myself by the fire while the maid dealt with my luggage. As my body gradually thawed, I felt an overwhelming desire to sleep. I was so tired after the long journey from Inveraray to Duart. But I thought of what Mama had said about making an effort. It was all very well for her; she'd once told me that when she had met Papa, it was love at first sight. Four years after his death at Flodden, Mama was still in mourning.

She'd told me recently that twelve was perhaps an excessive number of children, but it demonstrated how much they loved one another. This did not inspire admiration in me, but rather made me feel slightly sick. Though not as nauseated as I had felt last night, the first in our marriage bed.

I sat by the fire, trying to shake off the memory of it, but I could not forget the smell of him, and the pain. I stifled a sob and called for the maid to dress me for the first supper with my new husband in his castle. She held out a blue gown and a green one and I shrugged and pointed to the blue. I truly did not care how I looked before my husband – I simply had to please him until I had a child. Then surely the bond between our families would be secure.

My brothers' plan was that once this son and heir became the next Lord Maclean of Duart, he would be a useful ally to my Campbell family. I worried, though – when I met my husband, just before our wedding, I was surprised by how old he was and how dissolute he appeared. His had clearly been a life well lived and so it seemed rather strange that he had no sons already. My sister Jean said she'd heard he had mistresses all over Mull, but a son of these unions surely could never be legitimate. Why had he not married before?

Lachlan seemed so different from my brothers, whose manners were refined and who were all so well-read. I wondered if my husband even owned a library; I certainly did not see any books in the Great Hall. Just because we both had fathers killed at Flodden fighting for the King did not mean we had anything in common. My brother Donald was always telling me the Macleans and Campbells might have fought together against the English, but now we were the more powerful clan and the Macleans were jealous. My older brother Colin said my marriage would help prevent future feuds. But he would say that, of course, since Papa's death had made him the new Earl of Argyll.

I asked the maid to hand me a warm shawl and I smiled my thanks to her before heading for the stairs. As I climbed down the narrow stone steps, I took deep breaths to calm myself. I tiptoed into the Great Hall where I saw that at least the fire was lit, but the room was still cold. There were no tapestries or drapes on the walls or doors to help keep the cold out, and howling winds were whistling down from the high unglazed windows. I shivered and headed for the fire. I was just warming my hands when I heard a noise behind me.

"Catherine, my dear, come and sit over here. Supper is served." My husband gestured to the table at the far end of the room. Couldn't they have served the food by the warmth of the fireplace? I wrapped my shawl tight around my shoulders and left the meagre heat. I was about to sit down when the door was thrown open and a young man rushed in.

"Ah, Hector, I'm glad you could make it." Lachlan turned to the man, whose thick black hair was matted to his scalp. It was clearly still pouring outside, for he shook his head like a wet dog, spraying water everywhere.

Lachlan looked towards me. "Catherine, meet Hector Mor. He must go south to Islay tomorrow, so I wanted you to meet him tonight."

I gave him my hand and he grasped it with dirty, calloused fingers. He had deep-set brown eyes that bored into me and a face with a tawny complexion that was a pleasure to look at, dare I say more pleasing to behold than my husband's. The younger man's smile was unfathomable but gracious.

"Welcome to Duart Castle and to Mull, Catherine. I hope everything is to your liking?" As he spoke, I felt disappointment that his voice was as gruff as my husband's. It lacked the refinement of my brothers. And surely he ought to call me Lady Maclean?

"Yes, thank you," I said, polite in my lie; I was trying hard to settle in, yet the cold made the castle feel unwelcoming.

"Sit down, sit down, we must eat now," said my husband, who thumped himself onto a chair beside Hector and, before I had so much as adjusted my gown around my knees, reached over the table to grab a large game bird. Without even setting it on his plate, he ripped it in two and rammed a drumstick into his mouth. Grease ran down his chin as he chewed and I watched, aghast, as he proceeded to wipe his face with his sleeve. I reached for my empty goblet and raised it, still watching my husband. A servant appeared at my side to fill my glass with claret, and I drank deep, wondering how long it would be until I could give him a son then return to my own family.

"Catherine, you must try the roasted moorcock. The cook has a special way of doing it." Hector Mor lifted a platter and put it beside me. "What's that secret ingredient she uses?" he said, turning to my husband.

Lachlan shrugged. "Is it not just the fat from the cormorants she bastes it in? Gives it a good taste of the sea. Try it, Catherine."

I had been warned there might be sea birds on the table, for Mull is a large island and wild fowling provides essential food, not just for the poor. Indeed, when my family entertained the King at Inveraray just the year before Flodden, our chef had produced Solan goose, by royal request. Since there were so many of

11

us at table at home though, I was able to avoid it easily; the smell was off-putting enough. But here, as only three of us sat at this table, it seemed I had no choice.

"An even better bird to try is the roast fulmar. Give her some of that, Hector," Lachlan said, pointing to a large sea bird opposite me.

I nibbled on my barley bread and smiled. "Thank you. I will, but perhaps later." I glanced at the food before me. "Is that a roast heathcock over there? I am so very partial to that; I should like to start with it."

Hector Mor pushed the plate towards me and smiled. I looked into his eyes and was sure I saw kindness, something that was thus far lacking in my husband's. Hector Mor was about my age, and perhaps that was why I felt we might find more to converse about than I ever could with my husband.

It was unfamiliar for me to be at a table with fewer than a dozen people. Even when my sisters left to marry, my brothers were usually there, with their wives, and of course Mama and Grandmother, and always some kinsmen from nearby estates. Was this how it was always to be? Just me and my husband, with the occasional guest as a distraction? Were there no ladies to keep me company, to sew with, to walk with, to confide in?

A loud cough interrupted my gloomy thoughts and we both turned to Lachlan as he sat up straight in his seat and beamed at me, goblet raised high.

"Welcome to Duart Castle, Catherine. Here's to a fine and fruitful union of the Macleans and the Campbells." He downed his drink and a servant hurried over to fill it up.

I took a sip from my goblet and looked around the cavernous Great Hall. Everything was so different. But perhaps I just needed time to settle in. I was an optimistic person; I would find happiness here, surely. Mama said to be patient and courteous. I was determined to try, and if eating sea birds was part of that, then so be it.

Chapter 3

1517

Catherine

I stood at the tiny window of my bedchamber, watching the men down in the courtyard prepare to mount their horses. Grooms held the steeds steady while the bags were slung over the horses' backs, then the men swung themselves up.

At last, the rain had stopped, and the clouds were clearing from the east. I peered out and saw the sun was already low in the sky. Perhaps I would take a walk around the estate today. I was about to call for my maid to help me dress when I saw the last man to climb onto his horse turn his face up towards me. It was Hector Mor.

Of course – he was leaving to sail to Islay today, to settle some land issues on behalf of my husband. Presumably he worked for Lachlan in some capacity, perhaps as factor, but I was not told much about him at supper and I had been raised never to question guests, but rather to let them tell their own stories. I had intended to ask my husband later, but since I pretended to be asleep when he came to bed, I could not.

What I did know was that he lived on one of the islands off the west side of Mull called the Treshnish Islands. Over the rather unpalatable food at supper, he had taken some time to describe to me their beauty and the astonishing array of flowers all over the machair. He said there were sea pinks, bluebells, honeysuckle and violets; and a profusion of birds, the barnacle geese overwintering there and in the summer, thrushes, starlings and blackbirds. Many of the seabirds that the locals regularly eat were plentiful there: kittiwakes, fulmar, skuas, guillemots and puffins. This reminded me that I intended to speak to the cook about menus and try to persuade her to serve wildfowl less often.

Hector Mor told me also of the abundance of grey seals there, the waters around the islands making them a perfect breeding place. Then, with a twinkle in his eye, he told me stories of the selkies all over the islands. And all the while my husband ate on, hardly conversing at all, merely guffawing when Hector Mor began telling me tales of the seal folk. Despite his unrefined appearance – like my husband's – there was something beguiling, almost alluring about him. It was perhaps the way he looked directly at me when he was speaking, his eyes so dark they seemed almost black as they gleamed in the candlelight.

Hector smiled up at me from the courtyard and gave me a wave. I waved back and tried not to appear as if I was staring at his strong, muscular body as he turned his horse around. I watched the beasts trot off down the cliffs and head south, presumably for a boat to Islay. My husband said they usually sailed from somewhere called Lochbuie if there was a large party; otherwise the boat left from our own beach.

I turned to my maid.

"I shall dress in my heavier gown; I intend to go out walking today."

Elspeth bobbed and scurried off to fetch a dress as I watched the horses gallop out of the courtyard and round the bay, then up through the yellow gorse bushes at the far end. Once they were out of sight, I stretched my neck to see further, but there was nothing but the caw and the squawk of the seabirds as they swooped and dived around the cliffs.

I sighed. I was not used to silence. Duart Castle seemed to be far removed from the rush of activity of my own home. At Inveraray there was always a bustle of life from the nearby harbour. The noise of the weekly market reached the top tower of the Campbell castle, where my sisters and I used to stand and peer down to watch the flurry of activity as stalls were set up from first light. We would listen as the herring sellers and cheesemongers cried their wares, and dash down the winding, narrow stairs of the castle to cross over the lea to the harbour. Mama told all her daughters that we were forbidden from going to the market. It was not for ladies, she said, it is for our servants. But Marion, Ellen and I loved the atmosphere, the bustle and the excitement – and that was also where I would sometimes catch a first glimpse of Archibald as his boat was sailing into harbour from Auchenbreck. Only my sisters knew about him, though I was convinced Grandmother had guessed. They too adored him; but he was not theirs.

Once dressed, I went down to the Great Hall where I saw my husband already sitting, bent over the table, eating with gusto. It seemed that mealtimes were essential only for him to fill his belly; not an opportunity for elegant discourse, as I was used to.

"Good morning," I said, smiling politely.

"Ah, you're awake," he mumbled through a mouthful of bread and cheese. "Come and sit down. Eat." He pointed at the food in front of him.

As I took a seat, once more I felt a painful longing for my own family. The first meal of the day was a buzz of gossip about the previous night's supper and relaying to the others what the day had in store for them. Here on Mull, it seemed that it would only be me and my husband.

"I will be off soon to hunt. One of my kinsmen said the wolves were back on the west coast, over towards Ulva. It's quite a long ride and I may not be back for a day or two."

"Oh," I said, wondering if this happened to every bride two days after their wedding. "Well, I'm sure I can occupy myself." I took a small salted herring and began to eat, trying not to stare as Lachlan chewed noisily opposite me. I shivered. Even though the fire was lit, the room was still draughty and damp.

My husband was clearly one who preferred silence when he ate, but I was simply not used to this, and I burbled on. "Is there a library here at the castle? I love to read poetry and wondered where you might keep your books?"

He gave me a strange look. "My books?"

"Surely there must be some at Duart," I suggested. "At Inveraray we have some of the finest books of poetry, literary texts, tales of heroism. They are now printed in Edinburgh, my brothers tell me," I said, beaming. "And of course the prayer books."

"You read?" He frowned, as if not understanding my question.

"Yes, and all my sisters too," I said proudly. My grandmother had insisted we learn to read and write even if it was rather unusual.

He shrugged and returned to his morning dram. "No books here that I know of." He tipped the liquid down his throat. "Not much call for them. We use our voices to communicate," he said, chuckling. He stood up and came to my seat. He kissed the top of my head and patted my long tresses.

"I shall see you once we get home, my little redhead."

Little redhead? Did he think I was still a child? Besides, I was tall.

"Amuse yourself till then." And out he swept, tightening the belt around his plaid as he went.

*

I stepped off the earth floor of the kitchen and up onto the cobbled stones of the courtyard outside. I sighed: the castle's cook, Agnes, was clearly not going to change her menus any time soon. On hearing my request, she had pointed to a pile of seabirds in the far corner and a flurry of white, grey and black feathers. A young lad sat plucking them, presumably for supper. Could I feign illness? No, I was determined to try to fit in and somehow settle here at Duart. Agnes was not unkind, but seemed not to understand when I said I was not used to seabirds. "Perhaps mutton would be good at meals? Or beef?" I had asked hopefully. She shrugged and returned to peeling onions, as if doing this, tears streaming down her face, was preferable to talking to her new mistress.

I walked out past the castle walls and headed away from the sea and the cliffs. I headed over some grassy hillocks towards a clump of trees, then turned to look back at the castle. In the clear daylight, I had to admit it was rather impressive, perched high on the cliffs, with the sea now still and calm. Everything looked different from yesterday's storm. I was about to go into the woods when I heard something. I stopped and listened. It was music – a light, clear, flowing tune that was both haunting and beautiful. I followed the melody around the trees towards a tiny house at the edge of the woods.

As I approached, I saw before me a low stone cottage with a wisp of smoke coming from the turf roof. I sniffed the air and smiled; I loved the smell of peat. I walked through a bower of hazel trees, letting the music guide me. The sound was coming from inside. It was now almost ethereal, the high notes so utterly perfect in their tone that I found myself moved beyond words. I rested my hand against the stone wall of the cottage and leaned towards the unglazed window, closing my eyes.

At Inveraray we employed the MacEwens, a family of musicians and poets, to play solely for us. Hereditary harpists had been with the Campbells for generations. They played and performed for us on every occasion and sometimes even when there was none. John MacEwen had even followed my father into battle at Flodden and sadly, like Papa, had died. His body and his harp were returned along with father's, and his body is buried near Papa's grave. My brother had assured his family that they could continue to live on the lands granted to them and that, when young John, his son, was sufficiently experienced, he would take over playing at family gatherings as official harpist, using the MacEwen harp. He was only about fourteen, but it was already clear that he had a natural way around the brass strings.

As I closed my eyes and listened to the sweet, rich melody, I wondered if this was perhaps my husband's musician playing. This cottage was by no means a hovel, yet it was hardly any size at all, certainly not as substantial as the Campbell's harpist's house. But as I was becoming aware, nothing was quite the same here on Mull.

I did not want to interrupt the flow of the music by moving, so stood there for a while, listening to what I knew was a clarsach. This type of harp was one of the instruments that the Campbell musicians played, as well as lyres and lutes; but surely not even Old John MacEwen had ever played as beautifully as this.

The music stopped quite suddenly, as if a hand had just been placed over the strings. I thought it best to move away, for fear of looking like a mad woman, leaning against the wall, eyes tight shut, tears rolling down my cheeks. I sped towards the woods, turning to look back once, but the door remained firmly closed. I wiped my cheeks and wandered deeper into the forest, between the birch and hazel trees, listening instead to the songs of the birds.

Chapter 4

1517

Catherine

My husband did not return for six days. I was sitting at the table in the Great Hall when the door swung open, and in strode Lachlan on a blast of cold air.

"Ah, good evening, Catherine. They said you were at supper. I am completely famished; we rode all the way today without stopping. There's another storm due in tomorrow."

He unbuckled his belt and flung off his plaid, sat down on the chair and a servant ran to fill his goblet. He downed the wine and called for more, all the while surveying the food on the table. He rammed a thick slice of mutton into his mouth then sat back on his seat, looking over at me with a frown, as if he had forgotten who I was.

"Did you stay here all this while by yourself, Catherine?"

I raised my hands. "I had little choice. I thought you would be away only a day or two. Had I known you would be gone this long, I could have sent a message for one of my younger sisters to join me." I was trying hard not to sound as upset as I was.

He shrugged. "Well, the wolves – you know how they are."

"No, I'm afraid I don't. They are not something my brothers or my late father ever hunted."

"Ah, well, the stalking can take a very long time. They can lead us on a merry chase that ends with no quarry at all."

Though I was angry with him for being so inconsiderate, I forced myself to converse. "And did you get any?"

A broad smile spread across his face. "You wait and see, Catherine. We will have some very fine wolfskins to sleep under. We got four of the beasts, each one such a beauty." He grabbed a hunk of barley bread. "Very satisfactory journey, all in all."

I turned away and a servant filled my goblet. I took a sip, all the while wondering if he might ask what I had been doing during his absence. But when I looked back at him, he was slavering over a whole capercailzie, holding it down with one hand and ripping off a leg with the other. He gnawed at the meat like a crazed animal, as if he had not eaten in weeks. Well, I was not used to this silence. I would lead the conversation.

"You will, I'm sure, be interested to hear what I have done while you have been over on Ulva?"

He glanced at the walls. "Can't see any new tapestries or drapes in here yet." He winked. "What have you been doing, then?"

"I have taken walks in the woods, over the beach and along the cliffs. I took a horse one day to Craignure, but I did not find any company there."

"What were you expecting, Catherine? It's a village with a few crofts and an ale house. You could have spoken to the ale wife there if you were that desperate for company." He was chuckling.

"I am not desperate for anything, Lachlan, apart from some civilised conversation," I snapped, trying not to cry.

He leaned back in his seat and sighed. "Would you like me to plan a gathering? I could invite some folk to the castle, as a welcome for the new Lady Maclean."

"Yes, that would be wonderful, Lachlan." My thoughts turned to the parties we held at Inveraray. Clansmen and women came from far and wide for the grandeur and sophistication of the food, the wines and of course the lively discourse. Archibald and his family were at the last gathering, and I was enjoying the memory of our time together that evening when my husband's gruff voice broke the spell.

"I can't promise as elegant an assembly as you're used to at Inveraray, but we can get some of my clansmen's wives along for company."

"Thank you," I said, smiling. "Shall I speak to the cook about menus?"

He shrugged. "If you like. She does tend to prepare the same dishes though."

"Shall we have music?"

He turned to look at me. He had an almost tender, kind expression on his face. "The Macleans of Duart do music better than any other clan." He raised an eyebrow. "True, your musicians played well enough at our wedding – they seemed talented at the lyres and the lutes – but nothing is comparable to the sound of our clarsach. Our harpist is superior to all; you wait till you hear."

I was about to ask him about the enchanting harp music I had heard in the woods when he stood up.

"And now I must go and supervise the men treating the wolf skins. Last time the lad didn't do it right and they stank."

"Are you home for a while or shall you be travelling again soon?"

"Yes, that's me here for a while, I think. I won't be needed again so soon on the Treshnish Islands. It's all settled there."

"But I thought you were on Ulva?"

His eyes narrowed and he picked up his plaid from the chair. "Yes, of course – not Treshnish, but Wolf Island." He raised an eyebrow. "Ulva means 'wolf island' you know." And he swept out of the hall, leaving me to my silence once more.

Chapter 5

1517
Catherine

"Fetch my red gown, Elspeth." I gestured to my favourite dress, feeling I ought to make an effort for the soiree. "And if you can weave some plaits into my hair please?"

The girl was always so silent, I thought she was perhaps deaf or unable to speak, but she nodded and brought over my ivory comb.

I was so looking forward to meeting other people. The past few days had been exceedingly dull. Even at mealtimes, it was only Lachlan and me, and the conversation was limited – indeed, often non-existent while he chomped away at whatever carcass lay before him. Later, once he had finished with me, I thanked God he always left for his own chamber and I at least had the bed to myself. His body was repugnant, but fortunately he only came to my chamber in the dark when I didn't have to look at it.

Elspeth pulled another shift over my head then fastened me into my gown. I was continually cold in this draughty castle, and I wore as many layers as possible without looking fat. And as she tied the ribbons, I thought once more about Inveraray and how my sisters would all get dressed together before an assembly. We would discuss what the ladies would wear and how dashing some of the local men might be. I used to join in these discussions, talking about potential beaux, until Archibald came into my life. I sighed as I thought of him. Not only was his face beautiful and his manners impeccable, his skin was clear and unmarked by the pox, unlike my rough, hirsute husband's.

I'd asked Agnes to prepare any dishes other than the seabirds that graced our table at every meal. She scowled and told me that was what the guests would expect. I had come to realise she was in fact an unhelpful and invariably sullen woman.

"Well, that was before I became your mistress. I should be grateful if you could put some mutton, beef and fish on the table too."

I knew that sweetmeats would be out of the question in that dank, cold kitchen she lived in, but I did ask for some berries. She looked at me as if I were mad.

"What, you mean brambles or blaeberries?"

"I suppose so – or crowberries. You know that they're the plant that represents the Macleans of Duart, of course?"

She shook her head. "But you can't eat them."

"Are they poisonous?" I had to admit to myself that I didn't know that.

"No, just bitter," she muttered.

"Then have the boy fetch some blaeberries – they're sweet enough to eat as they are."

Of all the berries in the forests and on the moors, I know blaeberries well, as they are the plant the Campbell men wear in their bonnets. Our festive tables were often adorned with them. The French chef at Inveraray was far more accommodating to our requests than this stolid old cook.

But she did not even nod in agreement; she simply ignored me and returned to the pile of dead birds on the table. It seemed I had no authority in this kitchen, or indeed anywhere in my husband's castle.

The other details I tried to attend to turned out to be just as difficult. The tapestries I found in an old trunk were moth-eaten and could not be hung. The glasses I wished to use for the toasts were chipped. Really, my husband had no pride in things that mattered in my family. I spent the afternoon trying to make the Great Hall look better than the drab, draughty room it was by

23

hanging garlands of oak and ash. Lachlan swept into the hall at one stage, looked around and told me it appeared as if we were about to host a pagan ritual, not a small gathering of good Christian people. I despaired.

*

On the evening of the gathering, the fire was blazing, the candles burning and the table groaning with food. I peeked over to see what Agnes had prepared and saw with relief that there was a haunch of mutton and a side of beef, rather than just seabirds. She had even put some blaeberries and their leaves in a bowl. As for bread, there was not only the usual barley bannocks, but also some lighter wheat and oaten loaves.

As I surveyed the room, I sniffed the air. There was the smell of candle wax as usual, a lingering scent of the cinnamon oil on my hair and the pleasing waft of hot roast meats, all of which were redolent. But there was something else. Perhaps the maid had put too much lavender on my gown, for there was an unusual hint of sweetness. Lachlan came into the hall and looked around, smiling. I noted he had not bothered to wash; his nails were black and he had mud on his face. I went towards him and licked my finger to wipe the mud off his cheek.

"What are you doing, woman?"

"Do you not mind greeting our guests unwashed?"

He shrugged and gestured to a servant to pour his ale. While he quaffed this down, I shook my head. Could I ever change or at least attempt to civilise a man as stubborn as my husband?

"Who can we expect tonight, Lachlan?"

"I told you before, Catherine. Just the family, those near enough to ride over for an evening." He went to the door where two guards stood, swords at their side. I heard him instruct them to let in only members of the clan. "Anyone else, send your man to see me." I saw him patting the dirk in his belt.

The sweet aroma was distracting me; I felt quite light-headed, it was so alluring. I peered through the gloom at the dishes on the table one by one, until I noticed an unusual dish and I realised it was crowberries in a thick syrup. So Agnes had in fact followed my instruction and had cooked the tart berries in honey. I smiled; perhaps I had some authority after all. I went to re-position a couple of candles near the table so that the food could be identified, not merely guessed at.

As the first visitors arrived I joined Lachlan, waiting for him to introduce me. The ladies were dressed in fine gowns and capes or shawls and the men, like my husband, were in plaids tied with heavy leather belts. As we sat down to dinner, I touched my husband's arm and whispered, "When do the musicians start? I thought you had organised them?"

He frowned. "They will begin to play in good time, Catherine. Our ways are not the Campbell ways, don't forget that."

I presumed that meant they played after the meal, unlike my family whose harpists played throughout. Things were all so very different here.

At the table, I found myself beside Jean Maclean, and an ancient kinsman of Lachlan's, John Maclean. Since he was very hard of hearing, I talked mostly to Jean, who was perhaps about twenty years older than me and had the most striking black curly hair, flecked with silvery white. She was some distant cousin of Lachlan's and lived in a place to the west of Duart called Lochbuie. She invited me to visit her and though I did not take to her – for she was rather cold and aloof – I gladly accepted the offer. Any female company would be a relief after the enforced solitude here at Duart.

When I ran out of things to talk about, I asked her about Hector Mor, who I hadn't seen again. I had thought he might be here tonight, but could not see him as I looked around the table. I found myself feeling disappointment; he had represented a glimmer of hope somehow in this dingy, cold castle. Perhaps he was still on Islay.

She gave me a rather strange look when I asked about him. Leaning conspiratorially towards me, she asked, "Has Lachlan not told you?"

I shook my head. "I met him over dinner on my first night at Duart, but I have no idea who he is, other than that he hails from the Treshnish Islands."

"I see. Well then, it's probably best if Lachlan tells you," she said, sipping her wine.

And before I could enquire further, a hush spread down the table. On Lachlan's command, the music had begun. As I leaned back in my chair, I recognised the plangent sound of a harp. I looked around and saw a screen had been set up at the other end of the hall. The beautiful melody was coming from there. It was the same moving music from the clarsach I'd heard in the woods. It was captivating and enchanting. Everyone sat still and listened; even the servants stopped their bustling as the assembled guests turned their heads to appreciate the music, which seemed to cast a spell on the room. I closed my eyes and listened, as the cares of tomorrow began slowly to ebb away.

Chapter 6

1518

Catherine

I was taking my daily walk across the beach beneath the castle when I heard a familiar cry from above. It was a high-pitched noise, a staccato of friendly cheeps, nothing like the harsh cawing of the crows that fly menacingly around the castle every day at dusk. I looked up and saw an oyster catcher above me, circling, watching, then swooping down. His long red beak and red legs cheered me, and I decided to sit down on some dried seaweed on the beach and watch him for a while as he hovered and dipped. When he eventually disappeared, I stared out to sea, beyond the white crested waves, hoping I was looking in the direction of home.

I could never call this place home. Even after these long, wearisome months, Duart Castle was not (and I did not think ever would be) a place I could be happy. It was simply not where I wanted to be. It had a cold, unwelcoming feel to it, inside and out. My life was lonesome, I had no friends and a husband who spent most of his time travelling all over the island either on business or hunting. Or so he said. On the few days he was home, I forced myself to converse and appear interested in him, but little was truly said. He never seemed curious about me or paid me any attention, other than in the bedchamber. And that, thankfully, was swift.

I was slowly becoming convinced I must invent some pretext to go home to Inveraray Castle to visit my family. I had already written to Mama asking if she could send one or two of my sisters, but she said I ought to give myself to my husband for a while. What did she know about Lachlan's character? How could she know her daughter sometimes felt so miserable that she had had the urge – more than once – to pick up the dirk her husband laid on the table beside him at dinner and stab it through his heart. That seemed to be the only way out.

This betrothal had made me a mere pawn in the game of chance between our two families. And in that game, the dice was meant to roll in favour of me having a son to unite the Campbells and the Macleans. Well, after all these months of what seemed like captivity, I was not expecting a child and I had had enough. I wanted to go home. I felt a tear trickle down my cheek and was about to get up from the beach when I heard a noise and looked towards the woods.

Coming slowly down the track was a girl carrying a basket on her back. She was singing, and as she approached, I realised I recognised the tune from our Campbell musicians. It was lilting and uplifting, and I wiped the tears from my face and stood up. She saw me and gave a shy wave before walking over to the rocks. She sat down, pulling her shawl around her shoulders, then took a knife in her hand. She was hunched over the rock, busy removing something with a deft movement. I watched for a while then, starved of company, wandered over towards her. I now noticed her beautiful, thick black hair, which was even longer than mine. It was twisted down her back in a heavy plait. She turned on hearing me and smiled, her green eyes friendly.

"What are you collecting?" I asked, crouching down beside her.

"It's the limpets. There's a knack to getting them off the rock before they know you're there."

I watched her insert the knife between the shell and the rock, quickly ease it off with a deft twist and throw it into her basket. "If you tap them first, they clamp themselves onto the rock and you can't get them off. They're clever wee things." She grinned at me shyly, then returned her gaze to the shells.

28

"So how do you cook them?" I had never to my knowledge eaten a limpet.

She shrugged. "In the usual way, just boiled."

She lifted one up, ran the knife around the edge and held the shell above her mouth. "Or you can eat them as they are," she said as she tipped the glistening flesh down her throat. And as I watched her, I realised she was not as young as I had at first thought; perhaps she was more my age or perhaps my sister Ellen's – just a year or so younger than me.

I extended my hand. "I'm Catherine, from the castle."

She nodded. "I know who you are, my Lady." She glanced back up at me and took my hand in her wet one. "I'm Lorna."

The silence was filled with the sound of the waves gently lapping onto the shore.

"What was that song you were singing earlier?"

"Just something my father used to play. I don't know the name of it."

"Oh, I thought I recognised it. Is it a tune for the clarsach?"

She smiled. "Yes, it is."

"And does your father still play it?" I wondered if he was the person playing the harp so beautifully the night we had the gathering at the castle.

She shook her head and turned back to the limpets. "He died," she muttered. "At Flodden."

"Ah, just like my father," I said, sighing at the memory of the Campbell men returning to Inveraray in a slow procession after the battle, the family standard held low, their bleak expressions conveying the news to my mother and sisters before we even had to ask.

I shook my head. "Where do you live?"

"In that wee stone cottage at the edge of the woods over there."

I looked to where she was pointing and realised it was where I had heard the beautiful music in the first week after I had arrived.

"Do you play the clarsach yourself now?"

She looked directly at me, her green eyes steady, and she was silent for a moment. Then she leant towards me and whispered, "My brother does, my Lady."

There was a flicker of movement to the side and we turned to watch a tiny sandpiper run along the beach behind us, teetering along on its spindly legs. It raced along the sand to the far end where we heard a couple of high-pitched calls, then off it flew into the air and over the sea. We both smiled then she stood up and moved nimbly on to the next rock, her bare feet placed firmly on the wet seaweed. "Sorry, but I've got a lot more to collect before it gets dark. I need to pick some dulse too, for the soup." And she crouched down and turned her back to me to concentrate on the limpets at her feet.

I nodded and walked away, back towards the castle.

I knew I'd be facing the grim expressions of the servants, who would shake their heads as I passed. They clearly thought I was peculiar, wanting to go out for a walk every day; why was I not inside instead, sewing or embroidering, pursuing the pastimes of a lady? I looked up at the bleak grey stone walls and pushed back tears once more. I could not possibly live here forever. My husband was not an evil man – not that I knew him at all well – but we had nothing in common. He only needed me to breed. Worse still, he seemed to bring out the worst in me. I had never had thoughts of murder before, but now I fantasised about stabbing him to death or poisoning his ale, just so I could be free.

More than ever, I longed to see Archibald's beautiful face. I craved his touch. I had written to him, of course, but heard nothing back. Perhaps he thought it was improper; he was a man of integrity and I was, after all, a married lady. I sighed and clambered up the grass to the entrance to the courtyard. I swung the heavy door open and as I walked inside, a cold chill enveloped me.

Chapter 7

1518

Lachlan Cattanach

He met her in the courtyard. He'd just been to the kitchen to give Agnes the hares and partridge they'd shot up north. A rare smile had flickered across the cook's ravaged face as he'd handed them over.

"They may please her Ladyship. She still doesn't take to the seabirds, even though I cook them with those fancy spices she likes, your Lordship."

He burst out laughing.

"Agnes, you could cook with all the spices in Arabia, and she would still deem it unworthy. Or certainly not as good as the Campbell family are used to." He winked and went out the door where he caught sight of his wife blowing in through the west gate. She was tossing her hair around like a hound coming in from the rain.

"Good afternoon, Catherine."

She started and pulled her thick red hair back behind her head with two hands, fastening it with clasps, as if it was improper for him to see her beautiful hair down. Ah, these Campbells and their ridiculous sense of decorum.

She nodded, approaching slowly, and he saw she was forcing her pale, freckled face into a smile. As usual, it was clear she was not pleased to see him.

"Did you have a fine walk? Were you on the beach again?"

"Yes. I find it exhilarating to watch the oyster catchers, the herons and sandpipers. I envy them their ability to fly high in the sky."

31

This free-spirited wife of his puzzled him. "Now why would you want to fly when you have two good legs to walk?"

She shrugged and turned to go inside, then swung round. "Lachlan, I've been thinking. Would I be able to visit Inveraray in the next few weeks, before winter sets in?"

Again, she fixed a smile on her full lips.

"There are storms brewing in the east so I can't envisage a safe sailing any time soon. Why do you want to see them anyway?"

"They are my family." She sniffed. "I miss them."

"Your family is here now, Catherine. If you're lonely, then we can have another gathering like we had some months back. You can meet some more clanswomen."

She sighed and shut her eyes as if blocking out either the memory of it or perhaps his craggy face.

"Could we just have the musicians again, Lachlan, like before? Even just at our supper, the two of us? Their music is so good for my soul."

"If that's what you want, yes, I can try to arrange it before I go."

"Where are you going off to now?"

"I've business to do up in the Treshnish Islands. I'll be away tomorrow for a few days."

She opened her mouth to speak then changed her mind. Shoulders slumped, she turned around and headed for the main entrance.

"I'll see you at supper, Catherine."

And though it was obvious she had heard him, she continued up the steps, cocooned in her silent sulk.

Even had he wanted to, he would not cancel his trip to the Treshnish Islands, for his lovely Marion was waiting for him. Without any of the responsibilities or disagreements that seemed to come with his wife, there was always the lovely Marion Maclean.

He smiled as he thought of her. Yes, he had a mistress and she was fair and kind and loved him, unlike Catherine who thought she and her entire family of Inveraray Campbells were superior to the Macleans of Duart. Well, Marion Maclean of Treshnish had none of those affectations, and though she was nearly as old as he was, with a wrinkle or two on her fair face and even some streaks of grey in her fine black hair, she still thrilled him more than he could ever say. Even after these twenty long years, he sighed at the thought of her touch and the memory of her sweet lips.

*

At supper, she asked again about visiting her family.

"Lachlan, do you think I could visit Inveraray after the storms have passed?"

He put down his goblet and looked at her. Her shoulders were stooped, her head hung over her plate.

"Are you unhappy here, Catherine?" He leaned towards her.

"I am lonely." She sniffed.

"Did you not enjoy the company of my cousin Jean over at Lochbuie? I thought you went for a couple of days, a month or two ago?"

She shrugged. "Yes, it was fine. But she is much older than me and we have little in common, apart from books. There is no one my age. And I miss my sisters."

"Well, you do have rather a lot of them, don't you?" He was chuckling, but her face was like a stone.

Dear Lord, was there any pleasing her? She didn't like the food at Duart, she lamented her husband's lack of books, she resented his different ways and felt superior to the Macleans. Suddenly he remembered what she did enjoy, and Lachlan lifted his head to snap his fingers at Willie, who came bounding over.

"Your Lordship?"

"Tell the musicians they can come in now."

While the servant ran off towards the door, he glanced at his wife, who had raised her head. She had the look of a little girl about to ride her first horse.

"Did you ask them to play, Lachlan?"

He nodded and they watched them enter, wrapped in their cloaks, their instruments at their side.

As they began to set up, she leaned towards him. "Why do you not have them more often? Are these ones your hereditary harpists? The ones you had at that assembly months ago?"

"Yes, but there have been a few adjustments. You'll see."

Lachlan told them they did not need to play behind the screen as it was just the two of them at table, so she could see that, unusually, it was the girl who had the gift from her father, not her brother. As they started to play – young Angus on his fiddle and Lorna on her clarsach – he noticed she was frowning. Good God, what now?

"Do you not like the music, Catherine?"

"Oh, I do, I really do," she whispered. "It's beautiful." She pointed at Lorna, whose long black hair was tied up on her head with some twine. "But I know that girl. Is she the one from the cottage by the woods?"

"Yes, the family have lived there for some time now."

"I met her – Lorna – down at the beach, picking limpets off the rocks. She said her father died at Flodden?"

"That he did. Like my own father." He looked at her, remembering. "And yours too."

The gentle plucking of the harp and fiddle strings filled the room as they tuned their instruments. He leaned towards her and whispered, "Her father Angus was the best harpist in all the islands, indeed, in all the west. Now his daughter continues to play in his memory – and to his standard. But we'll need to get young Angus onto the harp soon, though he's only ten or eleven."

"Is that why they were behind a screen at the assembly? You don't want anyone to know the most beautiful tunes on that

34

harp come from a girl?"

Did she believe there was any choice? "Of course not. It would be unacceptable for Lorna to play in public. Don't forget, the clan's musicians must lead us into battle too."

"But could she not just play here while we live our lives at peace, ever hopeful there will be no more wars?"

He chortled. "No more wars? Are you mad?" He shook his head. "And I'm not sure your brother the earl would countenance a girl leading the Campbells into battle, would he?" She opened her mouth to reply, but she was cut short. "And neither would I."

She sighed deeply, turned back round to face the musicians and shut her eyes. The music now filled every nook and cranny of the Great Hall as the girl and her brother played the old melodies. Lorna really did have her father's gift; Lachlan had to concede, she was just as good as him now and it was obvious why some found her playing so moving.

How he would love his fair Marion to hear Lorna play. He smiled as he thought of his lovely mistress, then turned to see tears trickle down his wife's cheeks. Her shoulders shuddered and she shut her eyes and tipped her head back to listen. He looked away from her over to the musicians, wondering about the power of music; it was the first time Lachlan had seen his wife look interested in anything at all. He sighed. His life had surely not been this complicated before she had arrived at Duart castle.

Chapter 8

1518

Catherine

The music ended and the musicians lifted their instruments and started to leave the room. I stood up and went over towards Lorna and smiled.

"That was wonderful, thank you. I had no idea it was you who played so beautifully. You have such a talent."

"Thank you, my Lady, she said, and bowed. She looked up at me, an unsure smile flickering on her lips. I was about to invite her to join us for a glass of wine, even though I felt my husband would not permit it, but she turned and headed for the door, as if uncomfortable speaking to me.

"Perhaps I shall see you on the beach, Lorna," I shouted after her, but she did not turn her head.

I watched them go out the heavy wooden door with their instruments, then it clanged shut and I trudged back to the table.

"Lorna has a gift, Catherine," my husband said, peering at me over the rim of his goblet, "but she cannot be your friend. You know that, surely?"

I raised my shoulders high. "I shall pick my own friends, Lachlan, since I have no other company."

He opened his mouth to speak then shut it as he stood up and leaned in close towards me. He sighed then spoke slowly, enunciating each word as if to a fool. "As you know, Catherine, I shall travel tomorrow to the Treshnish Islands for a few days, and on my return, I shall spend a week or so here. Then – if the storms have abated – I could perhaps arrange a trip to Inveraray for you." He paused and stood up straight. "Sadly, I would not be able to join you as I must be ready to go to Islay for the Council. No firm dates are set yet – it all depends on the tides – but I must be prepared when I have word. We continue to meet at Finlaggan even though the regent for the boy king tries to prevent us." He turned his face away from the table and spat onto the floor.

The disgust I felt at my husband's manners were overcome by the relief I felt at both the prospect of a journey home and the fact my husband would not accompany me. I beamed with pleasure, hoping he would not realise the true reason of my joy. I must pray that those storms in the east would not come to much and that I could indeed sail home. I tried to suppress a grin as I thought of the journey without him. When he continued to speak, I listened with half an ear.

"For the Council, I shall sail with my men from Mull to Colonsay, then onto Oronsay, our last stop before we land at Nave Island, just north of Islay. There is a very fine monastery there where we are always well looked after. From there we await high tide, then sail past Ardnave Point and up Loch Gruinart. There the horses will be waiting on the shore and they will take us to Finlaggan, where we'll stay for the duration of the Council. It's a journey I have done many times, but never fail to enjoy."

I aroused myself from my daydream when I realised he was addressing me, not simply outlining his itinerary.

"You shall not accompany me on this occasion, Catherine, but perhaps on a future visit, you may come with me. I must determine from the other nobles, like the Macleods of Harris and of Lewis, whether the Lords take their wives along. The nobles in the Council take close kinsmen with them, but I've never paid any attention before as to whether spouses also attend. I know my cousin Murdoch from Lochbuie does not take his, for she is too old to travel, but next year you might come along with me."

"So you travel just with your servants or with kinsmen?"

"Hector Mor will of course travel with me."

Well, that seemed rather strange. He had dined with us at our table, so he was not a servant, and yet I had not been told he was kin. "As an attendant or a kinsman?"

He stared at me. "A kinsman, Catherine." He wiped his mouth on his sleeve. "Also, while we are both on Islay, I shall take the opportunity to start preparing his marriage indenture."

"Who is he marrying?" I was shocked that Hector Mor was to be married, not only because his kind eyes and his sensitive nature made his company so much more agreeable than when I was dining solely with my husband, but I also realised I would once again be alone, without companionship of my own age at the table.

My husband's eyes narrowed. "I shall give you the details once the contract is agreed." He leaned towards me. "But, Catherine, how could you have thought Hector Mor was a servant? He sits at our table and eats our fine fare. Would your brother the earl allow a hireling to dine with your grand family at Inveraray Castle?"

Despite my sorrow, I had to smile as I contemplated the words "fine fare" to describe the putrid seabirds that Agnes continued to provide. My husband reached back to his chair for his belt which he tied tight around his waist, then strode towards the stairs, while the servants scurried about clearing the table. I got up and followed him.

"Is he your cousin, Lachlan?"

He turned and stood, legs astride, his shoulders raised as if in defiance. "No, Catherine, he is not. Hector Mor of Treshnish is my son."

He was clearly waiting for me to react, but the shock of this was so great, I could not say a thing, so I simply stared at his retreating back and returned to the table, where I sat down once more and grabbed my goblet of wine. I drank it down in one long draught as I thought about what had just been said. Of course, how obvious it was now: they both had hair and eyes as black as a raven's. Their complexions were both swarthy, though one far more pleasant to behold. I leaned back while the implications of what Lachlan had just said sank in: surely I did not have to produce an heir, since he already had one. I could not ask if he had been married before or if Hector Mor's mother was one of his many mistresses my sisters had heard talk of.

I realised that my purpose to breed a son and forge an alliance between the Campbells and the Macleans was founded on lies. There is no way my brother could have known this when he arranged the marriage. He was surely duped into drawing up the indenture of marriage; all our family was. So why in God's name was I married to this negligent savage if I did not need to produce an heir?

*

The morning after this discovery, having established that Lachlan had departed for the Treshnish Islands, I went down to the beach to clear my head. I had hardly slept; my mind was so full of last night's revelation. As well as the fact my husband already had an heir, I mulled over what had happened to Hector Mor's mother. Had she died? Had they even been married? Then, just as a herring gull rose high above me with a jeering cry, another thought occurred: Hector Mor's mother was still very much alive and that was who Lachlan was off this very day to see on the Treshnish Islands.

I walked past the gorse bushes and onto the shore, where the tide was out. I sat down on a rock and looked north to where two boats were tied up at the jetty. Lachlan presumably would take one of those boats for his trip to Islay next week and, God willing, the second boat would be the one I would take on my visit home. I stood up and looked east to where Inveraray surely was. I had been miserable the day I arrived here, and the bad weather in the latter part of the journey did not help my mood; but I had presumed it would change once I got to know my husband and had children. Though the first had happened gradually and the outcome was less and less to my pleasing, the second was never going to happen, I would now make sure of that. Somehow. It had not happened so far, so why should it now?

I shivered and pulled my woollen shawl around me. There was a low mist and no sun, meaning I could not see any land beyond the sea, but I did see an outcrop of rock in the middle of the water which I had not noticed before. Perhaps it was a small tidal island that disappeared when the tide was high in the Firth of Lorne. I sighed as I wished I could somehow disappear, like the rock under full tide, from this godforsaken place.

I had no idea how long I sat there, in despair, dreaming of Inveraray. I remembered vividly the laughter that filled the Great Hall when we had banquets, the teasing between my sisters about everything: our dresses, our hair and of course the men we hoped to marry. I recalled the majesty of every dinner, whether we were entertaining other nobles or simply the local priest. Though, admittedly, when we had entertained the king that memorable day, Mama had the servants go to more effort to make the castle look even more beautiful. The fires blazed in every fireplace and candles were lit in every nook and cranny. I was thinking about the difference here at Duart, with its freezing draughts, wind howling around every chamber and never any guests, when I heard a noise behind me.

I turned around, hoping it might be Lorna, but it was one of the servants running towards me.

"My Lady, there is a visitor arrived. You are to come and see him – it is a holy man." The young lad looked agitated and so I followed him, trudging back over the beach to the rock, and climbed up towards the castle, all the while wondering which holy man would pay a visit to this castle at the end of the earth.

I went up the steps directly to the Great Hall and stood at the door. Over by the fire – which, thankfully, the servants had lit earlier – was a priest, his back to me. He was wearing a grey cassock, his hood still up. I walked towards him, coughed politely, and slowly he turned around. I gasped when I saw his face, and bit my lip as I tried to control my emotions. He inclined his head.

"My Lady," he murmured, a smile beginning to flicker on his lips, "I heard you were in need of ecclesiastical solace."

"Indeed I am," I whispered. "Shall we sit?" I gestured to the seats in the nook and turned to the servants hovering at the door. "Go and fetch refreshments."

My heart was beating fast.

And as they all hurried away, I grabbed his hand and leaned in to inhale his familiar, heady scent. "Archibald, I always knew you would come."

Chapter 9

1518
Catherine

The last time I saw Archibald was before my marriage had been arranged, at the fair on the feast of St Brendan. It was an annual fair, of great importance to the people of Inveraray. He was due to arrive with his two brothers early in the day and, as usual, my sisters and I were watching from the tower of the castle to see whose boat would arrive first.

My older sisters Margaret, Isabel and Janet were already married and Jean was already betrothed, but Marion, Ellen and I were carefree, without marriage contracts. Mary was too young at eleven to worry about beaux; she was more interested in watching the fisher girls gut the herring in record time than flirting with men.

"Look over there! Is that not the boat from Auchenbreck, Catherine?" cried Marion, jumping up and down.

I stretched my neck up and peered over the turret. It certainly looked as if the boat was coming from the direction of Tighna-bruaich, but most boats also sailed from the south of the loch to reach Inveraray in the north. I squinted in the morning sun to see who was on board and was sure I recognised Archibald's thick blonde mane, though all three brothers had similar hair. There were three men giving instructions to their servants and when I saw one of the men turn his head up towards the castle and wave, I knew it was him. I sped downstairs, followed by my sisters.

Mama was in the Great Hall, working on Jean's wedding dress with my aunts when she saw us fly past the door. She called out for a servant to bring us back in at once. Marion hung her head low and shuffled back inside, closely followed by Ellen, but I carried on running to the harbour. What did I care if I was punished? I would not miss seeing Archibald just because Mama thought it indecent for a lady to run. To appease her, knowing she would have a servant run after me to ensure I was safe, I slowed down, held my head high and walked over the road to the harbour. There I turned around to smile at poor Aggie, one of the kitchen maids, who had clearly been sent after me.

"Aggie, I'll give you some of those sweetmeats you like if you say nothing to Mama."

She bit her lip.

"It's all right, I'm not going to do anything bad!" I said, laughing at her anxious face.

I stood at the harbour wall and watched the boat sail towards me. There was another wave from the boat and this time I knew it was Archibald having sailed up the loch from Tighnabruaich. I watched the three brothers bring the boat to shore and Archibald was first off. While his brothers helped tie her up, he strode up the jetty towards me and I felt my heart begin to thump.

I hoped my face did not betray my excitement as I fiddled with my hair, trying to fasten it up with my clasp. He approached and I took in his beautiful face with his deep-set blue eyes, full red lips, and that golden hair. I held his gaze and tried not to swoon. Then, when he was in front of me and Aggie took a step back to bow, I stretched out my hand and he kissed it. That kiss will be forever ingrained in my memory as one of the most exciting moments I have ever experienced.

And so, all these many months later, as I looked up once more into Archibald's kind blue eyes, I felt an emotion that I had not experienced in all my long, sad months at Duart.

"Catherine," he said, leaning in. "I received your letters but could not reply. You understand why, don't you? But I had to come and see if you were as unhappy as you said."

I tried to suppress a cry. "Archibald, thank you for..."

There was a clatter as the servants entered the room bearing food and drink. They bowed and shuffled around Archibald as if they had never had a priest in the castle before. I tried not to giggle as I looked at his coarse grey wool cassock and wondered at how incredible it was that one simple item of clothing can transform a person. I took a deep breath and sat up straight as they laid down ashets of refreshments on the small table before us.

Archibald kept staring at me, as if trying to recall exactly what I looked like; or perhaps I looked different. It was such a long time since we had met, though I suddenly realised I must have been looking rather unkempt after my walk on the beach. If only I had known he was about to arrive, I would have at least tied up my windswept hair; I must have looked like some wild peasant. I tried to pat the unruly locks down around my shoulders while I gazed at the man I'd fallen in love with years before. Even as children, when his family came to our castle to stay, he and I had a special, unspoken bond. And now here he was in front of me, dressed as a priest, in the castle I would never call home.

*

After some stilted conversation over the ale and bannocks, while the servants hovered nearby, I stood up and addressed them.

"I shall be taking our guest on a tour of the estate before he begins his religious devotions. Please ensure his servants are fed and his horses taken care of." I swept out of the door and down the steps into the courtyard, hearing Archibald's footsteps follow.

We walked in silence until we were outside the castle and then I turned to him and smiled. "Let us walk on the beach. The sound of the waves and the gulls will mask our words." And as we climbed down towards the sea, I felt my heart soar. What did it matter that I was married to an unfaithful brute? The love of my life was with me once more.

When we got to the rocks, I sat down and patted a rock beside me. An oyster catcher dived low nearby. Usually I watched the birds with a sense of longing to be free. Today was different: I felt neither the usual sense of frustration nor resentment, merely joy.

"Catherine, I can't perch on a rock like a fisherman mending his nets." He grinned. "I am a holy man. Surely you can see that."

I chuckled and gazed up at him. He was looking around, at the waves gently lapping onto the shore, at the bracken that was gold in the sun and back towards Duart Castle that stood solid on the rock behind us.

"It really is beautiful here, Catherine. How lovely to live in such a place."

I frowned and followed his gaze over the sea to the gentle green hills of Lismore. They were not as impressive as the snow-peaked mountains over the water from Inveraray Castle, but I realised this view was indeed rather lovely.

"I suppose it is. I have only seen the mists and the rain and felt the damp in my bones." I turned to see a bird with a red throat swoop low over the sand; Lorna had told me this was called a diver and that these birds only visit in the winter, en route to a distant land. I had longed to be that bird and fly away from everything to another place where I might find joy. And now it seemed I had found it, or rather, it had come to me.

"Let us walk, Archibald. We can talk more easily."

And as we walked up and down along the sand, we talked of home, my true home, not this dark castle I was tied to. He told me about his last few visits with his family to Inveraray and how my younger sister Marion had told him she didn't think I was happy, and he confirmed that he had received my letter and therefore knew that. He said she had looked horrified that I, a married woman, was still writing to my former beau.

As he said 'beau', I shuddered all over. I gazed at him, trying to keep my emotions in check.

"Archibald, let us go to the woods, where we cannot be seen. Come, follow me."

"We must be careful, Catherine. I don't want any of the servants telling your husband."

"He is only my husband in name; he neither wants me, nor I him. It is a disastrous union. I hate him." I turned towards Archibald and looked into his kind blue eyes. "You are more my husband."

He smiled and walked respectfully behind me. As we passed the castle, I suppose there was a chance someone might see us if we were too familiar. Just knowing he was so close made me feel hot all over.

We came to Lorna's cottage where long strings of smoke puffed out of the roof. The door was ajar, and I put a finger to my lips as we passed in silence. We arrived at the woods where we walked under the hazel and birch trees, the leaves heavy and dripping with earlier rain, and the moss squelched underfoot. I strode on, dipping my head to pass under the boughs of the willows, pausing to hold up a branch for him to go underneath, inhaling his scent as he passed through. I turned and smiled as he followed. I had no plan; I simply wanted to get deep into the woods so we could be alone, unseen, and be close.

We came to a clearing. I leaned against an oak tree, and reached out my hands. He touched my fingers, then slowly bent towards me. Soon his face was level with mine and our lips touched. As I closed my eyes, I shut out all thoughts of this godforsaken place. Rather, I thought of the past we shared and of present happiness, my lover here before me in my arms. I never wanted it to end.

Chapter 10

1518
Catherine

Three days later, we sat in the freezing chapel, Archibald in his priestly robes and me shivering from the cold, pulling my thick wool shawl tighter around me.

"We don't have to keep up this pretence much longer," I whispered. There were two servants at the door with candles and tapers, so we had to keep our voices low. I was hoping they would leave us soon.

"Dominus vobiscum," he intoned. I could not look at his face, for fear I would giggle. Thankfully all the servants saw was a holy man dressed in priest's habit and their mistress sitting or genuflecting before him. *About time too*, I imagine they muttered to each other, since I had hardly been in the chapel at all during my many months here. It wasn't just the cold – there seemed no point in thanking God for anything, until now.

There were noises at the entrance, and I looked around as one of the grooms rushed in and bowed respectfully to us both. He stood, waiting until Archibald had finished reciting what he could remember of his Latin. Archibald stopped and looked at the servant.

"My Lady, I am sorry to disturb you, but there is a visitor – Hector Mor. He said he would like to see you now, or once you have completed your devotions, for he is only here for a brief visit."

I crossed myself and got to my feet, then nodded my head at Archibald, who stood, hands clasped in front of him, looking towards the door. I turned and saw Hector Mor standing there, his bulk taking up most of the narrow entranceway. His kind eyes crinkled as he smiled at me. He looked happy to see me after such a long time, and had my visitor not arrived days ago, I too would have been delighted to see him. But everything had changed. When I looked back towards Archibald I realised once more how fine, delicate and pale were my lover's features, how fair his hair, and his body so much slimmer than this sturdy son of my rugged, swarthy husband.

"Welcome, Hector Mor. Please go to the Great Hall, I shall be there presently."

But he remained standing, staring past me directly at Archibald, who had quickly pulled the cowl up over his head and had lowered his gaze.

"The servants will bring us refreshments. I shall not be long." I gestured to the door and watched as he frowned, then turned around slowly and headed outside.

"Do you know him?" I whispered as we walked out of the chapel.

"I think so. I'm sure I've seen him with your husband. Did he come to Inveraray when the marriage was arranged?"

I shrugged. "I have no idea – I was in such despair, I refused to attend any of the dinners or indeed even meet him. I told them I was ill, indisposed."

I recall Mama being so angry with me, but I simply would not leave my room to share a table with the man she and my eldest brother had chosen for me. It was only Grandmother who understood. She slipped in after dinner and lay down beside me on the bed, stroking my hair, telling me she knew why I was ailing and that sadly ladies were usually unable to achieve their heart's desire, but that I must never give up hope. In the meantime, I simply had to accept the arrangement and do my duty. And in the few weeks I had until the wedding, Grandmother was commissioned to talk to me about how life as a wife might be; as usual, Mama simply did not have much time to spend with

48

me. But now I was confronted by my lover and my husband's son – and in this cold, draughty castle I had come to loathe.

"I must leave now; your husband will be returning soon. I shall tell my servants to get the horses ready. If this younger man recognised me, Lachlan Cattanach might too."

My breath caught as I looked up at his clear blue eyes, but I knew there was nothing I could do. The servants were out of sight, and I reached up and stroked his face for one last time, closing my eyes as he kissed me. Then he yanked his cowl down over his head and retreated, bound for the stables. I watched him leave, biting my lip as I tried to stem my tears, then I walked up the stairs to the Great Hall where I knew Hector Mor would be waiting.

"Ah, Catherine," he said, his smile gone. His expression was stern. "I am sent ahead by your husband to say he will be back tonight and that you are to lay on a feast."

"Why?" I was still close to tears and now my sadness deepened.

"We have never caught so many wolves. He wants to celebrate with his kinsmen."

I nodded, realising I now felt neither anger nor despair, I simply felt indifferent to everything. All I wanted was Archibald back, in my arms.

Hector Mor began to leave, then turned at the door. "The priest – I am sure I know him. Was he at Inveraray?"

I swallowed. "Yes," I answered carefully.

"But he didn't look like the priest Lachlan described. He said the man who'd performed the marriage ceremony had been so short and stout, he could barely move."

"We have more than one chaplain at Inveraray, Hector Mor." He was looking at me strangely. "Is there anything else?"

He smiled – an odd, knowing smile, then bowed and left, slamming the wooden door. I turned to the fire and watched the wood glow then darken as the breeze whirled and the cold stone walls closed in around me.

*

After the usual difficult meeting with the cook about the preparations, I sent a servant to ask Lorna to bring her musicians with her later to play. At least my husband might be happy about something. Love of music – particularly the Duart harpists – was probably the one and only thing we had in common. I spent the rest of the afternoon in bed, feigning a headache, trying not to sob into my pillow.

Three days he had been here, only three, but how blissful they had been. Archibald and I had revelled in each other's company and in our bodies. I did not even care if I looked dishevelled when I returned from the woods, always a short while before him in case we were seen emerging together. My love had been rekindled to new heights, but now he was gone I must think only of the illicit joys of the past; I could not contemplate a future without him.

I was thinking I ought to get Elspeth to fetch my gown for the evening when I heard the howls and barks of the hounds beneath my window. Soon I heard the thud of steps on the stone stairs and the door swung open. Lachlan swept in and headed towards the bed.

"Catherine, how fortuitous that you are in bed. I was hoping that we might celebrate here first, before the dinner." He began to unbuckle his belt. Dear God, he was going to get into bed with me.

He stopped disrobing and turned his head. "You organised the harpist to play this evening, I presume?"

"She has a name, Lachlan. She is called Lorna. And yes, she is coming with her brother to play for us." I propped myself up on my elbows as something occurred. "I thought you were going to the Treshnish Islands, not wolf hunting."

"Both are possible, Catherine. Your husband is exceedingly versatile, as you know," he said, smirking.

I turned over towards the pillow so I did not have to look upon his large, hairy body as he undressed, and I did not see his face as I shut my eyes. I could only smell the sweat of several days' hunting and God knows what else. And even from a distance, his breath smelled of raw meat. I sighed and rolled over, as any dutiful wife would have done. I had no choice.

Chapter 11

1519
Catherine

I walked barefoot along the beach at Duart, looking out to sea. It was an unusually calm day, hardly a breath of wind, and not a cloud in the sky. I hoicked up my skirts a little to paddle in the cold water, then sat down on the rocks. A high-pitched wail made me look up. There was a red-throated diver high above me and I watched as it swooped towards the water then dived in with a great splash. I kept peering over to the spot it had dived into, but did not see it coming up for air.

"They can stay under the water for quite a while, my Lady."

I turned around to see Lorna standing behind me, a basket on her hips.

"I've never seen that before," I said, turning back to the spot where the bird had entered the water. Soon it emerged, shook itself off and flew away.

"That's quite some noise it makes too."

"Only at this time of year. It's when they breed."

"Oh, I see." I smiled up at Lorna, who sat down on a rock beside me. We often met here or in the woods, and one day she even played her clarsach for me. Once again, I was moved beyond words. I was mesmerised as I watched her pluck the strings, using the pad of her finger to pull the string into her hand. The skill she has is surely a gift from God.

"Lorna, I get so much pleasure listening to you play music for me, but I do nothing for you. Is there anything that I could do to help in any way?"

"My Lady, it would not be proper for you to do something for me."

She turned away, watching a couple of dippers preening their feathers on the rocks, then bent over, sticking her forefinger in the wet sand. She wiggled her finger to and fro, making patterns and figures of eight in the sand, then looked up.

"Could you write my name in the sand?"

I leaned down and spelled out Lorna with my finger in large letters. "It'd be better with a stick of some sort."

She was staring at the letters. "I've never seen my name written out. It's a grand mixture of loops and circles." She ran over to the trees at the edge of the beach. I watched her kick the leaves then bend down. She sprinted back to me, holding a twig aloft.

"How does yours look, my Lady?"

I drew my name in the sand, did hers again with the twig, then asked her which she preferred.

"Why does yours have that dot not joined up?"

"It's the dot above a letter i." I frowned at her as an idea formed. "I could teach you some basic letters, Lorna, if you'd like, and perhaps you might be able to read – then even write yourself?"

She gasped. "That would be wonderful, but it would not be permitted for someone like me. And a girl."

I snorted. "No one need know."

"Not even your husband?"

"Why should he?"

"He can be quite... traditional."

"Yes, but as much as I hate to admit it, also honourable." I smiled. "And I don't think this would trouble him."

"Honourable is a strong word, my Lady," said Lorna, glowering.

I could not believe I was defending my husband's character. "Has he offended you, Lorna?"

"Not directly, no," she said, looking down again at the sand. "Not really. But anyway, it's not important."

"Very well. So let's start down here on your letters the next time the weather's fine."

"Thank you," she said, smiling, staring at her name. She got to her feet then watched me rise carefully from the slippery rock. I was nervous I might fall.

She was looking at me with a strange expression.

"When is the baby due, my Lady?"

My mouth gaped and I felt my cheeks flush. "How did you know? No one knows, only my maid." I was cross; how dare she betray my confidence? "Elspeth should not have told anyone."

"No, no one told me, truly. I just know by looking at you."

"But I am not yet fat."

"My father used to say I had the gift his mother had. I can see things. Not all things, of course – but some things I can."

"Well, since you guessed, then yes, it is true." I smiled. "I think it is about four more months till the baby arrives. I spread my fingers over my belly, which still hardly showed, under my swathes of skirt. I was nervous yet excited about this tiny baby growing inside me.

"Oh, Lorna, with your gift of sight, can you tell if it's a boy or a girl?"

"Easily. There's no doubt, my Lady. It's a girl."

I beamed. That was perfect. I would have my baby and then – since I had not produced a boy to ensure the dynasty continued should anything happen to Hector Mor – I could escape back to Inveraray with my baby. Lachlan could take another wife to give him a boy.

Lorna began to ease her knife under the limpets to deftly scrape them off the rock, before throwing them into her basket. Without looking at me she whispered, "Will you be telling your husband soon?"

I swallowed. Part of me had realised I would have to do that soon, but of course I still hoped above hope that somehow Archibald would return. That was why I had not repeated to Lachlan that I wanted to return to Inveraray. It was easier to see Archibald here than at my family home, surrounded by all my sisters and brothers, and of course my mother, who would not be happy I'd come home without my husband at all.

Most of all, I hoped the baby was Archibald's, but how could I know? Presumably if it was pale and fair- or red-haired, then it was a Campbell; if it was swarthy and dark-haired, a Maclean. Would it matter though, since it was my child?

"I plan to tell him once he returns from the Council on Islay. That should be any day now."

"He will surely be overjoyed, my Lady".

I shrugged. Providing my husband with a child was the very purpose of this marriage contract. But now I was with child, I wanted to keep it for myself – I did not want my baby to be a pawn, a pledge between the Macleans and the Campbells.

"Yes, I am sure he will be, Lorna." I trailed my fingers in a rock pool at my side. "What is this seaweed called?"

"That is carragheen. It makes a delicious pudding, very nutritious. Cook will probably prepare some for you when you are lying-in."

I continued to drag my hand through the water in the pool while Lorna finished slicing the limpets off the rock.

"My husband told me your father was the best of all the harpists. Did he teach you from quite young?"

She nodded and we both turned to watch a large black guillemot soar high above our heads, then fly towards the far shore, where it landed on the rocks and preened its feathers. "He was the best clarsach player and the best teacher."

"And you told me he died at Flodden too."

"Yes." She let out a long sigh. She picked up her basket and stood up. "Did they bring your father home?"

I swallowed. "His men brought his body back to us, yes. He was laid to rest in the family plot. Where is your father buried on Mull?"

"He is not. He was left there on the battlefield, for the corbies to peck at," she muttered, scowling. She took a deep breath.

"Right, I am going back to my house now. Will you accompany me, my Lady?"

I got to my feet, glancing at her face and realising the conversation about her father was over. I went to join her, walking alongside as she pointed out the various plants and birds on the way.

At the edge of the woods was a purple flowering plant I had never noticed before. "What is this one, Lorna?" I said, reaching out to touch the petals of the hooded flowers.

"Don't touch it," she shouted, yanking my hand away. "It's poisonous."

I stood and looked at the pretty plant. "Really?"

"Yes, it's called Wolfsbane, though I've heard it also called Monkshood as it looks like a monk's cowl." She turned to me. "Like the holy man who stayed at Duart for a while a few months ago. Like his cowl."

How much did Lorna know if she had this gift of sight? Had she seen us together?

"Ah, I didn't know that. How poisonous is it?"

She shook her head. "It's so lethal, you don't even have to make it into a potion or a tea; even just smelling the flowers or brushing against it can kill."

"Well, well – thank goodness I know. Thank you, Lorna, for warning me to stay away from it." I turned towards the castle. "Shall I see you again soon? Will you come and play at supper when my husband returns?"

She nodded, gave a small bow and strode off through the hazel trees towards her house. I lingered by the Wolfsbane and stared at it, hardly believing something so pretty and harmless looking could be so deadly.

*

"So, Catherine, I imagine you will want to hear all about my stay on Islay. I don't suppose you have done much since I have been away?"

My husband sprawled on his chair opposite me while the servants hurried about, stoking up the fire and topping up his drink.

"I've done the same as usual, Lachlan. Just walking on the beach, watching Lorna harvest her family's food, and waiting." I yawned, knowing he was about to tell me all about his time on Islay, so fixed on an interested face. But then I decided to be bold and tell him my news.

"Actually, there has been something of interest I've discovered while you have been away."

He raised his head from a leg of some disgusting seabird, and I watched, trying not to gag, as he wiped the grease running down his chin on his sleeve. "What's that, then?"

"Certain things about me have begun to change." I intended to draw this out, perhaps even have some fun.

"In what way?" He looked at my hair, which was hanging loose, in thick coils around my shoulders. I no longer cared to coif my hair for him. He then stared at my bosom and waist and then suddenly his eyes grew big. "Are you with child, Catherine?"

"I am, Lachlan." I tried to suppress a victorious smile.

He closed his eyes and leaned his head back. "At last! What joyous news!" He stood up and clapped his hands. "Bring more ale!" he bellowed to the servants, who ran towards him at once.

He turned to me and grabbed my hand. "When? Do you know?"

I shook my head. How wonderful it felt to be the one in control, for once. "I think the baby will arrive in about four months, but dates are always difficult to predict as I'm sure you know from your kinswomen." I could not bring myself to mention his mistress, the mother of Hector Mor.

"We shall have Cook prepare your favourite dishes. Now, what was it you like? Mutton? Heathcock? What else are you partial to, Catherine?"

I smiled. "I shall speak to her myself, thank you."

"Your mother. When shall she arrive?"

"She does not know yet."

"Then I shall send word."

"Or perhaps I can write to her myself?"

He opened his mouth as if to contradict me, then shut it and smiled. "Of course, you are so clever, Catherine, reading and writing as you do. Yes, please do that."

He drank deeply from his refilled goblet. "My son shall unite the Macleans and the Campbells once and for all."

I was about to suggest the possibility of a daughter but decided to say nothing.

We both turned as the door opened and Lorna entered with her musicians.

"Ah, wonderful," he said, beaming. "Just what is required. Play on! Only celebratory songs if you will, no laments. For tonight, we are glad!"

I looked at Lorna when she lifted her head up from her deferential bow and she smiled, knowing. Soon, she began to pluck her clarsach and I leant back to listen, shutting my eyes which were for once not streaming with tears of melancholy, but dry-eyed in contentment. I had just four more months of assuming the prevailing role in this relationship. And it felt good.

Part 2

Chapter 12

1519
Catherine

It was not long till my baby was due. And as I had anticipated, Mama could not come. My sisters Isabel and Jean were having babies at the same time, and they lived nearer. All the women at Inveraray were convinced that Jean was having twins as she was so enormous, Mama wrote. She said she could send my youngest sister Mary to be with me, but the storms had begun, and she was still too young to travel such a long way by herself, even with servants.

I lay in my bed, the wolfskins over the blankets at the foot of the bed, to keep my feet warm as the cold winds howled around the castle walls and the chill air seeped through every crevice in the stone. I thought of Mama giving birth at Inveraray Castle twelve times. Since I was fourth youngest, I only remember my sister Mary being born, for I was about five at the time. But I do recall the celebrations and joy throughout the castle when the safe delivery of another child was announced, even if after the first much-heralded four boys, came eight girls. We younger children were of course not allowed to attend the celebratory feasts, but I remember Grandmother coming to tell me and my sisters about the new baby, Mary, and how we were to be permitted to visit Mama in her bedchamber to see our new sister.

Marion was a toddler and Ellen only a baby herself, but Grandmother brought us all to the room, which I vividly recall being warm and brightly lit with candles whose flames did not flicker as wildly they do here in this draughty castle. Mama's room was so snug, I remember wanting to get into bed with her and nestle in beside her warm body. But of course that was not allowed. Grandmother held my hand and pushed me gently forward when it was my turn to kiss both Mama and the baby. I thought Mary looked rather odd, with wisps of pale ginger hair on an otherwise bald head. Her ears stuck out and her chin was pointed, but her nose was the prettiest thing about her. I cannot say I was impressed at how she looked. Grandmother used to say that all babies, being a gift of God, are beautiful, but I recall thinking that God was perhaps having a bad day when Mary was born. Bless her, she was not a bonny baby.

I felt a movement in my belly and gently caressed the baby which was turning over inside me. It was such a strange feeling, and yet somehow reassuring. I looked around the cold, stark room from my bed and saw the maid sitting by the door, looking bored.

"Can you put more logs on the fire please, Elspeth? It's so cold in here."

She jumped to her feet and went to the fire, where she tried to make the frigid room a little less chilly. I turned to the books by my bed and opened the same one I had read over and over. Despite the fact I had nothing in common with Lachlan's elderly cousin Jean, she had brought me some books, knowing I would otherwise be bored. She told me she did not understand why my mother could not come, even though I mentioned the long sea voyage and the storms and my sisters' babies many times.

As I began to read, a thought occurred.

"Elspeth, could you come here?" The girl raced over and stood, looking as nervous as a kitten. Even after working for me all this time, she still hardly spoke and always looked as if someone was about to hit her. I had tried so hard since I arrived to make her less anxious, to no avail.

"Could you send Donnie up here? I need him to send a message for me."

She ran off and I shivered as I pulled my shawl around me. Soon the cook's son Donnie arrived and stood respectfully at the door. "Your Ladyship?"

"Donnie, can you go to the harpist's house and ask Lorna to come and play for me?"

He looked startled. "Should I ask his Lordship first?"

I sighed. "No, just go and do it!"

He bowed and as I listened to his footsteps fade on the ancient stone steps, I regretted shouting at him. That would get straight back to all the servants via his mother, Agnes, who already seemed to loathe me. But really, sometimes it was as if I had no authority in my own house. I don't remember when Mama asked a servant for something, that they queried her right to give commands herself without Papa's approval.

*

After I had dined, Lorna arrived. She set her instrument at the door and came towards the bed. She gave a short nod and smiled.

"You look well, my Lady. Will the baby be here soon?"

"I hope so – I can't stand much more of this, just lying here in bed with no one for company but the servants."

"And your husband?"

"Oh," I said, "yes, well, he only comes once a day, if that. He says he is far too busy, but what he does is a mystery. I can tell he is itching to leave on an expedition or go hunting, but he stays. Some sort of husbandly duty, I suppose."

"I just saw him, he looked pleased I was coming to play for you. He said he should have thought of that himself."

I patted the bed. "Come and tell me what you have been doing, Lorna."

She laughed but remained standing. "The same as usual, my Lady. Going to the woods and the beach to forage for our food, taking care of the house and my little brother. I've been practising all those letters you taught me last time we were on the beach, but I always do them just before the tide comes in, so it's all washed away. Imagine if anyone knew!"

"And do you think you've learned them all now?"

She nodded. "I hope so. I've also been practising my clarsach and I have played at a couple of gatherings your husband has had in the Great Hall. Apart from that..."

"What? He's had dinners – company – while I am marooned up here?"

She shrugged and asked me how I was feeling about the birth.

"Well, since there is a good chance I shall die, I'm not looking forward to it, not at all. But I do feel I want the baby to come out soon so that, should God spare me, I can begin to live some sort of normal life again."

"Is it Betty Maclean who will deliver the baby?"

"Yes, she arrives at Duart tomorrow, so I do hope the baby can wait till then. She is said to be the most proficient midwife on Mull."

She nodded and I pointed to her clarsach. "Never mind that, though. Play for me now please, Lorna."

She settled herself on a stool by the bed and began to play. At first the music was lilting and high, uplifting and beautiful but then, as the melodies changed into the old laments, the music became slower, more haunting, ethereal. I closed my eyes and listened to the notes and wept. Through wet eyes, I saw her look anxiously at me. She stopped playing, but I gestured for her to carry on. And as an overwhelming feeling of melancholy came upon me, instead of forceful kicks from within, I felt nothing. It was as if the baby was dreading coming into this troubled world her mother inhabited.

Chapter 13

1519
Catherine

The baby came late. The midwife said every day for three weeks it should be today. In the end, Lachlan was not even at Duart Castle when I delivered my beautiful, chubby little girl. The midwife said for such a big baby and for my first, I did well, in labour for only a few hours. So now I lay in bed gazing at her full head of thick black hair and her perfect, peachy skin, feeling only indescribable joy. When the wet nurse took her from my arms to feed, I insisted she stay right beside my bed so I could continue to stare at her in wonder. I had given birth to this little helpless baby and for once I felt nothing but happiness.

"In the absence of your husband, are you intending to send word to your family at Inveraray Castle yourself, or do you wish to wait until he has decided on a name?" the nurse asked. "I could ask for writing materials to be brought to your bed, my Lady and I could find someone to write if you dictated?"

"I can write for myself, thank you. So yes, I shall write to my family as soon as possible and the name can wait for another missive. But can you also ask downstairs if anyone knows when my husband might return?"

She nodded and headed for the door, her bulky frame swinging as she stepped, while the maids bustled around me, being more attentive than they ever had been in the two long years I had lived at the castle. I was beginning to understand what cheer a baby brings to everyone. Even the fire was stoked up constantly with wood, instead of me having to always nag and pester.

"Could you also ask them to send Lorna up with her instrument?"

The nurse frowned.

"She is the family harpist; the servants know where she lives. I should like her to play for the baby." I beamed. "Thank you." I watched her grab the rail and start to walk gingerly down the steep stone stairs.

I leaned against the bolster and lifted the goblet to my lips, sipping as I looked at the baby sucking noisily beside me. Her dark hair was certainly like Lachlan's and Hector Mor's, but she was thankfully not as swarthy as them. I closed my eyes and began to pray, muttering to myself, thanking God for giving me not only a beautiful baby girl, but also the product of true love. Please, God, she'll grow to look like Archibald.

*

Around a week later, the door creaked open and I peered up from my bed into the gloom. It must have been early morning for it was still quite dark and there were no candles lit. It could not possibly be my husband, for he always bounded in like a wild animal, bulky and strident.

I shut my eyes, thinking perhaps one of the servants was stoking up the fire, but soon there was a whisper at my side. Before I even opened my eyes, I could smell the stale wine on his fetid breath.

"Catherine, you have done well. Our daughter is bonny and fat." He kissed my forehead and in the dim light I could make out an expression I had never seen before: certainly not love – neither of us had ever felt that about each other – but something that resembled tenderness, perhaps.

"Thank you, Lachlan. So you've seen her?"

He beamed. "Yes, and she has such a Maclean look about her. Of course, it is unfortunate our firstborn is not a boy, but there is time, plenty of time."

I winced and sat up in my bed.

"Are you recovering well, Catherine? They said it was quick for a firstborn, and one so big."

"I am fine, thank you. Just a little sore, but that will pass. Nurse and the servants have been unnaturally courteous and kind. Even Agnes came up yesterday to see her and to ask what I should like to eat." I tried not to look surprised when Agnes asked how I was, in such a kindly manner. Gone was the sullen woman I always met in the kitchen; this was a happy woman who was desperate to hold the baby.

Lachlan nodded. "It's what they all wanted here at Duart – new life. Though how long she will live here, I will consider carefully."

"What do you mean, Lachlan?"

He shrugged. "There are customs, you know, traditions to be adhered to."

He held his hand up to my face as I tried to speak.

"But all that is for another time. Now let us first discuss the name of our daughter." He settled himself on the end of the bed. "And then you can let your Campbell family in Inveraray hear the news."

"Oh, I've already written to Mama and my brother to tell them about our daughter. I said I would let them know about her name soon."

He frowned. "That should have been my role, as Laird of Duart, to let the Earl of Argyll know."

"He is my brother, Lachlan." I sighed. "Besides, I had no idea when you were going to come back. In fact, at first I presumed you were in the Treshnish Islands, but then I was told you were on Islay for the Assembly."

"Indeed I was, and it was there I decided what name our baby – whether boy or girl – would be given."

"Well," I said, wanting to have my say. "In the Campbell family, the girls' names are usually Margaret, Isabel, Janet, Jean,

Marion, Ellen, Mary – and of course my mother is Elizabeth. And I rather like names such as..."

"Stop! I am quite aware of your family names, but I think you are forgetting who the baby's father is, therefore who chooses the name." He was scowling.

"I just thought we might give her something traditional, with perhaps my name or my mother's as second names?"

He looked at me as if I were a child; though, compared to him I was. He looked even older as the grey light of dawn seeped through the narrow windows.

"On Islay, there is a name which is very special as it was the name of the wife of the first Lord of the Isles."

"But we live on Mull. Why would you want an Islay name?" I scooped my thick hair up behind my head with both hands as I was suddenly very hot. I sat up straight.

"It is not a specifically Islay name, it is a noble name of both the islands and the Highlands. I have a fondness for Islay and hope that our daughter will have a connection with the island too."

"But..." I held out my hands, not understanding.

"She will be called Amie Marion Maclean." He grinned. "There. Doesn't it sound good when said aloud?"

"Amie, like the French for friend?"

"Yes, and Marion like one of your sisters." A smile played around his lips. He had never taken any interest in any of my sisters, so I was surprised he even remembered their names.

"Amie." I tried the name, even though I had never heard of it. "It's pretty, it will suit her well." I shrugged. What else could I do? The choice of name, like so much else, was not in my power. All I had to do was provide my husband with a healthy child and this I had fulfilled admirably; even if my greatest wish was that the baby was not his.

Chapter 14

1520
Catherine

I was coming down the stairs from the nursery, having helped the nurse put Amie down for her afternoon nap, when I nearly bumped into a maid who was rushing upwards.

"What are you doing, child? Why are you running?"

"They said to tell you the countess is here and you've to come now!"

Countess? Surely my mother had not deigned to visit? It certainly would not be my brother the earl's wife, for she was having another baby any day.

I followed the girl and entered the Great Hall. There in the corner nook sat my grandmother and my youngest sister Mary. I ran over to them and bent down to hug them both.

"You came! Thank you, thank you so much. I thought Mama said no one from Inveraray could possibly make the journey?"

"My daughter-in-law sometimes exaggerates. The weather is set fair for at least a fortnight and Mary and I have had such a pleasant journey – haven't we, child?"

My sister looked still very young, though she must be twelve or even thirteen by now. My grandmother was more lined than I remember, and her hair had flecks of white, but she must be nearly sixty. Tears of joy ran down my cheeks. I grabbed Grandmother's hands and kissed them. "I cannot wait for you to meet my baby. She is so beautiful."

Grandmother winked. "Did I not tell you all babies are beautiful, Catherine?"

A cough alerted me to the servants standing by. That was one thing I had hopefully changed during my time here at Duart Castle. The staff hovered by, ready to attend to our needs, rather than our continually having to ask.

"Bring some refreshments and ask Jeannie to prepare beds for my grandmother and sister."

"It is not warm in here, is it?" my grandmother said, shivering.

"Oh, sorry, the fire was blazing earlier but in this room there are always variations on less cold, never warm."

"Is your husband at home?"

"Yes, he is out at present, but you will meet him over supper."

She was studying my face. "Is he delighted with his child?"

"Yes, he really is. Since she's now six months old and can react and smile, he seems to adore making her laugh. Simple things seem to please him."

She gave me an odd look as the servants arrived and noisily set down goblets and pitchers of wine and bannocks.

"This doesn't look like the bannock at Inveraray, Catherine," my sister said, pointing to the grey beremeal rounds on the ashet.

"There's a lot here that is different from home, Mary." I poured the wine then beamed at my guests. "Tell me all about everyone at Inveraray then I'll take you up to meet Amie."

*

"My wife tells me you can only stay a week or so, Lady Campbell?"

Lachlan was on his best behaviour and had even washed his face before he came into the Great Hall to meet Grandmother and Mary. I had wanted Hector Mor to join us, but he was away again. I felt he had been avoiding me since Archibald's visit.

"Yes, one of my other granddaughters, Catherine's sister Janet, has just given birth and the christening is next weekend – Mary and I intend to be back for that. As you know, we hold rather magnificent gatherings at Inveraray." She looked around as if amazed that supper was only laid for the four of us.

"Yes, I do indeed." He gulped down his ale then raised his eyes upwards as if thinking of something.

"Is it your usual priest who performs the family baptisms? Presumably not the one who was here?"

My heart stopped. I knew where this might lead. Hector had obviously told him about his suspicions over the holy man he had met that day.

"I told you, Lachlan, we have more than one priest at Inveraray." I lifted my heavy hair off my shoulders, suddenly feeling rather hot.

My grandmother narrowed her grey eyes as she looked towards me, but she said nothing.

"Father Thomas is really fat and very funny, and he always drinks all the wine, Mama says," Mary said, snickering.

"Behave yourself, child. That is not talk for company." Grandmother held her head high. "We do indeed have more than one priest in attendance at the castle." She sipped her wine. "Now, Lord Maclean, let me congratulate you on your beautiful daughter. And such a pretty name, one I have not heard of."

"She is a joy, Lady Campbell. And looks so like a Maclean. All my relatives swear she is like my mother, who sadly died far too young."

"Well, she certainly is less pale of skin and her hair doesn't look as if it will become red like her mother's, but her eyes are the same shape as Catherine's." She shook her head and laughed. "But the main thing is that she is hale and hearty."

Lachlan raised his glass. "That is so true."

There was a clatter as the door opened and the musicians began to set up. "Catherine, I asked the harpist to play tonight, as a celebration. I thought that would please you?"

"Thank you, Lachlan," I muttered, wishing he were being more the brute I was used to and less the kindly, well-mannered gentleman before me so that Grandmother could see how I suffered.

"I notice you have a woman playing for you. Most unusual," Grandmother said.

"Yes, she is too good to hide. She used to keep away from us, behind the screens, but my wife pointed out how talented she was and how she ought to be treated as well as her father, my hereditary harpist, was."

"Catherine has always had strong views. Some of them are, however, eminently sensible." She took my hand and winked at me.

Mary was fiddling with her shawl and yawning.

"Mary, are you tired? I'll have someone take you up to your room?"

Grandmother stood up. "No, it's fine, Catherine, I will go up early too, even though the music is so soothing and pleasing to the ear."

A servant ran to pull back her chair and Grandmother took my sister by the arm.

"Oh, just one thing I forgot to ask," she said, leaning towards my husband. "The choice of names: Amie has been explained to me, with its rather tenuous Islay connection. But what about Marion? As you know, that is a Campbell name and Catherine's and Mary's sister has that name. Is it a common name for the Macleans too?"

Lachlan slowly swallowed the lump of fowl he was chewing. "Yes, it is a Maclean name, especially popular on the Treshnish Islands, where many of my kin live."

"I see. Well, it is perfectly charming and suits your daughter. Look after her well." My grandmother beamed at us. "Both of you. Keep her close."

And she swished out of the room, Mary at her side.

Chapter 15

1520

Catherine

"My dear Catherine, I am so pleased we came to see you and meet your beautiful daughter." My grandmother and I were walking down from the cliffs to the jetty for their boat back across to the mainland. It was a calm day and as we passed beneath the castle, we saw plumes of smoke from the tiny cottages blowing straight up towards the cloudless sky. Mary was skipping in front, like the child she still was. Perhaps it was the fact she was the last of twelve children, but she was so immature. The thought that Mama would try to marry her off in two or three years was terrifying.

"I'll miss you both," I said, pulling her to me as we walked arm in arm. It's been so good to be able to catch up on the news of everyone back home."

"But you do know this is your home now?"

I said nothing, but she continued, drawing nearer. "Also, Catherine, I have said nothing more about what your husband said on that first night, but am I correct in thinking that you have already had one visitor from Inveraray?"

I glanced at Grandmother. I never could lie to her; to my sisters and my mother, yes, but not to her.

I nodded.

"Be very careful, Catherine. You put into jeopardy not only the sanctity of marriage, but the bond between the Macleans and the Campbells."

"Can I ask you one thing, please?"

"Go ahead."

"Is he – Archibald – is he married yet?"

73

She shook her head. "He must no longer be of interest to you. And yes, his marriage contract was drawn up with some haste, for his father had been very unwell. I believe the ceremony was some six or seven months ago."

I opened my mouth to speak, but decided silence was best. She drew me into a deep embrace at the boat and whispered, "It may seem hard, but Lachlan Cattanach is your husband and Duart is your home now. The most important thing is the safety and health of your child. Do not do anything to risk his loyalty and her security." She kissed my cheek. "Now farewell, Catherine."

She took the boatman's hand and stepped into the boat, and Mary followed, waving coyly.

I stood watching them sail away from Duart and off into the wide stretch of water. I took a deep breath. I would not cry – I was determined not to. My life was here now. I had my baby, and she was my family. I looked up at the flock of oyster catchers swarming noisily above and once again wished I could fly. I watched them as they landed gracefully on the rocks near the shore, their red beaks only visible now they were wading in the water. I gave one last wave to the boat, a tiny speck on the horizon, already passing the tiny rocky islet in the middle of the Firth of Lorne, then returned to the castle and went straight up to the nursery to see my Amie.

*

I held her on my knee, tickling her chubby little chin and making her laugh, while thinking that there was surely nothing in the whole world as precious as the gift of a baby. I was just about to hand her back to the nurse for her nap when the door creaked open. I turned around to see my husband standing there, his pock-marked face breaking into a smile as his eyes came to rest upon Amie.

"Shut the door, Lachlan. It's cold out there," I said, quietly, so as not to alter the sleepy expression on my daughter's face.

He walked towards me and bent down to stroke her soft cheeks. I looked from the baby to the man and tried, as usual, to see no resemblance at all. It was always there, but I continued to hope that things would change, that over time her dark hair would become blonde and her skin paler.

"Is she going down for a sleep?" he whispered, and I marvelled at the tenderness he had come to show since her birth. It still made him no less repugnant to me in every other way, but at least for now, there was this.

"Yes, but she'll be up this afternoon. Did you say you are going away in three days' time?"

He nodded. "Yes, and there are things I wish to discuss with you. I shall be in the Great Hall when she is put down. Come and join me." He planted a gentle kiss on her dark curls and left the room, silent as a mouse; in her presence, the wild animal in him was gone.

I handed her over to the nurse, caressed Amie's warm cheek, then headed downstairs, closing the heavy wooden door quietly behind me. As I trod the worn stone steps, I thought about Grandmother and my sister, how they would soon be passing the southern tip of Lismore and heading for the shore before the long horse ride to Inveraray. The long journey did not seem to faze Grandmother. She was remarkable for her age – she told me she was 56 – but still so full of life and vigour. I know even she disapproved of me asking about Archibald and I felt desperate that he was now married. I had not even asked who his bride was – I could not bring myself to, I was so heartbroken on hearing the news.

"Ah, Catherine, come over and sit here by the fire with me," a voice bellowed, and I crossed over to join my husband on a chair at the hearth.

"Isn't she a bonny baby? I have high hopes for her."

I laughed. "Is it not a little early to start contemplating who she will marry when she is only six months old?"

"I am not thinking of marriage yet, Catherine. I am concentrating first on her foster family."

"What?"

"Her foster family. She will be going away to a foster family for seven or eight years before returning to us already well versed in those skills girls must learn and..."

"What are you talking about? We are her family, I shall supervise her education and her upbringing, just as Mama did with my sisters and me. I am her mother."

"And I am her father. And I have decided her foster parents will oversee her upbringing for the first few years."

I stood up and glowered at him, trying to keep my hands behind me for fear I would strike him.

"I don't understand. Explain what exactly you mean, Lachlan."

He gestured for me to sit down, and I perched on the edge of the seat, jaws clenched.

"You have clearly not heard of Celtic fosterage."

"When a child becomes an orphan and is taken on by a kinsman's family?"

He shook his head. "No. Under fosterage terms, a contract is drawn between two noble families whereby a child is brought up by a family who is not his or her birth family. They are usually aged seven or eight, but sometimes babies are given foster families too."

I felt an icy chill flood through my body, and I stared at him, eyes wide, terrified where this conversation was heading.

"It is a custom among clan chiefs – especially amongst those under the Lordship of the Isles, so perhaps less known to your people in Argyll – to consolidate and forge pacts between families. The child remains with its foster family for a specified number of years then is returned to its own parents. And in so doing, there is a close bond – surely no stronger link between two families, not even through marriage."

None of this made sense, but I was so overcome, I could not even speak. He continued.

"Fostered boys learn skills such as the art of battle and swordsmanship, but also – as well as girls – poetry and playing musical instruments such as the harp.

The bond created by foster child and foster family can be great and these affectionate links are hopefully maintained for life."

I felt faint and gestured to a servant to bring me wine. Once I had the goblet in my hand, I gulped it down.

"As you know, in a few days' time, I leave for Islay. As well as attending Hector Mor's wedding, my main purpose is of course to be at the Council, but..."

"So Hector Mor's marriage will take place soon?" I welcomed the change to the conversation; perhaps Lachlan would forget about this ridiculous idea of fosterage.

"Yes, it is all arranged. He marries Mary Macdonald next week. They will live some of their time at Dunyvaig Castle on Islay, but of course he will continue to do my bidding here at Duart when required."

I was still considering that news when my husband continued. "While on Islay I shall also be completing negotiations with Mary's father, Alexander Donald Macdonald, for his fostering of our Amie. My ancestor, Lachlan Lubanach Maclean, married John of Islay's daughter Mary Macdonald some 150 years ago and it was because of that marriage the Macleans were given Duart Castle." He smiled, as if what he was telling me was normal. "And so, this fostering arrangement will continue the bond between the Macdonalds of Islay and the Macleans of Duart."

I was so shocked; I still could not speak. My mouth gaped open, and my heart seemed to stop.

Then I came to my senses. "No!" I shouted. I could see the servants' horrified faces as I bellowed at my husband, leaning towards his smug face. "I will not allow this!"

Lachlan shrugged. "It is all arranged. And besides, as I said earlier, I am her father. I am the one who decides. When I was on Islay the last time, we made provisional plans, depending on whether it was a boy or girl."

"And what difference would it have made if it had been a boy?"

"None. I might have waited until he was a little older, but possibly not."

I started to remonstrate again, and he held up his hand in front of my face.

"After I've undertaken this visit to Finlaggan, Amie will stay here at Duart till she is about a year old, then I shall have Hector Mor take her over with the nurse and her own servants. We shall bring her back here again when she is seven or eight, though I may choose to see her when I am over on Islay on business. They are one of the most noble families on Islay and it is an excellent contract; of course, we need to give a number of cattle and in return we are given cows and bulls, so…"

"Cattle? For my precious baby?" I was yelling but did not care. "This will happen over my dead body!" My fists were clenched in fury. I wanted to kill him.

"It is not your decision, Catherine. It is mine." His ugly face remained void of emotion. "She is my daughter and the negotiations have already been made. Whenever she is weaned, she will be on her way to Islay."

I jumped to my feet, knocking the chair over in my haste and spilling the last of the wine in my goblet. I ran out of the room, through the solid wooden door and started down the steps with heavy dread. By the foot of the stairs, I knew what I had to do: I must find Lorna immediately. Once in the courtyard, I slowed myself down to a steady stride so the servants would not think me mad. Though what I was about to ask Lorna to do for me was not the request of a sane person. As I emerged from the castle walls, I could hear the wolfhounds baying, howling as if closing in for the kill.

Chapter 16

1520

Catherine

"Lorna, Lorna!" I shouted, banging on the flimsy door to her house. I was puffing, having run all the way from the castle entrance to the woods. As I tried to slow my breath down, I tilted my head and heard the music suddenly stop.

There were swift footsteps, then the door opened. Lorna looked at me askance. "What's wrong? Is it the baby?"

"No, she's fine, but..." I gulped, trying to stop myself sobbing.

"Come away in, my Lady," she said, opening the door fully and bowing as I entered.

The room was dim, and smoky from the fire in the middle of the floor. A pot hung over it and there was steam coming from it. The smell was not enticing at all. In a dark corner I could make out the clarsach, laid against the wall. I had looked closely at it the last time Lorna played in the Great Hall and marvelled at the smoothness of the wood, which was willow. Lorna had told me that in some families the harpist's instrument also had carvings of animals and scroll work, but the Macleans preferred simplicity and so hers only had one small carving of a crowberry and its leaves, at the top of the soundboard.

"I must apologise for barging in like this. And in the middle of your harp practice."

"It's fine, I was just going to stop and add an onion to the fulmar in the pot."

I sniffed the air and tried not to grimace.

"Sorry, it's not what you're used to," Lorna said, gesturing round the room before dragging a chair over to me and sitting herself down beside me on a wooden stool.

She peered up at my face and took my hand. "He wants to remove the baby, doesn't he?"

"How do you know?"

"I just know." She was staring at my face. "How long do you have?"

"Well, he said when she's weaned so another few months, but he leaves for Islay in three days to arrange things, so it could be earlier. I just can't believe it. I've never heard of such a barbaric idea – that I should hand over my baby, my own flesh and blood, to complete strangers for years on end." I shook my head.

She shrugged. "I've heard some of the clan chiefs do that."

"Thank God the Campbells do not. We can look after our own quite adequately." I wiped my eyes. "And all for a few cattle and a bond of friendship. It's inhuman."

She patted my knee. "So what are you going to do about it, my Lady?"

I swallowed and leaned towards her. "Poison," I whispered.

Her eyes opened wide. "What?"

"Yes. My husband cannot do this. I will not let him and so I intend to poison him then escape with Amie back to Inveraray." I let out a long breath. Having said the words I had been formulating since he told me his plans, I felt shocked myself, but still determined.

Lorna began to twist a loose ringlet of long black hair around her fingers, head bowed, as she thought. "And you need my help."

It was a statement, not a question, but still, I nodded.

"My grandmother used to make potions from some of the flowers and herbs, mostly to cure, but once I know she did it to poison."

"Really?"

Lorna bent towards me, though there was no one else around to hear.

"There was a groom at the castle who took advantage of her

80

granddaughter – one of my older cousins. He refused to marry her when she discovered she was with child. He was found dead soon after, having spent his last hours sweating and convulsing, then paralysed in agony till his heart stopped." She shrugged. "Not a good death."

"What happened to your grandmother? And your cousin? Were they ever found out?"

She shook her head. "He had done the same thing with several other girls and he was not liked. No one mourned his loss."

I shivered. "So will you help me, Lorna?"

She took a deep breath and turned to the fire, which she jabbed at with a poker till the embers flared and glowed. I bit my lip, saying nothing, until she shifted back towards me. "You know the battle where our fathers were killed."

"Flodden," I said, and she nodded.

"Well, I heard an account from a kinsman of what happened to my father. As family harpist he died alongside the Maclean chief, your husband's father, soon after the king was killed. Your husband's grief was so great he thought only of bringing the body of his father home." She gritted her teeth together. "So when we all gathered in the courtyard of the castle some days later to accept our dead, my father's body was not there. Lachlan Cattanach's men had brought as many of the dead home as they could, but my father's body was not there. When we asked, one of your husband's men said they had tried to find him but had been prevented by your husband. It was his *men* – not him – who tried to get as many of the Maclean bodies home; Lachlan Cattanach only wanted to return here as fast as possible."

"But you play your father's clarsach?" I said softly.

"One of the men found it just as they were leaving. My father must have been separated from it in the turmoil and chaos of the battle."

I swallowed. This did not sound like my husband. For all I hated him, he was loyal to his men; and he was certainly no coward. I thought back to that day in September 1513: though I was young, I remembered the procession of horses with carts full of bloodied corpses rumbling into Inveraray Castle courtyard, the horror of seeing my father's body draped in the Campbell banner. But his men had managed to bring home the bodies of the Campbell harpists as well as their instruments.

"Did you speak to him about it?"

She guffawed. "I was only a child at the time, but the hurt of my family festered for a long time. He asked my grandmother forgiveness on her deathbed; he said he'd done it because he had to get the survivors of the clan home before more were killed. The borderlands were wild, there were thieves everywhere. They'd withstood the artillery fire and the cannons, but then had to ride through the dangerous lands where the reivers lived." She paused and let out a long breath. "We of course understood that he had to get as many of his kinsmen home alive as he could, but to abandon my father so far from home..." She glanced over to her harp. "I just thank God that I have his clarsach and that when I play, I feel he is with me."

She sighed. "Remember I said perhaps your husband was not always honourable? That's what I meant."

She bowed her head as if in prayer and was silent for a while, before looking up. "And so I will help you. Not only because you have started teaching me my letters and you are a fine lady, but also," she paused, "it will go some way to avenge my father's abandonment. My grandmother forgave him and so did the rest of the family, but I can never forgive Lachlan Cattanach for leaving him behind..." her eyes narrowed, "... to be pecked by corbies and eaten by the wolves."

She stood up and walked towards the door. The skies were becoming grey, and the wind was getting up. She frowned as she stood, deep in thought.

"I think we must act soon, before the rain arrives." She pointed at my hands. "Do you have sturdy gloves?"

"My husband has his hawking gloves. I could get those?"

"Do that and bring some sort of bag or receptacle that will not be missed."

"I will. What is your plan?"

She peered out the door and looked up into the gathering clouds. "If you meet me here just before the light fades, I will tell you what we'll do."

I got to my feet and went to join her at the door. "Thank you, Lorna."

I sped through the wood until I caught sight of the castle, then I slowed down to a saunter, as if I had not a worry in the world.

*

I clasped the bag and gloves to my chest and wrapped my shawl tight around my shoulders before tiptoeing down the stairs from the Great Hall. Lachlan was going down to the jetty to supervise the arrival of some supplies from the mainland and on past experience, he invariably was gone a good couple of hours, talking and drinking with his friend the captain – sampling the claret in the shipment – before staggering back up to the castle in the dark. I felt safe for now, and stole out of the castle's main entrance, nodding at the sentry guard on duty as if it were perfectly normal that the mistress would be going out by herself as the light was beginning to fade.

When I reached the woods, I turned around; there was no one visible outside the castle, and I hoped the guards suspected nothing. I ran towards Lorna's house and saw her waiting in the doorway.

"This is what we're going to do, my Lady."

Lorna had a look on her face I could not quite pin down. Was it anger? Or perhaps just determination.

"Have you got the gloves?"

"Yes," I said, handing them to her. She put them on and grinned; they were far too big for her tiny hands.

"Follow me," she said, pulling the door behind her.

"Are you going out for long, Lorna?" a young voice shouted.

"No," she shouted back, presumably to her younger brother. "I'll be back to give you your broth."

She pulled her cape up over her head and strode towards the edge of the wood, where I followed her, still carrying the bag under my shawl. Soon she stopped and peered into the undergrowth. The trees were silhouetted black against the dying light.

"D'you remember I told you this was called Wolfsbane or Monkshood?" she said, pointing to a tall plant with purple flowers. "And I said it was poisonous? Well, this is the one my grandmother used. It's lethal."

I gulped. This was all becoming real. "Is it the flowers you use?"

"You can, but the leaves and roots are most poisonous. I'm going to take some of the root, a few leaves and a handful of flowers too then dry them all and grind them up so you can sprinkle it into his food. What kind of dishes would he eat lots of?"

"Everything." I sighed, remembering how my husband attacked food as if he had been starved all his life.

"Or if I grind it up fine, you could add it to his wine – that might be easier. I think you could also steep some of the flowers in oil and apply it to his skin, but that could be more dangerous to others if he touches someone. Eating or drinking it is best."

I felt I was in a trance, listening to this fatal plan, which started with Lorna and ended with me administering the poison.

"It should take a couple of days to fully dry, so I can grind it up then I'll give some to you in a small vial to use whenever you can. He travels in three or four days, you said?"

I nodded and she turned to look at me. I could just make out her expression in the dying light. Her brows were furrowed; she looked driven, indeed slightly possessed, but it was probably just the darkness descending. Leaves were rustling on the trees in the dark woods behind as the wind got up.

"How will it affect him? Can you tell me what will happen?" My heart was beating so fast, yet I tried to speak slowly, as if everything was normal.

"The effect should be quite quick; he'll start to feel numb then will probably vomit and maybe have difficulty seeing. His chest will start to tighten then his heart will just stop. It shouldn't take long – a few minutes, hopefully."

My eyes were wide as I played out the scene in my head. She nudged me, hard, as if bringing me back to the present. "Hold the bag out wide so the plant doesn't touch you." There was no doubt who was in charge. I was no longer her mistress; she had me in thrall.

I took the bag from under my shawl and held the handles out fully. I watched her uproot a tall plant with the huge gloves. She laid it on the ground then carefully sliced off some of the root with her knife and stripped off some of the leaves. She piled these, with a handful of flowers, into the bag then threw the rest of the plant deep into the woods. Then she grabbed the bag from me.

"I'm going home now, but come back in two nights' time and I can tell you if it's been dry enough and if I've got the powder ready. All being well, it should be, and you can do it just before he is planning to leave."

I nodded, still feeling as if I was in a trance. Lorna was taking control of everything, and I was simply a willing accomplice. More than just willing: I wanted him dead. And soon.

Chapter 17

1520

Catherine

"Try to add it to something creamy or liquid, the same sort of colour," Lorna told me when she gave me the ground up Wolfsbane. It looked so harmless – a dull, greyish powder that she handed to me at her door.

"I washed the outside of the vial thoroughly so you can handle it with your bare hands." She pointed to the stopper in the slim bottle. "Just be sure you don't touch the bottom end of the bung when you remove it."

I took it from her gingerly and put it in one of the fingers of a pair of slim gloves I had brought along. I could carry it unseen in these.

"Thank you, Lorna. I owe you so much." I tried to smile but was still so terrified that what I was about to do could go wrong. I found myself trembling. I had spent much of the morning with my beautiful Amie, playing with her, kissing her dimpled cheeks and tickling her to make her laugh, and this reinforced that this was the only way out. I would not give up my child. Not for anything.

"Once this is done, we'll continue to do our letters on the beach, and everything will be fine and…" I stopped. How could anything possibly be fine after this?

"I'll see you later," Lorna said.

"Oh, are you playing?"

"Yes, he's invited me over with the other musicians, but he might not be around by then, I suppose." She had a steely look in her eyes, and I wished my resolve was as strong as hers. But poor

Lorna had lived a hard and burdensome life – she was used to misery, whereas I had lived a life of luxury and privilege. Something like this was alien to me. Well, it was about time I faced reality. I reminded myself I would do anything for my daughter.

I turned to go, and she pointed to the vial in my glove. "Remember not to touch anything it goes near. Just in case there's any spillage you don't see."

I was nearly out of the woods when I heard her running after me. "I forgot to say, if there's any left, you must get rid of the vial at once."

I hadn't thought of that. "Where should I put it?"

"If I see you tonight, give it to me. Carefully. Wrap it in something. But if that's not possible, then throw it as far away into the sea as you can. From high up on the cliffs."

I nodded and trudged on under the hazel boughs and past the tall ash trees towards the castle. As I emerged, I looked down at the pair of gloves I was carrying in my hand, one finger bulging with the vial. I would have to keep it hidden under my shawl until this evening.

I pulled my shawl around me as I walked past the tiny turf-roofed cottages on the way up to the castle entrance, nodding in response to the people at their doors who bowed respectfully. If only they knew what I was carrying with me.

*

"Are you sure you will need a shawl tonight, my Lady?" Elspeth asked as I grabbed it from her hands. "It is really quite warm, and the fires have been lit for hours."

"I find I am a little chilled, but thank you for your concern."

She stood by the fire, looking at me. I still had to pick up the vial.

"Please could you go and tell the nurse I shall be looking in later to see Amie, before her bedtime."

"But you always do, my Lady," remonstrated the surly girl.

"Just go and do as I ask, will you?" I was feeling so irritable and anxious, I couldn't even try to be civil. I could not plan how this was going to pan out until I had seen the food on the table, which is why I wanted to get downstairs early.

I grabbed my glove, wrapped the shawl around me and headed towards the door. At the sight of the wooden crucifix on the wall by the door I stopped suddenly. Please, God, forgive me for what I am about to do. I stood staring at the cross for a moment, entranced, then shook my head. "But I have no choice," I muttered as I went out, slamming the door.

On entering the Great Hall, I was pleased there was no one there apart from the usual huddle of servants by the door. They scattered as I entered, and I went to inspect the table. I had asked the cook for broth tonight, made with mutton and bulging with barley and kail. He liked broth and I thought that would be the easiest food to stir the powder into. But as I peered at all the dishes, I saw there was also some crowdie, the soft cheese made in the crofts all over the island. Though it had never been served at Inveraray, it was a favourite of my husband's and was often on dinner and breakfast tables here. And I admit, eaten with a barley bannock, it was not unpleasant. Perhaps I could mix some into that as it was creamy, which was what Lorna had suggested. I worried that the servants might become ill too, as they always ate the leftover food from our table – but surely by that time, they would know of the poisoning?

"Ah, Catherine, you are here already." I swivelled around and saw Lachlan at the entrance, a tall wolfhound by his side. "I must go and deal with one of the grooms. He needs disciplining after the way he treated one of my horses. I won't be long."

And off he went, followed by his loyal hound. Right, act now, Catherine, or your chance will be gone!

There were now three servants in the room, one near the table and two by the fire, stoking it with more wood.

"Go and ask the cook for more crowdie," I commanded the

servant at the table. "My husband likes it very much."

And as he ran towards the door, I turned my back on the other two attendants by the fire and removed the vial. I tipped some into the broth and sprinkled a little on top of the crowdie, then mashed it into the soft cheese with a knife that had been placed beside one of the vile roasted seabirds. It would have been easier to disguise the powder in one of those – the smell and taste was so rank, it would be impossible to detect another flavour. But visually, it would not have been difficult to spot. I replaced the stopper, taking care not to touch the end.

A noise behind me made me turn around, quickly secreting the vial first. There was the servant with the new dish of crowdie, which he put in front of the chair I always sat in. Heart thumping, I took my seat and a servant rushed over to fill my wine. I generally drank very little, for my husband's wine is not as refined as those in our cellar at Inveraray, but tonight I needed a drink. I took a gulp and watched the entrance, trying to stop my hands from trembling.

Soon Lachlan arrived, clattering through the door while a flurry of servants hovered nearby. The hound rushed in with him and went to sit in front of the fire, his tongue lolling out of a mouth that was dribbling with saliva.

My husband came to sit opposite me and drank a full goblet, which was immediately refilled.

"I asked the musicians to come tonight, Catherine." He looked towards me and smiled. I smiled back and thought how the last time we both had been in here, I had shouted at him and slammed the door as I ran out towards Lorna's house. What a lot had happened in three days. I must keep calm.

"So, have you had time to consider what we discussed about the fostering?"

I said nothing. I was watching him stretch across the table for some bannock and a seabird. Then I realised he was looking at me, waiting.

"I have, Lachlan. Yes, I have." Eat the crowdie, I urged from within.

"And?" The grease ran down his chin and he wiped his mouth on his sleeve.

"I find I now realise all your decisions, dear husband, are for the good of the family." I forced another smile.

"That's the spirit, Catherine. On my instructions, Nurse has already begun to wean Amie and that is working very well; she will be ready soon for this voyage to Islay." I bit my lip as he surveyed the table, deciding what next to eat. "Unusual to have broth in the evening, is it not?"

"Oh," I said, trying to steady my racing heart, "I asked Cook to make it for you as she said the kail was good at the moment and I know you like it."

He began to serve a bowlful for himself then turned to me. "You like Cook's broth too, don't you?" and he began to dish some out for me. I held my hand up then decided that was futile, so I took the bowl. Do not eat the broth, Catherine.

He had his bowl in both hands, ready to sup when he put it down with a thud as he peered in front of him. "Crowdie – well, well. You are spoiling me tonight, Catherine."

"Oh, that was Cook's doing. She said one of the tenants had brought it along earlier for you." He dipped his knife into the bowl and spread it onto a thick chunk of bannock. Then he bit into it – a huge, ungainly mouthful, his lips smeared white.

And I waited, hand poised over my own dish of crowdie. I tried to look away, but could not; I felt as if I was under a spell.

He screwed up his face then lifted the bowl of broth in both hands and took a deep swig. "Something doesn't taste right with the crowdie. Is yours all right?" He said, pointing to mine. I took some on my bannock and nodded, terrified even to speak. His face suddenly contorted into a grimace then he picked up the bowl of crowdie and flung it across the floor. "Poison – that's what it is. Someone's trying to poison me." He gestured for a

90

servant and he got to his feet. "Find out who sent Cook the crowdie!"

The dog had bolted over from the fire and was now slathering over the broken dish of cheese and licking it up noisily. Soon it began to howl and at the same time, I heard a low, animal-like noise – a guttural cry of agony – from my husband. I turned around and saw he was on all fours, writhing like the dog. His face was covered in sweat. "Ale, fetch me ale!" he bellowed to the servant, who brought him a goblet. Lachlan tipped his head back to take a drink and then vomited. I watched in horror as he began convulsing on the ground, his body jerking around in torment.

The door swung open and Hector Mor was there, his men racing in behind him. "They told me he's been poisoned. How much has he had?"

I could say nothing, I just stood there, hands outstretched by my sides. I shook my head.

"Drink – get drink down him to flush it out!" he commanded the servants. I watched them try to hold his writhing body and pour the ale down his throat, most of it dribbling down his chin and beard. He was convulsing and thrashing around, and in between, he kept scratching at his face. Hector Mor's expression was grim as he gave his men commands. I was immobile as I watched the convulsions become less pronounced and soon Lachlan lay completely still, as if paralysed. I peeked around to see his face, which was now deathly pale, no longer sweaty. It looked as if it had been numbed. Dear God, was he dead already?

"Is he...?"

Hector Mor gently kicked the limp wolfhound at his side. "The dog's dead."

He knelt beside his father. "Don't die, Lachlan Cattanach Maclean!" And I watched as my husband's eyelids flickered. "I need to be sick," he whispered.

"Get cloths!" his son bellowed at the men, then he held his

father's head as the sickness came out in a rush.

Another bleary eye opened and I heard him mutter, "Hector, find out who did this to me."

"I will, you can count on me."

My heart seemed to stop as I pulled my shawl tight around me, hiding the vial.

"You! Help me carry him gently up to bed," Hector Mor shouted at a burly servant. "And bring up pitchers of ale and wine. As much as you can carry. We've got to get the poison out."

The room now stank of vomit and excrement – clearly the hound had emptied its bowels. I stood watching the scene unravel before me. The hound was dead. But had Lachlan taken enough of the food with the poison in it? Lorna had said an older plant might not be as effective, but how could we know how mature the plant was? Dear God, surely he'll die soon too?

There was another noise at the door as the musicians entered, their instruments at their sides.

"Out of the way!" Hector Mor bellowed, and they all jumped to one side as he passed, supporting Lachlan's head and shoulders, the servant holding onto his legs.

Lorna gave nothing away, but her eyes flickered over to me. She clutched her precious instrument to her chest. I could neither move nor speak. What if I had failed and he was about to recover? Dear God, where would that leave me – and more importantly, my daughter Amie?

Chapter 18

1520

Catherine

I sat huddled by the fire in my husband's room, trying to block out the noises behind me. There was wailing and groaning and retching, interspersed with splashing and sloshing as the ale was poured into him. There were loud shouts, mostly from Hector Mor as he bellowed his instructions to everyone, whether to keep forcing drink down Lachlan or holding the bucket under his head, mopping his brow with cool cloths. I could hear my husband's teeth chatter together in between his spewing. He was clearly hot but also icy cold. Surely his body could not last much longer?

A servant came over to ask if I required anything, which was unusual; normally they would have ignored me, but they must have thought that, like everyone else in that room, I feared losing Lachlan. Little did they know I feared *not* losing him.

"No, thank you," I whispered, trying to make myself invisible.

I had not had time to get rid of the vial and was trying to formulate a plan for what to do. Lorna presumably would not still be downstairs with her instrument, so I could not ask her to help; besides, she had done so much already. I turned around on hearing footsteps approach.

"Catherine," Hector Mor strode over to me, his face distorted with fury, "did Agnes say who handed in the crowdie as a gift to my father?"

I shook my head, the rest of my body somehow unable to move.

"Go and ask her." He gesticulated towards the door. "The man must be found and punished."

He marched back to the bed where Lachlan lay, calmer now, possibly sleeping. Unless – pray God – he was dead...

"Go! Go now, Catherine! The poisoner cannot be allowed to make his escape!" he hissed.

Under normal circumstances, I might have admonished a younger man of lower status for such insolence, but clearly nothing here was normal. As I stood up, he commanded two of his men to accompany me, presumably to bring the man to him; or perhaps to ensure I carried out his command. Could he possibly suspect?

I tried to breathe normally, but my heart was racing. I walked down the winding stairs, clutching the vial to my chest under the shawl. At the bottom of the stairs, there was a noise of barking and braying and I turned to see two of the hounds racing around the courtyard, a groom running after them with chains.

"They're the young dogs," said a gruff voice beside me. "Their father was Lord Maclean's hound, who died."

I gulped. So far, I had killed one dog and for all I knew, also my husband. And did this procession of the three of us to the kitchen mean an innocent man was about to be slaughtered too?

"Excuse me, Agnes," I called into the dingy, cold kitchen. I waited till the cook sauntered out from the larder and glared at me, sullen as usual. "Can you remember who gave you the crowdie?" I tried to make my voice sound normal.

I hoped that perhaps she would not, and then the matter would end.

"Aye, of course I do," she said, scowling. "But Robert would not harm anyone, certainly not his master."

"Robert Maclean?" one of the henchmen asked.

Agnes nodded.

"The one who lives on the path towards the woods?"

She nodded again and wrung her hands on a filthy cloth. "I know he wouldn't do that, it can't be him. It must be someone else." She bit her lip. "He's my cousin, I know him well – he'd never harm anyone."

"It's Hector Mor's command," the stout man said and swept out, waiting at the door for me. I looked at Agnes, whose eyes narrowed as she stared at me. She knew, I was sure. The other man gestured for me to follow his fellow guard. I went out, feeling the cook's eyes bore into my back.

"We're off to get him; you'll want to return to your husband, my Lady." At last, some sort of civility.

I nodded and headed for the stairs before turning around and tiptoeing after the men, through the main entrance to the castle. I then went in the opposite direction, heading for the cliffs. Now I had to be quick, and I ran, gasping for breath as I rounded the back of the castle and started up the cliffs, grabbing onto clumps of grass as I climbed. I was puffing all the way; I was going up so fast. At the top I looked down onto the waves crashing against the jagged rocks.

Everything was grey – the sky, the water, the stones – and this suited my mood. I felt a combination of anxiety, panic and sheer despair. I had been given no choice though; I had to kill him, for the safety of my daughter. But perhaps I hadn't thought about the consequences clearly enough. All I had considered was how I would soon be able to escape with Amie. But now that hope seemed remote.

I took the vial from under my shawl and flung it out to sea. I listened for a tinkling or a smashing as it landed on the rocks – or a splash as it fell into the water, but I heard nothing, and I had no time to linger. I clambered down the cliffs, hands sore on the scree as I stumbled and slipped. At the foot, I sprinted back to the castle where I slowed to a saunter, brushing my hands together to remove the dirt, and I entered the courtyard once more. The groom was dragging away the two hounds, now chained together. Their heads were down, and I could hear their growling, low and menacing.

*

I began to climb the stairs to Lachlan's bedroom, taking my time while my head whirred with plans. On the top step stood the priest, clutching his cross to his chest. His expression was bleak. Dear Lord, had my husband just died?

"My Lady," he said, breathless. "I am not as fit as I once was to climb all those stairs."

He breathed slow and steady, while staring at me. "They said it would not be long. I am here to guide His Lordship on his way to meet his Maker." He took one last deep breath then pushed open the door. I followed him inside.

The room stank. When I left, the smell had been sweat and vomit, now it was also excrement – and this time not from an animal. I covered my nose with my shawl and approached the end of the bed, trailing after the priest. Two servants were changing the soiled bed clothes One of them, a young girl, screwed up her nose as she ran past us to the door with them. I stared first at Lachlan, whose body was now still and his face white as milk. I could not tell if he was breathing. I then raised my head and looked at Hector Mor, who stood at the top of the bed, legs wide apart as if guarding the occupant. His face was grim, and I noticed he was looking at me with a cold, distant stare.

He gestured to the priest to begin to recite the last rites over Lachlan, then came towards me. Bending down, Hector Mor whispered in my ear. "Do you have any idea why Robert Maclean might have done this?"

I shook my head but did not trust myself to speak.

"And do you agree he must be put to the sword for trying to kill my father?"

His stare was unsettling, but I took a deep breath and thought of Amie.

"If he poisoned my husband, then yes." I could hardly believe I was condemning an innocent man to death.

"You will want to be with me when I execute him, I imagine?"

His stale breath was hot on my neck. I swallowed. "Of course,"

I said and tried not to shudder.

"Hector Mor! Come here!" A cry from the bedside and he rushed over. I followed, heart beating fast.

"There was movement, he took a breath!" An eager servant was pointing at Lachlan's chest, which did seem to be rising and falling.

The priest stepped back and allowed Hector Mor to lean in and put his hand under his father's nose, holding his fingers steady. "He is breathing!" Hector Mor stretched both arms heavenwards in supplication. "God has answered our prayers."

The priest crossed himself and withdrew a little as I stepped forward into his place.

"God be praised," I mumbled, glancing at Lachlan's body, which looked as if it was indeed coming to life. The deathly pallor remained, but there were slight movements, twitches around his face and arms. Dear God, he was alive. What was I to do now?

"We shall let him sleep, and then the minute he wakes, offer him wine," Hector Mor told the servants. "I shall be back presently. Lady Maclean and I have business to attend to."

He took my arm and walked me to the door. All the way downstairs, I felt I was in a dream, or rather a nightmare.

"Must this man still be executed, Hector Mor? Now that my husband is hopefully recovering?" I mumbled.

"Of course," he snapped.

The two of us descended first to the Great Hall where a guard handed Hector Mor his sword. He beckoned for two other guards to follow us and then together we walked down the steps to the courtyard where, instead of the two braying hounds, there was a man tied to a stake. He sat slumped on the ground, sobbing. As we approached, he tried to stand. "Hector Mor, I don't know what they're talking about. I would not poison his Lordship, you know that. You know me. I am a loyal servant!" His pleading eyes were filled with tears.

"I thought I did, Robert Maclean. I will give you one last

chance to confess your sin before you are punished before God."

I turned to see the priest standing beside us.

"I did not poison him! I tell you, I would never do that, I've known him since I was a boy and..."

Hector Mor strode over to the man and stood before him. There was a clamouring at the gate as guards tried to control the crowds gathering.

"Bring them in, all of them. They must see what happens to a traitor."

The gates opened and the people streamed in, congregating around the courtyard, some wailing, others with mouths wide open in horror. This was their kinsman, someone only he and I – and Lorna – knew was innocent.

"Stand up, man!" Hector Mor commanded, and the poor wretch struggled to his feet. I shut my eyes tight and took a couple of steps back, but still I could hear the awful piercing of the skin and the rip as the sword went in and out of the man's heart. I heard the guttural cry of agony then listened to the thud as he sank back down onto the ground. I opened my eyes and peered over to see him fall forward, the blood seeping all around. His body now lay on the earth and Hector Mor cleaned his sword, wiping it on his plaid.

I clenched my hands together to try to stop them from trembling and looked around at the crowd, who were quiet, incredulous. Most of them were shaking their heads, in deep shock, many were sobbing without inhibition. As my gaze turned to the kitchen, I noticed Agnes. She was staring at me with a disdainful and cold look in her eye. She knew. She definitely knew; of that I was now convinced. I looked away and a heavy feeling of foreboding swept over me. I took a deep breath to try to stop shaking. Dear God, what had I just done? Made an innocent man die. What a wretch I had become: but I had no choice.

I breathed in deeply again. Yesterday I had to plan to save my daughter; today I had to plan to save both Amie and me.

Chapter 19

1520
Lachlan Cattanach

He lay flat on the bed, eyes shut to concentrate. It was easier to think when he did not have to listen to his men or the servants asking if he required anything, if he could manage a little more ale. Good God, he must have drunk pints upon pints of beer and wine since yesterday – surely the poison had left his body? And yet he still felt weak – in body, but not in mind, thank God.

All he was able to think about was Marion. He so wanted her here to look after him and tend to his needs. She should be the one mopping his brow, rather than the servants. But when he asked Hector Mor to bring his mother to him, he said it was impossible – her presence would be neither appropriate, or at all pleasing to his wife. As if Lachlan cared about what she thought. His wife was an occasional presence at his bedside, and he wondered what she was truly feeling. She had always been an enigma, but her eyes were wide and blank – inscrutable – as she stared down at him. He could not decide whether she was simply traumatised about what had happened and being witness to Robert Maclean's execution by Hector Mor, or if it was the realisation that she herself could have eaten the poisoned food as easily as he had.

The nurse had brought his beautiful daughter to him in the morning and the little one cooed and smiled and cheered Lachlan up immensely. Her hair was now a little fairer than most Maclean babies, but her skin had his family's tawny hue, and her sparkling eyes were so like his son's, deep-set and dark. The minute his wife entered, he had them take the bairn away;

he could not even explain why, but there was something worrying about Catherine's demeanour.

The priest had been asked to stay in the chamber, his presence bringing Lachlan some kind of solace. As he blinked open his eyes to see him sitting by the window, he thought back to the curate who Hector Mor told him had stayed here for some three days while he was away. Hector had said he was sure he'd seen him before, perhaps at Inveraray, but not as a priest. Lachlan told him they were so excessive in the way they ran that household; they'd have had a veritable brigade of priests to tend to their spiritual needs. But he'd insisted there was something not quite right about the man. It worried Lachlan a little now – it had somehow come back to haunt him, but as his son kept saying, he must rest and not worry about things that could wait.

"Lachlan Cattanach, are you asleep?" came a soft, deep voice by his side.

It must be a kinsman coming to assess his health, for no servant addressed him in this way.

He blinked his eyes open to see a young man with thick, black curly hair.

"I'm here on behalf of my grandfather, John Maclean of Lochbuie. He is too infirm to travel but wanted me to come and pay my respects."

Lachlan nodded and he continued. "My father is away on Iona at the moment, otherwise he would have come."

"Send my best wishes back to your family. And thank you for riding all this way." He beckoned to a servant. "Be sure this young man is given refreshments before he returns home."

The young kinsman shook his head. "My men have brought our own provisions, do not worry. But thank you," he said, withdrawing after a respectful bow.

Even trying to sit up on his elbows was tiring, and Lachlan slumped back down. And then the realisation dawned. Of course – the lad did not want to eat at the Duart table, even though the poisoner was dead. Thinking about Robert, he wondered if there was a chance he hadn't been the one who'd added the poison to the food. He shut his eyes once more and recalled everything he had eaten yesterday. First the fulmar and some bannock. Then Catherine told him to try the crowdie. Then she said she had asked Cook to make the broth especially as it was one of his favourites.

A cold shiver ran through his body as a thought occurred, and he reached out to grab a servant. He turned as Lachlan hissed an order at him.

"Fetch Agnes the cook up here. At once!"

*

They propped him up on a pillow and he watched Agnes enter the room, puffing away; she was clearly not used to the stairs. Her domain was downstairs. She grasped the back of the chair beside his bed and wiped her sweaty brow, pushing some stray strands of grey hair back into her tight bun.

"Sorry, Your Lordship, I'm not as young as I used to be."

"Take your time, Agnes. Sit down." He looked at this chubby woman who had served his family at the castle all her life. What age would she be now – 45? 50? Who could tell? She had always been here, in the kitchen, at first helping and now in charge. Her nature was by no means ever cheerful; indeed, she was often surly, but she was solid. And loyal – or so Lachlan thought. He had always treated her and her family fairly, and he was convinced she bore no grudge.

Once her breathing became steady again, he stared directly at her.

"Agnes, you will know that Robert was executed for attempting to kill me with poison. They think it must have been either a deadly mushroom or Wolfsbane that was used. I obviously hadn't taken enough of it, thank God, but the poor hound did. He was my favourite dog." He sighed; the animal's demise still saddened him deeply. "Robert's cottage was on the way to the woods so he could easily have got either of those and mixed it into the crowdie he gave you for me."

She shook her head. "I just don't see why he would do that. He's one of us – a Maclean. Loyal to you and everyone here."

"What happened to the rest of the food on the table, do you know?"

"It was taken away with great care, then burned round the back, up towards the cliffs. We didn't know what else might have been tarnished."

"So it might not have been the crowdie that did it."

"No, of course not." She bit her lip. "You know her Ladyship sent down for another dish of crowdie? She said you liked it."

"No." Suddenly he remembered that she had her own dish of crowdie. "But Catherine did say she had asked you to make broth for me as the kail was good just now."

"That's not right." She frowned. "When she told me she wanted broth on the table, I said it wasn't usual at supper time and that the kail wasn't good as it was too early. We've not yet had the first frosts."

"So why would she tell me that?"

Agnes opened her mouth then shut it and looked down at her hands.

"What?"

She clasped her fat fingers together on her lap and lifted her head slowly.

"I watched her at Robert's execution. She had a look about her I'd never seen before. Normally there's a – forgive me, your Lordship – haughty air to her. But yesterday there was a different manner about her."

"In what way?"

"She looked scared, horrified and..." she glanced up at him, "guilty."

He stared at Agnes as realisation dawned.

He leaned in to draw close to her. "Say nothing of our conversation. Not a thing."

"Of course not, your Lordship." She clamped her lips tight together.

"And thank you. It's all becoming clear now." He gestured to the door. "You may go."

He watched her waddle towards the door and he beckoned one of his men over. "Bring Hector Mor here at once. Tell him there is no time to delay."

His voice, previously feeble, was raised as he shouted, "Go now!"

Chapter 20

1520

Catherine

I watched Hector Mor and his men storm out of the courtyard from the tiny window in the nursery. I handed the baby over to the nurse and tiptoed downstairs, trying to see where they were going. My stomach was churning with anxiety and even cuddling Amie and watching her gurgle with delight when I tickled her had failed to ease this feeling of dread.

From the courtyard I could see the three men stand by one of the turf-roofed cottages just outside the castle. This was where, just the day before, they had dragged poor, innocent Robert Maclean out from his home and Hector Mor had killed him for a crime he did not commit. A man with a long white beard came out and stood at his door speaking to them, then I saw him pointing up towards the cliffs. Could he have seen me go up to throw away the vial? Well, at least they would not find anything: it had landed in the water, surely. Though one of my constant nagging doubts, one that made me feel physically sick, was that I had not been able to throw it far enough, and instead of floating away with the tide, it was still sitting on a rocky ledge somewhere, waiting to be found.

I watched as the man went back inside, then emerged with a hooked wooden staff and all four men began to head towards the crags at the back of the castle. I remember Lachlan explaining to me how secure the Macleans had made Duart Castle when it was first built, with its position on top of the rocky headland, the cliffs preventing any possible assault from the sea. He said that the front of the castle was also impregnable as it too was built high up on the bluff.

I pulled up my shawl over my head and began to follow the men round to the sea side of the castle. I watched them begin to climb, pulling themselves up with their hands, just as I had done. The older man with the wooden crook was up first. He was obviously used to getting animals up and down the hills. I realised I had seen him before, herding goats when I was down with Lorna on the beach.

I clambered higher, but tried to keep my head down, then at the top I lay flat on my stomach to see what they were doing. They had spread out along the cliffs and were each staring at the rocks and grass at their feet. They moved slowly downhill towards the sea, one of them slipping on a rock and landing on his back. The others turned around as he yelped, and I lowered my head fast.

The man with the crook was down nearest the sea. He was probably only a few feet above the water, but higher than the waves at high tide would reach. I heard him yell to the others, who came towards him, one with hands outstretched as if asking a question. They knelt around a rocky ledge while the older man seemed to be poking something with his wooden staff. I could just about hear them above the noise of the waves. "Don't touch it!" cried the man with red hair, who I thought was Hector Mor's main attendant.

I watched him take a cloth from his belt and use it to pick something up from the rock. Dear God, they must have found the vial. Well, there was no way it could have been linked to me. They would surely presume poor Robert had run up here and thrown it away after he had poisoned Lachlan. Now I had to get back to the castle before they saw me.

I had just got onto one knee when I saw another of the men reach down to pick something else up. It was a pale brownish colour and looked like a small bird or a piece of cloth or... My mouth gaped as I realised what it was: it was my glove. I must have dropped it as I rushed back up the hill. Fool! How could I have forgotten about my glove? He held it up and they all looked at it then back up the cliff. They were going to give it to Hector Mor, who would easily discover it was mine. Unless I got rid of its pair.

A high-pitched, throaty cry above made me look up to see a black guillemot circling above my head. Accustomed as I'd become to the songs of the seabirds, today the cawing noise sounded mocking, as if its quavering cries were somehow presaging disaster. I shivered then began to clamber back down the cliff, stumbling over tufts of grass and rocks in my haste, and sprinted back to the castle entrance.

I turned back to see the guillemot flying high over the cliffs, where the heads of four men appeared. I slowed down to a steady pace and raised my head to try to look nonchalant. The guards nodded respectfully at me and I strode over the courtyard and climbed the stairs two at a time. I flung open the door to my room and saw Elspeth laying out some of my things on the bed.

She curtseyed and pointed down. And then I could see they were my gloves. A sudden chill ran through my body.

"I can't find the pair to this one, my Lady. I was just checking I hadn't misplaced it with the others. It was your nice goatskin ones."

"Oh, don't worry about it, Elspeth." I lifted the single glove. "There's no point keeping this one, so I'll take it for now."

She looked up at me, frowning. "Shall I not keep it and see if the other can be found?"

I shook my head. "No, it's fine. Thank you. You may go."

As I listened for her feet on the stairs, I heard the noise of heavier footsteps and knew it would be Hector Mor and his men, rushing to find my husband and give him the vial and glove. I went towards the table to find my rosary, returned to the bed and slid the glove under the covers beside me. I then lay down on top and closed my eyes. There was absolutely nothing I could I do now, apart from pray.

*

There was a loud knock on the door, and I sat bolt upright.

"Who is it?"

"Hector Mor," a gruff voice said. Though he had always been kindly towards me, and his manner fairly civilised, his voice could be brusque like his father's.

I sat back against the pillow. "Come in," I said, holding the rosary between both hands to try to stop them trembling.

He marched towards the bed and stood, legs astride, peering down at me. Any vestige of civility had left him.

"Lachlan Cattanach is well enough to come down from his chamber to eat. You are to join him. Now."

What an insolent manner he was now adopting. And as I looked at him, I saw that the kind eyes I used to admire were now filled with hate. I was scared.

"I am not sure I feel up to it, I am..."

"Get up, Catherine. Your husband requires your company." He turned towards the door. "We shall wait for you in the Great Hall."

I placed a foot on the cold floor and got up, placing my rosary on top of the bed, in case Elspeth came in. The glove under my bed covers was safe: I knew she would not touch a holy rosary. I swept my hair up and tied it at the back of my head with a wooden clasp then took a deep breath. I could do this. They did not know either the vial or the glove were mine.

But as I shut the door behind me, I realised that if I denied all knowledge of the vial, they might be able to blame it all on Lorna. Lachlan would remember how her grandmother had used poison in the past and that time, it had worked, unlike my failed attempt. And it was bad enough to have witnessed the cold-blooded murder of a stranger, poor Robert Maclean; I felt sick when I thought of his unnecessary death. But I would not let Lorna die. My mind was frantically thinking what to say as I entered the Great Hall and saw Lachlan at the table. I stood at the door for a moment, trying to gauge his mood before approaching, cautious. Then I was aware of someone coming out of the shadows behind me. I turned and there was Hector Mor, his sword tucked into his belt at his side. He must have come down from the stairs outside my room too. He gave a slight nod, as if remembering I was superior to him in rank, though what use was that now?

"Dear husband, you look well. How are you feeling?" His usual ruddy pallor had gone, and he was now pale and frail-looking.

"I find that I am not only fine, I am also ravenous. But I should like you to help choose my food here."

Hector Mor sat beside me, and I could smell the ale on him. I turned to him to offer a feeble smile. He ignored it.

"Here on the table are my favourite foods that Cook has prepared especially, but I wonder if you could assist." I looked at the dishes before us – the seabirds, some bannocks, mutton and the other usual dishes.

"What can I give you, dear husband?" I asked, stretching for his wooden plate.

But he drew it away from me.

"Catherine, there is a special condiment Hector Mor has found and we would both like you to try it first. Then, should you like it, I will try it too, perhaps with the roasted fulmar." He smiled, his black teeth making him more sinister.

Hector Mor was unfolding the cloth on his lap and as he held it out to me, his fingers touching only the fabric, I saw it was the vial, half empty. I felt my mouth gape open as I tried to think what to say.

"Could that be the vial of poison that made you so very ill, Lachlan?" They were both silent, both staring at me. I shook my head. "Please get rid of it, Hector Mor. It could still be lethal."

His lips twisted into a cruel smile. "Do you know where we found it, Catherine?"

I swallowed and wished I had had a goblet of wine before I came down here.

"No. Was it in the poisoner's cottage?"

He shook his head and looked at Lachlan.

A strange silence enveloped the room, only interrupted by a growling and yelping from the hounds outside. Then my husband spoke. "Catherine, this is indeed a vial of poison. It was found on the cliffs on the sea side of the castle. Someone had thrown it away, to try to get rid of the evidence." His eyes narrowed. "You were correct – it is lethal, and I should be dead, but clearly I did not ingest enough. Also, my dear son and my kinsmen tended well to me so that I have recovered fully."

"That is such wonderful news," I said, attempting a smile.

"But this was also found nearby." He lowered his hand and brought up the glove. And my heart began to race. Dear Lord, they had my glove.

"Is it not yours, Catherine?"

Take your time, do not say anything foolish. "May I see it?"

And he handed it to me as if giving me a charming gift.

I took it in my hand and turned it over. "It certainly looks a little like one I used to have, but I have not seen it – or indeed the complete pair – for quite some time."

Both men were silent and continued to stare at me. I felt so vulnerable. But I was a Campbell, I would not be cowed by bullies. "I am not sure what you are implying, dear husband, but I can avow that I have not seen the glove for a long while; and I have certainly never seen that vial." I sat up straight and raised my chin.

"Ah, Catherine, Catherine...haughty to the end," said Lachlan, sneering. He flicked a finger at me, then towards the door. "Since you have no desire to try this new condiment on your food, you may go up to your room." I stumbled to my feet, unsure of his intentions.

"Hector Mor, go and fetch her maid, Elspeth. Let's see if she can recall whatever might have happened to the pair to that glove."

I walked across the floor towards the door, as if in a trance. When I was outside, I could hear their voices. They were deep and low, like the angry growling of the hounds outside.

I climbed the stairs and passed my own room, heading up to the next landing. As the stairs narrowed, I looked up and saw, in front of the door to the nursery, a burly guard standing there.

"What are you doing here?"

"My Lady, I am here to prevent anyone but His Lordship or Hector Mor entering the room."

"But my daughter is in there. I need to see her. Move out of the way."

"I'm sorry, my Lady, but that's the order I was given."

"By whom?"

"By Lord Maclean," he said, shifting his feet wider apart, now obstructing the entire door.

"My daughter Amie is in there. Do you understand? I need to see her, she needs her mother."

He began to tap the sword in his belt and looked over my head, ignoring me. His expression was inscrutable.

"Please," I said, trying not to weep. "Please help me see my child." I reached out to touch his hand, but he swept it away and continued to stand there, his massive frame blocking the door.

As I turned back down the stairs, I began to whimper like a child and by the time I reached my door, I was weeping. The room was empty, and I walked to my bed, heaving with sobs. The rosary was no longer there and when I ripped back the covers, the glove was gone. I flung myself on my bed and covered my head with my hands. What could I possibly do now to save my child – and myself?

Chapter 21

1520

Catherine

I must have fallen asleep, as when I awoke, I was still on top of my bed, and it was cold and dark. I was about to get under the blanket when I remembered what had happened and leapt out of bed. Surely the guard would not be outside the nursery all night. I desperately needed to see my little one. I ran to the door and pulled the handle. I tried it again: it was locked.

I shivered, with the cold and with the realisation of what this meant. Now that Lachlan and Hector Mor knew I was the poisoner, my fate was in their hands. I let out a long breath as I remembered Hector Mor killing that poor, innocent man in the courtyard. Was that just yesterday? Surely my husband would not murder me too.

As I walked back to the bed, I had another nagging worry. They would know I could not have obtained the poison myself, so would Lorna also be implicated? The only thing I could do was ask for his pardon; otherwise, I risked never seeing Amie again. I would wait until the morning then go to see my husband and express my remorse. I had to get word to Lorna to lay low for a while. But how could that happen if I was stuck here? My maid would arrive at dawn – I would get her to help. Though surely Elspeth had been the one who'd found the glove and had given it to them?

I tossed and turned for the rest of the night, running through the apologies I would make and how I would beg for forgiveness. At some stage I was sure I could hear the hounds baying and the noise of horses down below in the courtyard, but when I ran to the tiny slit of window to look out, I saw nothing.

Noises outside the door awoke me from a restless slumber and I shouted 'Enter!' as usual, before remembering I was locked in. I stole over to the door and raised my fist to bang on the door, then stopped. I could hear voices just outside – perhaps I could discover my future if I listened.

I pressed my ear against the wood, but I could hear very little, so I got down on the cold stone floor, lying flat, my head pushed against the gap along the foot where the cold draughts swirled. I could not hear who it was, but one of the men sounded like Hector Mor. I kept hearing the word "tide". Someone said low tide, then another high tide. Then there was silence. I got to my feet and banged on the door.

"Let me out!" I shouted. "I need to get out!" Then I remembered I'd decided to be remorseful. "Please. Please can you open the door?"

As I listened to the footsteps disappear, I felt my shoulders slump. I had no idea whether the steps were going up to the nursery or down towards the Great Hall. I hoped the latter and that no one was going to see my darling girl before I, her mother, was allowed. I grabbed a shawl from the drawer, wrapped it around my neck and sat at the door, cross-legged, waiting, while hoping and praying that the mention of tides did not mean my baby was about to be taken across the sea to Islay even sooner now.

*

Sometime later – it could have been minutes; it could have been hours – I heard footsteps. Instead of passing my room, they stopped outside and there was the sound of a key turning in the lock. I got to my feet. I would not be cowed by whoever was at the other side.

I did not recognise any of the three men who entered, though they all wore the colours of my husband's clan.

"Yes?" I asked, raising my chin. "What is your business here?"

The older man, who was very short and stout, stepped forward and looked directly up at me. "We're here to take you on a short journey."

"What manner of journey?" Perhaps the talk of the tides was for me, not Amie.

"You'll see when we get down to the boat."

"What boat? Is my daughter travelling with me?"

One of the other men was stretching out a long piece of rope between his hands.

"No, she is not."

Where were their manners? Why were they not addressing me correctly as *My Lady*?

The man with the rope stepped forward and grabbed my hands.

"What are you doing? Get your filthy hands off me," I cried, but while one tied my hands behind my back, the other was wrapping a foul-smelling muffler around my mouth. I yelled loudly behind the fetid material, to no avail. He tightened it in a knot around my head.

"Right, get her out and down the stairs now. Then carry her to the boat."

Dear Lord, where were they taking me? I was incensed; how dare they. Surely as we headed for the stairs, someone would intervene – my husband, Hector Mor, the servants – but as they pushed me onto the landing and two of them clamped their massive fists around my elbows, I saw no one. It was as if the castle was deserted.

We passed by the Great Hall, but the door was shut and even in the courtyard, all doors were closed. I tried to shout under the thick fabric, but no sound could be heard. They had tied it so tight, my head hurt. As we passed the kitchen, the door was ajar and I tried to peer into the gloom, hoping that perhaps even Agnes would save her mistress. I was sure I saw movement inside, a person outlined in the smoky haze, but the men forced me forward, an animal going to slaughter.

I stumbled over the rough terrain outside the castle, but they did not stop. Instead they dragged me on, almost carrying me. I kicked out at them as we walked. They were guffawing, as if they were enjoying torturing the mistress of Duart Castle like this. We turned not towards the woods and the cottages, but the other way, towards the sea. And there, on the little jetty, instead of the usual bustle of small boats and fishermen, was no one. Under the murky mist hanging over the water I was able to see just one small boat sitting there. Where was everyone?

At the jetty, I was so exhausted, I stopped kicking and slumped in misery against one of the men. I realised I was powerless to do anything. One of the group shouted to the man whose firm grip was surely making marks on my elbow; it was so sore. Suddenly I was thrown into the tiny boat, as if I were a carcass. Two of them leapt in beside me. The third untied the rope at the jetty and flung it into the hull, its knotted end hitting me with a slap on my foot. I took a deep breath to try to stop myself breaking down in tears and wondered if I ought to just resign myself to my fate, whatever that was. But then I remembered where I had come from, that I was a proud Campbell daughter and now sister to the Earl of Argyll. I would not let these thugs treat me like this. Besides, I had a baby that needed me.

I started kicking out at them again and wriggling around with as much strength as I could, feeling the boat rock under me, until the older man jumped in and slapped me. Hard. It stung, but I could not even free my hands to rub it.

"If you don't sit still, you'll get worse than that." And he gestured to the other two to start rowing as I snivelled into the foul scarf and turned my head to look back through the gathering mist towards the shore. I was sure I saw a figure running onto the beach, fling down a basket and gaze out at sea. My heart missed a beat. Could it be Lorna? But if so, would she recognise me? Of course she would, she would surely see my long red hair swinging around my shoulders as I threw myself around the hull. But then I realised that, even if it was her, there was nothing she could do to help me.

As the boat lurched off from the jetty and the figure on the beach grew smaller, the mists enveloped us. I felt the tears stream down my cheeks as I sat, still and silent for the first time since they abducted me from my room, and wished to God I could simply die.

Chapter 22

1520

Catherine

We did not travel far. They were muttering to themselves in low voices as they rowed, but even though I was thrust close to them, their sturdy thighs touching mine, I could not hear their words. The ties from the scarf around my mouth had covered my ears and I could hear very little; and all I felt was my heart beating fast. My hands were cold, but I could not shift my shawl around my shoulders to cover them. I could no longer feel anger or terror, just despair that I was being taken away from my baby. Before I had Amie, I never thought I could possibly love another human that much – but my feelings for her were so powerful, I could simply not contemplate life without her.

The mist had become fog and we could hardly see a thing, but I felt the boat turn a little to the right. We must be in the Firth of Lorne, which I knew was where we had sailed over two years ago when I had first arrived from Inveraray. Apart from those blissful few days with Archibald and the joy of being with my baby, nothing had made me even remotely happy.

The sea was becoming choppy, and I sat with my head bowed low and not moving, for fear the tiny boat would capsize. But soon they slowed the rowing down and the boat turned again to the right. Were they lost? I could not see any land. Suddenly the older man stood up and pointed ahead, and through the fog I could see something.

"Is that the rock, Billy?" one of the men asked.

He nodded. The boat moved slowly towards it, then he lifted the rope and raised one foot onto the side of the boat. He jumped onto the rock, which looked no bigger perhaps than the inner courtyard at Duart Castle.

Two hands pushed me up, and I was thrust towards the edge of the boat. Trying to scream that I was terrified of water, my arms were yanked over the side. The man – Billy – dragged me to the highest point on the skerry and sat me down.

"We have orders to leave you here, tied up as you are," he said, removing his dagger from his belt. I drew back but he held me tight and brought the dagger close to my face. "But I am going to untie you so that before the tide comes in, you at least have a chance to find someone to rescue you."

I could not attempt speech, I was in such shock, as I watched him cut through the rope around my hands. They were red and sore, and I rubbed them gently.

He held the knife to the scarf at my face and I stood immobile as he sliced through it. At last, I could speak.

"I don't understand," I whispered, reaching out for his arm.

"The Master said to leave you here, tied up, but he isn't to know Hector Mor told me to untie you, just in case you can swim to land, or you could wave at a passing boat for help."

"What? My husband wants you to leave me here? On this tiny rock without food or water or..." I gasped. "Did you say tide? How high does the water reach at high tide?" I realised this was the tidal rock I had seen from the beach.

The man looked down, saying nothing while continuing to wind the rope into a tight ring.

"So you mean the tide comes up here, even to this higher point?" I was now shouting.

He shrugged. "Just keep yelling like that and wave your arms. There's nothing more we can do. We're obeying his Lordship's orders."

I threw myself at his legs, pulling at them, but he shook me off easily and quickly jumped onto the boat, which was bobbing in the choppy waters alongside.

"No, don't leave. Please. You can't abandon me – I'll die! My husband has clearly gone mad!" I was yelling. "I have a baby. She needs her mother. Please, help me!"

But none of the three men even turned as I stood on that tiny rock, shouting after them – pleading, begging – and they rowed off into the mist.

Suddenly, I realised what my husband's plan was. As my punishment for trying to poison him, he decided that I had to die, but not in public like that poor crofter killed by Hector Mor's sword. How many boats were likely to be passing in this thick fog?

I sat down, caressing my sore wrists, and began to weep. I was cold and scared – and alone in the middle of the sea. And there was absolutely nothing I could do.

*

It was when I had gone around the skerry for the second or perhaps third time that I realised the tide had begun to rise. My feet were slipping on the wet rock, and I tried to think what to do. I sat down by the edge and shut my eyes, hoping that somehow this would help inspiration come. So my husband had hired those three thugs to take me over here to this rocky islet in the middle of the Firth of Lorne to die. He had not even wanted them to remove my bonds in case I could swim. How could I possibly have known how to swim? I was a lady.

I opened my eyes and realised that the fog was lifting a little. Thank God. At least now I could see how near I was to land, even if I could not swim. Though surely swimming could not be that hard. I kept thinking of my little Amie as I walked around the tiny outcrop of rock again and again, hoping somehow that I could get myself back on dry land. I sat down, aware I was pulling myself up higher as the water rose. Dear Lord, what was I to do?

The tide was coming in fast. I scrambled up the slippery rocks as the water began to lap over my feet. Soon the only place to sit was the top of this jagged, rocky outcrop in the middle of a tempestuous, grey sea; I knew there was nowhere else to go. I turned towards the east where I believed Inveraray must be and thought longingly of my childhood there – the joy of my family and the fun and laughter. I thought of the long table set for dinner, the flickering candlelight making my mother's and sisters' jewels gleam as the log fires blazed. I remembered the assemblies in the Great Hall with our harpists playing in the corner, and the food that was so tempting to the palate. I recalled too the gentle smile of my grandmother as she sat looking around at us all, proud that she had helped create this strong, close family; a civilised family who cared for each other in times of need, unlike these savage, primitive Macleans.

And then I thought of my time at Duart Castle, of how cold I always was and how none of the food pleased me, apart from the crowdie. After using it to poison Lachlan, though, I did not think I would ever eat it again. If I survived. But I shook off such thoughts and considered the few happy times at Duart. My friendship with Lorna was good and her music was so perfect – the sound of her playing her clarsach so soothing, those ethereal notes that never failed to move me to tears. And of course the best thing had been becoming a mother and gazing at those dark eyes and long black lashes of my beautiful Amie. Even if I managed to return to Duart for her, how could I prevent her being taken away to Islay to be fostered? What a cruel tradition this was.

The water was up to my ankles. All I could do was stretch my head up high as I implored the heavens to save me: please, God, spare me! I promise to do anything – enter a nunnery, be a loving wife to Lachlan, even give up my child for fosterage on Islay, as long as I can survive. I hoicked up my skirts as the waves splashed onto my legs. The water was freezing cold, and I wondered how much longer it would take to die.

My eyes were streaming with tears as I peered into the distance. I looked around and felt myself panting for breath as panic set in. A sudden noise made me jump. I looked around but there was nothing there. My heart was racing, but then I tipped my head back and through the low cloud I could just make out two large birds flying overhead. They were herring gulls, squawking their high-pitched cries, and once again I felt envious of their ability to soar high in the sky.

My shoulders slumped once more as I realised how desperate my situation was. My feet were so cold, I could hardly feel them. Would I die of the cold before I drowned? Or would it be the freezing water filling my lungs that would take me?

Suddenly, shocking me out of my misery, I thought I saw something through the mist. I wiped away my tears and stared towards the east, where a pale sun was emerging. Was that a dark shape I could see in the distance, or were my eyes deceiving me? Had God indeed answered my prayers and was that a boat I could make out on the skyline? Perhaps I had begun to hallucinate, such was my state of despair. Of course it served me right – I should not have poisoned Lachlan; but it seemed at the time the only way out. But killing is wrong, so surely God was now punishing me too. And now I had ruined it for everyone; well, perhaps not for my husband, who would likely marry his mistress on the Treshnish Islands. Whatever happened next, I had no choice but to accept my fate. All I could hope and pray for now was that my little Amie was loved and cared for; that was my only desire.

I looked down to see the freezing water was now up to my shins. I raised my head to gaze once more at the horizon, then dropped my skirts into the water as I reached my arms high and waved my hands with wide, frantic gestures, trying to attract attention, my whole body swaying from side to side. I could feel my long hair flying in the wind like fluttering sails. And as the water lapped higher up the rock, I continued waving and muttering my frantic prayers, pleading to be spared, begging for someone to rescue me.

Chapter 23

1520

Lachlan Cattanach

He stood on the jetty watching the men row to shore. Thankfully the fog was beginning to lift, so he could now see them as they approached. There were only three people in the boat; they had done it.

Hector Mor was beside him, peering into the mist. "What will you do now?"

"We will wait till we know there is no hope she has survived then send word to the Earl of Argyll. I plan to do this later today." He raised his chin. "These Campbells do not intimidate me – we are equals. And so I must relay the tragic news of the sad and sudden demise of their dear sister and daughter."

Hector turned to face him. "But they will want a body, surely."

"And if that is what they insist upon, then they will have a body; or at least a coffin."

Hector Mor bit his lip. "How can you be sure she is dead?"

"The water rises over the entire rock twice a day at high tide – you know this, Hector Mor. She will drown. There is no escaping the power of the tides."

Hector Mor was becoming irritating. He had not been keen on the idea, even though he agreed it must surely have been Catherine who had done the poisoning.

"But she is so clever, she could have found some way to..."

"To what? To swim to shore? Do you recall how far offshore that skerry lies? It is impossible."

Hector Mor let out a long sigh. "Do you need me to accompany you to Inveraray when you go?"

"No. We need to have Amie safely installed on Islay before the winter. And since your marriage is now arranged, you can take the child to her foster father, Alexander Donald Macdonald at Dunyvaig Castle. Then you will have your wedding to his daughter Mary, as planned. This can all be done within the next few days. The child is being weaned, but she is to be accompanied by the wet nurse as well as her regular nurse."

"So you will not be there?" He was frowning. "I thought you had promised to attend the wedding."

"I have other things to do, you know that." Dear God, had he raised a warrior or a weakling? "It is all arranged. I will deal with the Campbells; you will deal with the Macdonalds."

The boat had reached the shore. Hector Mor caught the rope that was flung over the side and tied it up on the jetty.

Lachlan nodded at Big John as he came ashore. "It's done. She is on the rock and there's no boats anywhere around."

"But in the fog you couldn't see if there were any vessels on the water. We can't even see the rock from here," said Hector Mor.

"You can hardly see it from here anyway, it's so far east," Big John said, gesturing with his hand.

Hector Mor was now truly bothersome; Lachlan had often wondered if he had actually liked that shrew of a wife, if he was soft on her. The sooner he was married to Mary Macdonald, the better.

"She won't last long, that's for sure. Now, let's go up to the castle and eat." All three men had left the boat and were now on the jetty. "I feel a ravenous hunger for only the second time since that wicked wife of mine poisoned me." He was beginning to feel stronger now, thank God. Considering all his body had been through, it was nothing short of a miracle.

Clapping Hector Mor on the back, he strode along beside him. "They say the winds look set fair for the day after tomorrow. That is when you leave for Islay. And once word has reached Campbell, I will leave it a few days as he will surely send a message back demanding her body for burial amongst her own people."

"But surely we are her people now?"

"Hector Mor, has she ever acted like a Maclean or even shown any willingness to become a Maclean?"

His son shrugged.

"I am therefore happy for her family to have her buried at Inveraray with her own kin. And so I shall start the long journey over there with a coffin, to convey our condolences. The carpenters will soon begin fashioning a fine casket of best oak." He was chuckling. He felt no remorse for putting his wife on the rock; she had tried to poison him, for God's sake.

"We will land at Connel and then process with great ceremony along the many miles over the moors to Inveraray with her coffin. The bond created when I married Catherine will endure; they will be pleased we have undertaken such a journey to return her body."

"But you won't have her body. Won't they open the coffin?"

"No one opens a nailed-down coffin. It's bad luck. And we will ensure it feels heavy, as if there was her corpse inside."

He looked around at Hector Mor, whose jaw was set rigid, eyes glazed over, expressionless.

"It was the only way. You know that."

Hector shrugged and they entered the castle courtyard, where Lachlan raised his head and sniffed the air. The wonderful aroma of roasting seabirds was coming from the kitchen. "Come, let us eat. A celebration is required."

*

Two days later, Lorna stood in the courtyard with her clarsach at her side. She had a cloth bag at her feet.

"Are you ready for your first trip to Islay then, Lorna?" Lachlan asked. What a lucky girl she was. For a young woman to take on the role of the Maclean of Duart harpist on this voyage was prestigious. She did not, however, look grateful; rather, there was a sullen air to her.

She shrugged. "Your man said we'd be gone some two to three weeks?"

"Perhaps, depending on the tides. There's Amie to settle in at her foster family and then the wedding of Hector Mor."

"It's just that I need to let my wee brother know when to expect me back. I've left broth for a few days then Jeannie in the croft will feed him." She glowered at her master. "I still think he should be coming with me."

"One child on this trip is enough; that is my daughter Amie." Was there an undertone of ingratitude? Good God, either she wanted this opportunity or not. "You realise you are fortunate to be undertaking this voyage, Lorna – a mere woman? The Macdonalds of Islay have fine harpists, but I wanted you to show how accomplished the musicians of Duart are."

"I won't let you down, your Lordship. I just wanted my wee brother to come along too."

He shook his head and turned around at the kerfuffle behind them.

The nurse was there, carrying bonny little Amie all wrapped up in shawls and blankets for the journey. The maids bustled around behind her, carrying her bags.

"Meggie over there isn't going with them then?" said Lorna, pointing at the smallest maid.

"I have no idea about the arrangements of my domestic servants. What is it to you?"

"Meggie is the same age as my brother." She continued to scowl, clearly forgetting that she was addressing her lord and master.

Then she raised her head as if trying to gain Lachlan's height. She leant towards him and whispered, "I was wondering where her Ladyship was heading when I saw your men take her away in the boat a couple of days ago. I've not seen her since, and we usually meet down on the beach." Her eyes were unblinking as she stared directly at him.

He lifted his hand to slap her. But he dropped it when he saw her standing firm, unflinching. And suddenly he understood what she wanted.

Lachlan sighed. "All right, Lorna, go and fetch your brother, but if Hector Mor tells me the child has been any bother, then you will pay for it. Do you understand?"

"Yes, of course," she said, laying her clarsach gently on top of her bag and sprinting towards her home.

"Get him to bring along his fiddle!" he yelled at her back.

"Why is Lorna leaving? I thought she was accompanying us." Hector Mor appeared at his side.

"She has gone to fetch her brother." Lachlan shrugged. "I didn't want another child on this trip, but so be it. There is just about room on the vessel. He plays the harp too – not as well as she does, but he is a fine fiddler, so he might be useful anyway."

Hector Mor nodded and picked up Lorna's bag and clarsach, then they headed towards the jetty. From the top of the hill Lachlan could see his galley, where the men were loading provisions on board.

Down at the jetty, he took Amie in his arms and beamed. His heart melted as she gurgled up at him, blowing bubbles. How blessed he was, having his daughter near him for so long. He had never experienced that when Hector Mor was little, since he was brought up with Marion on the Treshnish Islands. Amie had given him so much joy, even if she was not a boy; or perhaps it was *because* she was not a boy, he felt even more protective. He wiped away some tears then kissed her on her soft, plump cheek. He felt emotional, but tradition must be adhered to; that was what had kept the Macleans of Duart strong and powerful for so many years. Fosterage had been in the family since anyone could remember, and so it would continue. Bonds would be strengthened because of this.

Lachlan watched as the nurse and the wet nurse stepped onto the boat, then he handed Amie down to their open arms.

"Take good care of my daughter," he said, his voice breaking a little. He would see her in a few months at the next Council; why was he feeling so sentimental? He cleared his throat and straightened his back.

The other servants boarded and he turned around to see Lorna and young Angus flying down the path, a fiddle under her arm. She grabbed her bag and clarsach from Hector Mor and jumped onto the boat. It was not hard to detect the difference in Lorna's demeanour; indeed, it was quite remarkable. Perhaps it was because she had her closest kin with her; or perhaps it was because she had seen into her master's soul and knew the truth.

Finally, Hector Mor stretched out his hand, which Lachlan took in his and beamed. "Take care to arrive safely on Islay. Ensure Amie is cosseted. And once you are back home at Duart with your bride, we will celebrate here too." He leant in to whisper, "By then I will have been to Inveraray Castle and back."

Hector stepped down off the pier into the galley. As they rowed away out of the bay, the servants on board nodded their farewells. Lorna glared at Lachlan, jaw set firm. There was no doubt about it – she knew.

He watched the boat head towards the east, where it would then turn south for Islay. He felt sorrow at the temporary loss of his daughter, and disquiet at the memory of Lorna's words and her expression. But as he walked back up the path to the castle, he forced himself to think of the many things that needed attending to, the first being to consult the carpenters on how much wood was required for a fine box worthy of a Campbell burial.

Chapter 24

1520

Catherine

I peered up through the clearing mists, sure I heard a noise overhead. I wiped the tears from my eyes to see more clearly. There was a bird with orange legs and an orange beak flying above, tweeting in a high-pitched call, sounding more and more frantic as I watched it pass directly overhead. I recognised it as a redshank; I had learned so much from Lorna, not only about music and foraging, but also about birds. I thought about those afternoons on the beach, me watching while she collected the limpets from the rocks or some dulse to make soup. She told me about which time of year different birds visited Mull and when they set off for warmer climes. She also told me the traditions and stories surrounding the birds; and my shoulders slumped as I remembered what she had said about this one. Redshanks are the birds that sing to the souls of those who are departing into the next world.

So there was no hope; I was going to die. No one was about to rescue me. I might as well give in and wait to be fully submerged in the water, which was now almost up to the tops of my legs. I was so cold; my teeth were chattering. Perhaps I could plead one more time with God to save me. I took a deep breath, then looked up again. The bird was gone, perhaps back to the shore to join its family down on the beach that had become such a happy place for me. My tears flowed once more as I realised I would never see my own family ever again – my beautiful baby and my dear sisters, brothers, mother and grandmother in Inveraray.

I contemplated what it was going to feel like to drown. Would my body surrender fast to the water as it flooded into my lungs? Or would I suffer long and slow as I spluttered and gagged and choked under the sea? I shut my eyes and took another long, deep breath, muttering one last little prayer. *Please God, let me live, somehow, and I will lead a quiet and holy life, devoted to You. I will take the veil, I will ask my husband's forgiveness. I will hand the care of our beautiful daughter Amie fully to him; I will not interfere with her life, provided she is safe. Even if she stays on Islay forever, I will be content just knowing she is free from harm and healthy.*

I was about to say a final Amen, but stopped as I thought I heard something. I opened my eyes and saw a boat through the clearing clouds. Surely it was an apparition. I waved my hands in the air, as frantic as a gull about to be taken by an eagle. The sky was now clear, and I peered towards the sound, yelling as loudly as I could. Yes! It was a boat, and it was sailing towards me. My heart leapt as I continued to flap my arms wide, though I was having difficulty standing upright, with the water being up to my waist. I steadied my feet on the two flat pieces of rock under me and stared ahead. The boat was travelling in from the east towards me. I turned to look in the other direction, where I could now see the castle, but it was so far away that I was sure no one would notice the vessel.

Soon I could see there were two men in the small boat, and I panicked – was it the men from Duart who had brought me over here and abandoned me to my fate? I stopped waving for a moment until I could see it was a fishing boat; between them I saw a willow basket like those I'd seen fishermen unload at Inveraray market. Also, these men did not wear the colours of the Maclean plaid. They both had red hair, the same colour as mine. I began to gesture once more and as they approached, I could see their faces, confused and shocked. They must think I was a madwoman. Oh God be praised; I was not going to drown.

Muttering a prayer of thanks, I shouted over to them and

soon their small boat bobbed alongside. One man put down his oars and stretched out both hands.

"Take hold," he shouted, "and I'll pull you in." The other man steered the boat as near as he could to the rock and I threw myself into his outstretched arms. The boat wobbled and tilted to one side, but then righted itself as I sat down with a thump, my sodden skirts heavy as if an anchor was tied to me.

I looked up at the men and began to cry. "Thank you, I was about to die. I..." My voice trailed off as my shoulders began to heave with sobs and I found I could no longer speak.

One man patted my hand while the other pulled off his mantle and wrapped it around my shoulders.

They both stared at me, open-mouthed. They shared similar features, and I presumed they were father and son. The older man spoke softly. "We thought you were a bird. Your arms looked like the white pinions of a large sea bird." He shook his head. "How did you get onto the rock?"

I took a deep breath and swept back my hair, which was falling over my face. "I was put there," I said. I glanced round to the castle, where – thank God – there was no sign of life on the shore.

"Please can you row away from here, fast, so they cannot get me."

"Who?"

"Please, can we just leave here?" And I began to cry once more.

The men took up their oars and since the boat was so small, I was nudged on one side by an elbow, while the basket of fish pressed into my other side, but I did not care. I was safe – I was not going to drown. I sighed deeply as they began to row in the opposite direction from the castle. I bowed my head and vowed that I would never return there.

Chapter 25

1520

Catherine

"Where are we heading?" I eventually asked of the two men, once Duart castle was barely a silhouette. The rock I had been left on was not even there; it must now be fully submerged in water. I shivered, with cold and with the understanding of what might have been.

"We're heading home." The older man peered down at my hands. "My Lady?"

I nodded. My fingernails were neat and clean and he had obviously noticed my hands lacked the callouses servants had. And perhaps my accent was different.

"Lady Catherine..." and I stopped. I did not want to even mention the name Maclean, so loathsome was it to me. "Lady Catherine Campbell."

"Of Inveraray?" He looked aghast. "The earl's family?"

"Yes. I am the earl's sister." I attempted a smile. "And where is your home? Where are we going?"

"Connel, a few miles over in that direction." He looked at the sun, which was now low on the horizon. "We cannot take you to Inveraray, but we will make sure you are somehow taken home safely." He looked at me again, a kindly look on his ruddy face. "Rest awhile, you've been through a terrible ordeal."

I tried once more to smile but could not, my face was so cold. "Thank you," I whispered as I huddled into the coarse plaid.

I turned to look round at the younger man behind me. He now wore only his shirt over his breeches, since he had given me his mantle. "You must be cold, I'm so sorry."

"I'm fine, he said, shrugging before looking straight ahead, pushing his head down every time he pulled the oars back.

"Might I ask the names of my rescuers?"

"I'm John and this is my son, Murdo. We're Campbells too." He grinned. "Though not clan chiefs like your family."

"My brother will ensure you are rewarded. You have been so kind. I was about to die, I was..."

"Rest if you can, my Lady" the older man said. "We've got a while till we get home."

I shut my eyes and thought of Inveraray and how my family would react when I told them what had happened. My brothers would want Lachlan's blood, there was no doubt about that. But as I mused over that welcome thought, I realised that in truth, that could not happen. As well as the fact that I did not want them warring again when they had all finally found peace, there was also Amie to think of. Surely if they were fighting, I would never get her back. No, this all had to be considered very carefully.

I gulped as I remembered my desperate pleadings and the prayers raised to heaven as I stood on that rock while the tides rose around me. I had promised God that if He saved me, I would leave my daughter's care to my husband – if he were dead, what would happen to her? Surely she would remain on Islay with her foster family – and lost to me forever.

I sighed and opened my eyes. It was more pleasing to watch the sea birds swoop and circle overhead as the little boat sailed on, away from the castle which had been my prison for the past two years. I could see the mainland on the horizon and for the first time in many hours, I felt a surge of joy.

*

I opened my eyes and saw a dim, dingy, smoke-filled room with a fire in the middle. I remembered I was inside the fisherman's tiny home, which was more hovel than cottage. And yet as I breathed in, I smelled only clean bedding. After we had arrived here yesterday, John's wife Annie had looked after me as if I were a child, helping me change out of my sodden, ruined gown and then dressing me in one of her coarse, simple smocks. She brushed my hair and tied it up with a wooden clasp, singing a lullaby to me as she brushed. I felt such an air of calm and peace as she did so, tears trickling down my cheeks. She insisted that I sleep in their bed – the only one in the tiny cottage. She said they would sleep by the fire, and I was too tired to continue my protestations.

I must have slept for many hours, as when I woke, I saw Annie stirring a pot over the fire in the middle of the room. She turned around on hearing me stir and smiled. Like her husband and son, she too had red hair. I got up and walked over to her, where she bade me sit on a stool by the fire.

"I'm just finishing the dulse soup." I watched her sprinkle a handful of oatmeal into the pot and stir again. "It'll be ready in a couple of minutes. I'll fetch a bowl for you, my Lady."

"Thank you, Annie. You have been so kind. Did you manage to sleep at all?"

She shrugged. "I sleep very little; it doesn't bother me though." She smiled at me. "You had a good, long sleep though."

I nodded, smiling back and watched her ladle some steaming soup into a small wooden bowl before handing it to me.

I knew Lorna often made soup from the seaweed she gathered on the shore, but I had never eaten it. I expected it to be green, but this was sludgy brown. As I supped, I realised how hungry I was and though it was not a familiar taste, I gulped it down. She nodded and offered me more and I was about to take it when I realised it was possibly the only food they had for the day, so I declined. She sat down on the other stool and poked the fire with the poker.

"The priest has sent news to the castle that you are here."

"What priest?"

"The village priest. He is the only one here able to write and so he sent off a letter to your brother, the earl. My son says Inveraray is about half a day's ride from here so hopefully he has received the news by now."

"Thank you," I said, watching the old woman as she got up and took some dishes outside to wash. I followed her out and sat on a wooden bench by the door. She was probably only my mother's age, but she looked older than my grandmother; these people had such hard lives, it was etched upon their faces.

As I watched her swill the bowls in a basin, I thought about the past few hours and realised she had never once asked what happened or who put me on the rock. Just like her husband and son, she simply wanted to help another human being in need. Again, I felt tears of gratitude run down my cheek.

The afternoon was pleasantly warm, and I sat outside watching the leaves on the trees flutter in the light breeze while she sat beside me, mending nets. The boat was due back soon, she told me, and she hoped there might be fish tonight. I looked out to sea where there were a couple of small boats bobbing about in the water and another thought occurred to me: I had stopped the men fishing yesterday – surely they had lost a day's income of fish to be sold at market. I would ensure they were recompensed for their losses in some way or other.

After about an hour (though it might have been longer), she got up and waved. I followed her gaze and saw two men clamber out of a boat and tie it up. One lifted the basket from the hull. They strode up the beach towards us and Annie went inside to stoke the fire and heat up the soup.

Just as they set down the basket of fish at the door, there was another noise and we all turned to see a stout man dressed in a grey cassock hurrying along the path from the village. Behind him were two horses trotting along slowly. The priest was puffing when he arrived at the door and the fishermen stood staring at the fine horses approaching their cottage. I got to my feet and

133

gazed over at the riders and noticed they both wore the Campbell colours. Just as the priest was gesturing to the cottage, I gasped. One of the riders tipped his hat and the other smiled; God be praised, it was my brothers, John and Donald.

Annie rushed out of the door and clapped her hands.

"They've come, my Lady. They have come to take you home."

And as my brothers dismounted and hurried towards me, I began to sob, this time tears of joy, not sorrow. As we hugged, I wiped the tears from my eyes and saw Annie and her family standing behind us, smiling at the reunion. I burbled to my brothers how very kind the family had been, not only rescuing me from a terrible ordeal, but also welcoming me into their home.

"You will be rewarded for your kindness," John said.

"What happened to you, Catherine?" Donald asked, pointing to my plain smock. They were both used to seeing me in fine gowns and jewels. "Where is your husband? And your child?"

And as more tears flowed, I shook my head and muttered, "Later. I will tell you everything later. Please, can we just go home now?"

Part 3

Chapter 26

1520

Lorna

I awoke to the noise of the boat shuddering to a halt. I looked around and saw the men stowing their oars then jumping overboard onto the beach to secure the vessel. I remembered Angus was nestling in my arms, and I bent down and tousled his hair. He blinked open his eyes and looked up at me, confused.

"Where are we, Lorna?"

"I don't know. It could be Islay." I turned and shouted over to one of the men. "What's the name of this place?"

"Somewhere called Claggain," one of Hector Mor's men yelled over the noise of the instructions being given by his master, who stood at the prow of the boat.

I shifted Angus from my arms, picked up my clarsach to prevent it getting wet and stumbled over the passengers towards him.

"Hector Mor, where are we?" I looked up and down the long beach and out towards the crystal blue water. I had never seen such a fine stretch of beach; ours at home near Duart was so much smaller.

We had had two brief stops after leaving Duart, one at another island called Colonsay then at a smaller one called Oronsay, but the rain had been so heavy, we had not left the shelter of a cave by the beach at all. The men had restocked the boat and given us some bannocks to eat, but we had seen nothing of these places. Since I had never left Mull before, nor indeed Duart, I was disappointed, but hopefully I could see more of this new place.

After leaving Oronsay, we had sailed down a narrow channel between two islands, one they said was called Jura, the other Islay. And at some stage I must have dozed as the heavy rain and wind had given way to misty calm. Surely this was our final destination. I stretched my arms above my head and yawned. I was stiff with the cold and being cramped on a boat with so many people.

Hector Mor turned to me, a worried frown etched into his brow. He swept back his lanky black hair.

"It's Claggain Bay, which is a short way on horseback from Dunyvaig Castle. But our hosts are not here yet. We'll have to wait till they arrive to greet us." He scowled. "They should have been here by now. I said we'd be at the south end of the beach, the sandy part."

We both turned around at the sound of a baby crying. Little Amie was bawling and wriggling in the arms of her nurse, while young Meggie was delving into the bags alongside. They were probably both hungry, the poor wee souls. Why was Amie's wet nurse not feeding her? Then I remembered the woman had lain prone, her head overboard, terribly seasick all the way from Duart.

I shook out my skirts, trying to remove the damp from the rain that had poured down on us for so many hours. At Colonsay, they had taken buckets to the inside of the boat to try to rid it of water. But we had all still got soaked, water slopping at our feet as we took our seats on board once more. Amie's nurse had been brought to the front by Hector Mor and told to crouch under two of his men, who had made a sort of canopy from cloths over the baby's head. As I'd watched him on the voyage here, I realised he was in fact quite a kind man, courteous to the servants and caring about everyone's needs. Had he known what Lachlan Cattanach had done with my Lady, I wondered. Surely not, I could not imagine he would countenance anything evil.

The more I thought about it, the more worried I was about

her. Had they removed her back to her home in Inveraray after the unsuccessful poisoning? I still blamed myself for that. I was not careful enough with the potion; I must have used too many of the flowers and not enough root of the Wolfsbane, or perhaps I'd taken the leaves from a plant that was too mature. I sighed. Nothing could be done about it now, but I did worry about Catherine. Had they just taken her to Lismore to live out her years there in a nunnery, to repent? Perhaps during this voyage I could ask Hector Mor.

Cries from further along the beach made us all turn around. Angus and I began to clamber out of the boat, lugging our instruments which we had tried to keep dry under our clothes. As I gazed down at the white sand, I was eager to set foot on it; Duart's beach was all shingle, so it was always rough underfoot. As my foot landed on the sand, I felt a strange joy. Even though it was cold, the feeling was welcome. It felt solid yet moving; it was a delight to wiggle my toes in it. I put my other foot down and stepped up the beach, Angus by my side. He had stretched his hand down and was picking up handfuls of the white sand, which trickled through his fingers.

The noise of horses' hooves followed the cries and we all looked south towards the end of the beach. Hector Mor strode up the sand to greet the riders and I watched them talking and laughing, while everyone else got off the boat. The baby was still crying; did she somehow know her mother was gone? Before Catherine had disappeared, she had explained the practice of fosterage, which she called barbaric – obviously she did not agree with her husband about sending their beautiful wee baby away. But she was only a woman, what power did she have? He made all the decisions. I still don't understand this fostering tradition the noble families seemed to favour. Why was that necessary when people had their own kin to care for them?

*

I was squeezed on a horse between Hector Mor's belly and Angus's back. It was not comfortable, but there was no more room for us in the cart, which was already full of provisions and the men. And of course Amie and her servants had pride of place in a litter, pulled by two horses and covered by a broad canopy of cloth. We trotted along, my brother and I clinging onto our instruments as we followed a woodland path under drooping branches of oak, birch, and hazel. Soon we came to a large chapel and Hector and the other riders brought the horses to a halt.

"We can rest here for a few minutes, Lorna," he said, as one of his men helped us down.

"What is this church?" I asked.

"Did you not used to be a silent one, Lorna?" He shook his head. "Catherine has been a bad influence on you. You used to know your place."

I ignored this and asked again.

"Kildalton. It means the church of the disciple or foster child."

"Why?" I asked, but he looked at me in a curious way then strode off towards his hosts to take a drink.

I turned around to see a tall stone cross with many carvings on it. I pulled Angus alongside and gazed at the engravings. I had never seen anything like it. I stepped round and round it, taking in all the carvings of people and snakes and angels and birds – and some strange, unfamiliar beasts. It was one of the most beautiful things I had ever seen. It was so tall and intricate, each panel telling a story.

I peered forward to count the big beasts round the middle circle. There were four; I could not tell what animal or monster they were, but they were big and somehow scary, with huge heads. There were snakes underneath, coiling round towards the base. I went around to the other side and saw a large-plumed bird feasting on some small round fruit. There was a lady with a baby and an angel by each side. I wondered if it was the Virgin Mary and baby Jesus – my grandmother told me that when he was born, there were angels and shepherds nearby. I was standing staring at it in wonder when I felt a tug on my skirts, which were still heavy and damp from the storms on Colonsay.

"Lorna, can we go and get a drink over there? There might be a bannock too. I'm really hungry."

"Sorry, Angus, of course you are. Go on over, I'm coming too."

I dragged myself away from the cross and headed to where everyone was gathering, just outside the chapel. I pushed him towards the crowd, to eat something, and peeked inside the door. It was gloomy, no candles were lit, but there was some light coming in through the tall slits of windows at the far end. I looked to my right and saw another tiny window, high up in the gables.

It was much bigger inside than I had thought, and I peered up at the wooden roof, high above my head, wondering how this would feel when there was a priest and a congregation inside. Would it feel cosier than it did now? Surely it would, with the warmth of the candles. Even though it was a chilly afternoon, I had a warm feeling of contentment. There was something about this place that made me feel secure. I wondered again why it was called the church of the disciple or foster child. I think I preferred the latter as if Amie was to be living nearby with her foster family, she would feel secure here too. I began to walk towards a grave slab on the ground when I heard the noise of boots.

"Lorna, come out of there – get up on the horse!" Hector Mor bellowed from the door. I followed to see him swinging a leg up onto his steed and Angus running towards him. I quickly gulped down some ale from a servant then headed towards him, my clarsach at my side. He took my harp and helped us up in front of him. I held on to Angus and then I felt a strong arm move around my waist to keep me steady.

"The next stop is Dunyvaig Castle, where Amie will meet her foster family. And I will meet my wife."

He clicked the horse into a trot and I asked, "Have you not yet met your bride?"

He sighed. "Lorna, try to keep your mouth shut once we are at the castle, even if spoken to. Remember you are but a harpist, even though you are the best in all the islands."

I had never heard those words from either him or his father; they made me feel glad.

"And no, it is not customary for a man to meet his bride till the eve of the wedding, which is tomorrow. That's when you shall play. Then after the several days of festivities, you and Angus shall return to Duart. Is that understood?" I nodded and mumbled agreement, then sat completely still as I realised he was touching my hair. He pulled my thick plait gently over my shoulder. It must be annoying him. "Was your hair always this long, Lorna?"

I wanted to turn around and look at his expression – surely he was mocking me – but he sounded genuine. And the gentle touch of his large hand on my hair disconcerted me.

"Yes," I whispered, "I've always worn a long plait down my back, Hector Mor," while looking straight ahead at the path ahead through the alder and willow trees. Then as the trees cleared, I gazed out towards the sea which was sparkling in the morning sunshine.

Chapter 27

1520

Catherine

I turned to wave goodbye to the fisherfolk who had not only rescued me from the rock, but who had also offered such kind hospitality, without any questions. My brothers had asked them to keep the incident a secret for now and when they looked confused, Donald told them it was a delicate situation and their silence would be appreciated. He insisted upon leaving a bag of coins for them, though they said they wanted nothing in return. They had done no more or less than anyone would have, in the circumstances, they'd argued.

John and Donald had asked only one further question of me before we left.

"Was this Maclean's doing, Catherine?" John had whispered to me while Donald was forcing the money upon my hosts. I nodded and he set his jaw firm as he muttered, "We will speak more about this on the journey."

Murdo reached out his hand to help me up onto the back of Donald's horse. I nodded in thanks to my hosts and we set off towards the hills.

As we trotted along the banks of Loch Etive, Donald asked me to explain what had happened. I began to relate the whole story, from the ruffians who had removed me from my room to being abandoned on the rock; I could feel the muscles of his chest tighten under the grasp of my arms. But still he said nothing and so I continued my tale of woe, sniffing away tears as I relived the moment of horror when I was convinced I would die, drown under the water that was lapping over my feet then up my legs until it reached my waist. I took a deep breath and explained how the frantic waving of my arms attracted the fishermen and how, without them, I would be dead.

I wiped my wet face on my sleeve and dissolved into tears as I told him how much I missed my beautiful baby, dear little Amie. Though Donald had only married two years before, he already had two little ones; when he said he could feel my pain, I knew he truly could.

"I cannot imagine being separated from my little ones for long. They bring such joy in this world that is burdened with sorrow."

We travelled in silence until we slowed to a stop to have some food. I stood against a tree in a forest overlooking Loch Awe, nibbling on the coarse barley bannock Annie had given us for the journey. I glanced to my right and saw Donald speaking in a huddle with John, voices low, heads close. He was clearly telling our brother what I had just told him. At one point I heard John cry out in fury and stamp his foot, only to be hushed by his younger brother, who was shaking his head.

When it was time to mount the horse to continue our journey, Donald spoke to me in a voice that sounded more like John's.

"We will avenge this act, Catherine. You and I shall say nothing more till we speak to Colin, but be assured, Maclean will not have his sorrows to seek once we find him."

He kicked his heels into the horse and we cantered forward to join the others.

As we sped between the ancient oaks, I wondered what the earl would decide to do. I would have to caution him – for all I loathed my husband and wished him dead, I did not want to jeopardise getting Amie back, so clearly battle was not an option. What did I know, though, of men's quest for revenge and capacity for retaliation? As usual, I was simply a pawn in the middle of a man's world.

*

As we approached Inveraray Castle, I could not help but smile. I looked up at the tall stone tower and the old ramparts where my sisters and I used to watch the boats down at the harbour. I realised that, despite all that had happened to me and the trauma of being separated from my child, I felt pleasure: I knew I would be safe here. For this was always my home, not that cold, draughty castle on Mull. We trotted into the courtyard and John shouted at one of the grooms to go and let our brother the earl know we had arrived.

When they'd received news from the priest that they must come at once to Connel for there was a family member there, needing urgent help, Donald said they had no idea it could be me. They thought it would be one of our cousins who had gone on a hunting trip. Our horses came to a stop and we dismounted and headed for the stairs, then to the Great Hall. I pulled my hair back off my face; it was matted and tangled. I must look such a mess. I was still wearing the fisherwoman's smock, a plaid from Donald, and my feet were bare.

We entered the hall and my brothers strode ahead to greet Colin. I stood by the door, beaming as I gazed at the walls of my childhood home. Then I looked at my eldest brother; there was something about him that did not look right. Clearly he had just received bad news. His face was ashen and even from the far side of the room I could see his eyes were red, as if he had been weeping. Someone must have died. Dear God, please let it not be Grandmother; but she was so healthy when I saw her just a few months back. My brothers were speaking in low, sombre tones. Then Donald clapped Colin on his back and turned around to point to me. Colin's mouth opened wide and his expression changed from deep gloom to joy. He rushed over to me and held my face in his hands.

"He wrote to me that you were dead, dear sister." He shook his head. "I don't understand."

"I was meant to have died, that's for sure," I said, trying not to cry. He pulled me towards him and embraced me, and my tears began to flow.

"Maclean told me you had died, tragically. He didn't say what happened, only that he was on his way here from Duart to pay his respects – and that he was bringing your coffin so you could be buried here."

"What?" I shook my head in disbelief.

John and Donald joined us and John raised his hand.

"Colin, we shall speak of everything later. It is a good three days' journey for them to arrive from Mull. Maclean cannot be here before tomorrow at least. Let Catherine go and rest." His eyes were wide. "Were Mama and Grandmother told the news too? If so, she must go at once to see them."

"Fortunately not," Colin said. "I only received the letter a short while ago. I was contemplating how to tell everyone such ghastly news. But now there is no need." He turned to look at me and smiled. "Yes, go and rest, dear sister. I will send Mama and Grandmother to you."

He gestured to one of the servants. "Take Lady Maclean to her old room. Have the maids attend to her, bathe her, dress her in her fine clothes once more. Then, once you are refreshed, we shall dine together later. Is that suitable, Catherine?"

I nodded. "But please do not call me by the name of my husband. I am back in Inveraray Castle where I belong; I am a Campbell."

My brothers all smiled. "Still the feisty sister we've always known," said Donald, grinning. "We will see you once you are refreshed."

And as I began to follow the servants towards the stairs, I heard Colin mutter to his brothers, "What in God's name happened to her? Was this Maclean's doing?"

"We shall tell you everything," I heard John say as Donald called to a servant, "Bring us some claret."

And as I stepped onto the stairs that led up to my childhood bedroom, I breathed the familiar scents of home once more, and I felt glad.

Chapter 28

1520

Lachlan Cattanach

The horses at either end of the wooden litter whinnied as the bridles were tightened around their flanks. The men lifted the coffin and placed it on the narrow boards before strapping the ropes tightly around it. What a beautiful wood the coffin was made of – the carpenters had done a splendid job.

They had tried to persuade their master that elm was best but, since it would take a couple of days to get the best wood, Lachlan had opted for the oak as it was already there in the workshop; it just needed to be cut. Besides, it looked very grand and surely Campbell would not complain his brother-in-law had stinted on the casket for his sister when he saw how splendid this one looked?

"Watch what you're doing, man!" he shouted at one of the servants who was trying to tighten up a loose rope. "That's a fine lady you're carrying there." He had to suppress a chuckle as he thought how gullible these servants were. Only Hector Mor – and of course Big John and the two other men who had taken her out to the rock – knew how she had died. And they were also the only ones who knew that inside the coffin was not the body of Lachlan Cattanach's red-haired beauty, but a mature she-wolf that his men had caught on Ulva. They had packed lots of sweet-smelling heather around the body and hammered in the nails so tight, no one would be able to remove the lid, even if they wanted to defy superstition and attempt to do so.

They had come ashore from the galley after sailing from Duart and were setting off on the long journey from Connel to

Inveraray. They were just mounting the horses when a couple of fishermen came towards them. They had been watching them drag their boat up onto the beach.

"Are you travelling far?" The older one said, a gruff tone in his voice.

"Inveraray," Big John said, gesturing to Lachlan Cattanach. "His Lordship is taking the coffin to be buried at the family home."

"I will do the speaking, John!" Lachlan shouted and trotted alongside the fishermen, who were glowering at the party.

"That's a long way to carry a casket," said the younger man, who was now standing in front of his horse.

"It's always worth the journey, however long it might be, to bury a loved one with due ceremony," he said, gesturing them to let the party proceed.

"That's a really fine coffin you have there," the younger man said.

"It is indeed. Now move along, you are blocking my path."

Big John steered his horse over to them. "This is Lord Maclean of Duart Castle. Be on your way, both of you!" he shouted, taking his dirk from his belt.

The older fisherman leaned in close to Lachlan and even from high up on his steed, he could detect the rank odour of rotting fish. "I heard there was a fine Lady Maclean used to live at Duart. Is she still there, then?"

He opened his mouth to speak but then saw a fisherwoman running down the beach. She was shouting at the two men, presumably her husband and son. She must have been watching from one of the hovels up on the shore. "Come away, John. Come home, Murdo, I'm needing your help up there." She stopped at Lachlan's horse and looked up at him, a look of fear in her eyes. She glanced down at his sword then repeated her anxious pleas to her family. "It's dinner time, let this gentleman on his way."

Lachlan laughed. "Thank you, we have just been talking,

nothing more. But now we must leave." Lachlan drew his horse's reins into his fist and watched her tug the hands of both men, clearly desperate to get them away. "Might I enquire your names?"

"Campbell," the older man said.

"Yes, we're all Campbells here," the younger one growled, and turned around to follow his mother home.

*

As they approached Inveraray Castle, Lachlan thought back to the last time he had been here. His young bride was both beguiling and beautiful and he remembered his first sight of her, with her thick, red hair and her tall, full figure. And then he recalled those first few weeks when he'd even thought he was in love with her, before realising that it was just lust and that there would never be anyone to rival his Marion of Treshnish.

"My Lord, there's horses ahead. I think they're coming towards us. Shall we wait here for them?"

He tried to see if they looked like the Campbells, but it was difficult to recognise the riders.

"We will wait for them here. Even if they are not our hosts, they will see we have a coffin with us and surely let us pass."

They stopped their horses and waited under the rowan trees, each of them with a hand on their dirk.

The approaching party had more horses and men than the Macleans, and as they got nearer, Lachlan saw that two of them had red hair like Catherine's.

"I think it's the Campbells," he whispered to Big John.

"Let's wait and see," he said, still as a bird of prey before it pounces.

"Maclean, is that you?" shouted one of the red-haired men.

"It is. Lachlan Cattanach of Duart. And are you Campbells?"

One of the men trotted near. "Yes, Donald Campbell of Inveraray. That is my brother John over there," he said, grim-faced, pointing to another red-haired rider. "We come to greet you and take you to the castle. Our brother, the earl, awaits."

"Ah good, so he has received our sad news?"

There was a silence as John approached. Lachlan stretched out his hand to greet them but both brothers' hands clung to their reins, even though their horses were still. Perhaps they were too grief-stricken to remember the niceties of civil greeting between noble men.

One of their men approached and whispered something to John, who nodded.

"My men will escort the coffin to the castle," he said, directing his men into position alongside the casket.

Lachlan noticed Donald peering at the lid and muttering under his breath.

"It's made from the finest wood Mull has," he said, trying to raise the tone from this grimness.

"You've certainly hammered the lid on well. Our mother and sisters would have hoped to see her one last time." Donald stared directly at him, unblinking.

"We wanted to be sure it was secure, for the journey; so, sadly, that will not be possible," Lachlan said, affecting a look of sorrow.

"I see," Donald said, lifting his horse's reins. "You may ride between my brother and me. The earl will be waiting to greet us in the Great Hall of the castle." He clicked his tongue. "Come, follow me."

They did as they were told, though Lachlan found his tone rather strange, since they were speaking one nobleman to another. But as they trotted under the willow and hazel trees, he had to keep reminding himself that they thought their beloved sister was in the casket. When he met the earl and Catherine's mother and grandmother, he would do his best to appear heart-stricken. The bond between their two families must continue to thrive and flourish, whatever had happened.

Chapter 29

1520

Catherine

Grandmother and I sat by the fire in her room, holding hands. She kept shaking her head, incredulous at what I had just told her. My brothers knew everything I'd been subjected to by now, and Colin had called them away for a conference to discuss what would happen. Their expressions were a mixture of grim and bellicose. Donald declared that he was going to get his men and travel to Mull while Lachlan was here so they could bring back baby Amie to be with her mother and her family. But she could already be on Islay, under careful watch with her foster family, I told them, sobbing. We must do nothing to jeopardise her being recovered to me.

Mama had taken the news in her own inimitable way, immediately turning the situation to herself, wailing that she was so bereft as she had almost lost of one of her precious children and that she must take to her bed at once. But Grandmother had simply pulled me to her in a long embrace and wept. And now here we sat, watching the wood crackle as the flames leapt in the grate. How much warmer it was here in Inveraray than at Duart. The fires were always lit and the wall coverings and tapestries hanging everywhere seemed to keep out the chill.

"What will you do now, Catherine?"

"I don't know. You saw my brothers want vengeance, but I cannot risk it for fear the Macleans keep Amie forever. Though Hector Mor would take over Duart Castle if Lachlan was killed, his contacts on Islay are about to be strengthened, with his marriage to the daughter of Amie's foster father." I sighed.

"What manner of man is Hector Mor?"

"He can be kind and thoughtful, sometimes very considerate; he is not the brute Lachlan Cattanach is, but he is a Maclean – he will do everything he can to take Amie over to Islay to be fostered, as that is his father's command. I don't know when that will happen." I shrugged. "But I don't see what can be done."

She tightened her grip on my hand and turned towards me. "Your brothers will find a solution."

"But for them, the only way is to fight. I can't have that; they must let Lachlan somehow think he has won." I bit my lip. "That he has got away with it. Then we can, by some means, get my baby back."

We both turned to see a servant rush through the door towards us. He bowed and my grandmother put down her goblet.

"Lady Catherine, the earl has a message for you," he said as he passed me a note.

"Your Ladyship," he said, nodding at Grandmother, "he says your presence is required at table as soon as you can."

"Very well," she said, getting to her feet. "Catherine, I shall see you later. Please rest if you can. We can organise supper to be brought up for you." She kissed me on my cheek then strode across the room, with the gait of someone half her age. How I hoped I would have her energy when I was her age.

I unfolded the note and read it. Then I re-read it for I could not quite believe what it said.

I beckoned over the maid. "Come with me to my room, I must change at once. Hurry, there is no time to waste."

*

I stepped down the stairs from my room, taking care my tresses remained tucked under my veil. I had chosen one of my sisters' finest gowns and the maid had coiffed my hair carefully so that it could not be seen under the white veil. I stole into the Great Hall, which was less light than usual. From the nook by the door,

I looked around and saw that not all the candles were lit. My brother had planned this down to every last detail.

There was a feast laid out all along the tables. There were great haunches of mutton, sides of beef, pies and bannocks – not a sea bird in sight, thank God. There was already much chatter and the noise of everyone's goblets being filled. No one had yet touched the food; they were waiting for the earl to begin to eat before they all did.

I could see Colin sitting in the middle of the table, his back to me. And there was a seat vacant beside him, to his right. On his other side, I recognised the back of Lachlan Cattanach, his unkempt hair matted to his head, his shoulders swathed in his plaid as usual. I looked around the table and recognised most of the guests as Campbell family or near kin. Lachlan's men clearly had not been invited to our table with him.

No one had seen me enter. I approached my brother and stood behind, just near enough so I could hear the conversation between him and my husband.

"I am so sorry to have had to bring your sister's coffin to Inveraray. On Mull, we all deeply lament her sad demise, but I felt it right to bring her back to her childhood home."

"Indulge a grieving brother, Maclean – tell me, was her death as painful as it was sudden?"

I could not see Lachlan's expression, but I found it difficult not to cry out in anger at his response. "It was a terrible and sudden illness, but I pray God she did not suffer."

"And you were there? At the end?"

I held my breath.

"I held her in my arms as she took her last breath."

My body was so tense, I was fearful the beating of my heart could somehow be heard. But then I noticed my grandmother staring at me from the opposite side of the table. She looked incredulous at my presence. I shook my head and put my finger to my lips.

"And was she able to at least say farewell to her child?"

I saw Lachlan take a long swig from his goblet; he was clearly thinking carefully what to say.

"Catherine had indeed said farewell to our darling Amie. Yes." I had to clench my teeth together for fear I would scream out loud.

My brother John, who was a few seats down from Colin and Lachlan, turned around and saw me there. He lifted his hand to tell me not to move yet and I pulled my veil over my face. I leant in to hear what my brother said next.

"Excuse the delay. We can eat soon, but there is still one guest due to arrive." He pointed to the seat to his right.

"Ah, a guest of honour perhaps; I see he is to be seated at your right."

"She. It is a lady."

Lachlan looked around. "I can see your mother – and your wife too..."

Colin ignored him and turned around to see me standing there. "Why, here she is." He beckoned me over. "Come sit, my Lady."

And I stepped slowly towards the table, pulling my veil up around my face. My eldest brother stood to greet me, taking my hand and guiding me to my seat to his side.

I did not look around but could feel Lachlan turn towards me.

Colin turned to the servants. "Fill up my Lady's goblet!" I stared at the pitcher of claret as it was being poured. My heart was pounding.

"Let us all raise a cup to our esteemed guest. Welcome home, dear Lady." He smiled at me, raising his goblet, and I turned slowly to face him. I could now see Lachlan, his expression one of complete incomprehension. His eyes grew wide as I threw back my veil so that my red hair – those long red tresses he used to admire so much – tumbled loose. He leapt to his feet, his cup falling from his hand.

"How is this possible?" he stuttered, looking from me to the earl, whose face was now grim. "You are not dead?" He looked back to me and attempted a smile. "My love, my Lady, my..."

Colin stepped in front of me, and I glanced over at Grandmother, whose mouth was open in horror.

"Maclean," he said, "You are my guest, and Campbells pay high regard to the rules of hospitality – you will leave my table unharmed, but be assured that you are no longer welcome in my house."

Lachlan, a look of terror on his face, scanned the table to see my other brothers leap to their feet, hands on dirks, their faces full of hatred and contempt. My husband pushed back his chair and fled to the door.

Donald and John flung their chairs aside and started after him, but Colin shouted, "Stop! We have a feast to enjoy. Our sister has returned. Let us eat and drink – we have much to celebrate."

Chapter 30

1520
Catherine

I watched aghast as Lachlan reached the door and two hefty guards caught hold of him. He attempted to struggle with them but more of my brother's men joined them and he was marched away, men at his side. The assembled company too were watching in astonishment – amazed not only that I had returned, but also that my husband had just been taken by the guards. Most had no idea what had happened to me, but surely the news would spread fast, as the claret and ale flowed.

"What will you do with him, Colin?" I asked my brother as we both took our seats once more.

"Your brothers and I have it all in hand, Catherine. You need not worry about a thing. You are safe back home in Inveraray and your child, God willing, shall be with you soon too."

My heart leapt.

"How is this possible?" I took a gulp of my wine to try to help calm myself; I was trembling.

"This is what is about to happen, Catherine," Colin said and leant in towards me.

"Maclean will leave Inveraray shortly, but without his men. They are already in our castle's dungeons."

"All of them?"

"Yes, and I can assure you, it is not the most pleasant place." Colin nodded. "Two of your brothers – John and Donald – will travel with Maclean back to Duart Castle. There they will deposit Lachlan Cattanach and return home to Inveraray with your baby. His men are imprisoned here as hostages, to ensure that will happen."

"But Maclean is dangerous. He is wily, and I fear for my brothers."

"They will have some kinsmen with them. They will be fine." Colin tore off some of his bannock and started eating. "And Maclean knows he must hand over the child to them; otherwise he will never see the men in our dungeons again. They will be put to the sword."

"But he doesn't care for anyone else's life – he will never hand her over."

"Let us see."

"And what if Amie is already on Islay?"

"You said that had not yet happened."

"Certainly not when I was put on the rock, but I don't know…" I began to cry. "I am worried, Colin: for my brothers, for my child, for the stability of relations between our two families. I was meant to strengthen that bond and now look where we are."

"Catherine, that man tried to kill you. Had it not been for your child, I would have run him through with my sword this very evening as he sat beside us; even the Campbell pledge of hospitality would have been abandoned. But this is the only way I can think of for your baby to be returned. And then you will be as good as divorced from him and we can find you another husband."

I sighed then took a deep breath. "Colin, I have to tell you something: when I stood on that godforsaken rock with the water lapping over my feet, then up to my knees, then to my waist, I prayed to God, imploring Him to save me."

"Of course you did, Catherine, the ordeal must have been dreadful."

"But as I begged God to save me, I promised Him that I would return to my husband, be a dutiful wife." I wiped away my tears. "I even pledged that I would give up my child, if only I could be saved that awful death."

Colin took my hand. "You did what any of us would have done. You were put there to die. And I am sure that God in his good grace will forgive you for such desperate vows." He gestured to the laden table. "And now enjoy yourself, dear sister. You are alive, let us feast till late."

I looked over the table to where Donald and John had just risen. Donald came over to us while John headed for the door.

"We leave presently. Can you tell me where in the castle your child sleeps, Catherine?"

I told him where her room was and how the castle was laid out. "Be careful, both of you, please," I murmured. "He is capable of anything, anything at all. He is used to having his way."

Donald smiled and joined John at the door.

A servant appeared behind Colin and whispered to him, at length. Eventually the earl shook his head and leaned in towards me. "On my command, my men have hacked their way into the coffin."

"Was there anything in it?" I asked, worried Lachlan had placed another body in the casket.

He nodded. "I have just been informed that the beautiful casket held the body of a fine she-wolf, with sweet-smelling heather and herbs tucked around to try to prevent the stink." He turned to the servant again. "Have them remove the skin. And ask them to have a fine cloak made with the fur. We shall surely have something good and abiding out of this sorry mess."

*

My mother moved along the table to join us after my brothers had left. Colin had clearly told her what had happened, and she turned to me with accusing eyes.

"Catherine, your ordeal has been so bad for my delicate constitution. I was nearly recovered and now I find that your husband has been banished from our table and his men to our dungeons." She sighed. "What did you do to provoke Lachlan Cattanach? Surely such a good man would not attempt to drown his wife without grounds?"

I felt hurt at the implied accusation. "Mama, what makes you think he was a good man? He's had a mistress on the Treshnish Islands for years and years, he already has a son, which means I did not need to marry him – and, most importantly, he wants to send our darling daughter to Islay to be cared for by a foster family. How can any of that possibly make him good?"

My mother had the knack of making me incredibly angry; no other person has ever incited such feelings in me, not even my husband. My mother has been pandered to by all my brothers and even most of my sisters; only Marion and Ellen understand that she is thoroughly selfish and thinks only of herself. Even though she professes to care about everyone, she is always turning the attention back to herself. I sighed and tried to push thoughts of my own role in this awful business aside. I could never forgive myself for Robert Maclean's death; but my desperation at the prospect of losing Amie had made me slightly detached, unhinged. I saw that now.

"Sweet child, I told you before you married Lachlan Cattanach that we women have to make compromises – a lot of compromises. But whatever befalls us, we must keep loyal, devoted and—"

"Mama, are you seriously suggesting he was right to have his men row me to an island in the Firth of Lorne and abandon me to the tides and seas...to die?" I could feel the blood rushing to my face. I took a large swig of wine.

"And perhaps you should remember, Catherine, that a lady does not gulp down wine in that manner; rather, we sip."

I was lost for words. What could I possibly say that would make her understand what I had been through?

"I truly thought that he was the man to tame you, curb your wild tendencies, but it seems the opposite has happened and—"

"Curb my wildness?" I realised my voice was raised and as I shook my head in despair, I saw Grandmother opposite beckoning me over to sit beside her.

"I shall see you later, Mama. I do hope you recover from your most dreadful shock."

"Thank you, darling. I shall try," she said, clearly oblivious to my sarcasm.

Grandmother patted the seat beside her and took my hands in hers as I sat down. "You must pay no attention to your mother," she whispered. "Sadly, she is so self-centred – she only sees things through her own narrow perspective; and she is getting worse." There had never been much love between my grandmother and her daughter-in-law. The only time they seemed to be united was when my father was so tragically killed at Flodden.

"Now, tell me what you plan to do while you await the safe delivery of your beautiful Amie to Inveraray."

"I don't know. I am still so confused, and I feel it will take time to recover."

"Of course, sweetheart. You have been through so much."

"Colin is suggesting I should take another husband; and Mama is telling me I should return, tail between my legs, to Lachlan Cattanach as a loyal wife." I spread out the palms of my hands in incomprehension.

"You must simply rest and take your time. Leave the men to deal with your husband and bring Amie here; then you can decide what you want to do. There will be plenty of beaux lining up for your hand if you do decide to marry again." She smiled.

The noise around the table was increasing, all the diners were relaxing and celebrating after the earlier drama. Now it was just family and close kin, without the intrusion of a Maclean. I looked towards the far end of the table and realised there was a face I did not recognise.

"Who is that lady over there, sitting beside my sister Janet?"

Grandmother looked down the long table.

"That is Margaret Campbell," she said. "She has become a good friend of Janet."

"A Campbell? But why do I not recognise her? She is not married to any of my brothers. I know their wives."

Grandmother let out a long breath. "She is your cousin Archibald's wife. Did you not see him leave with your brothers to journey to Mull with your husband?"

I could not speak. I simply shook my head, mouth open in disbelief. I stared at the pretty young woman with glorious fair hair tumbling around her shoulders.

"When did you say they married? Where…" I broke off as she got to her feet, attended by Janet, who held her arm as if she were an invalid. She turned around and I could see she was wearing a huge gown. Was she very fat? With a gasp, I realised she was expecting Archibald's child. I stared at her as she waddled out of the room, helped by Janet and my sister Isabel.

Grandmother patted my hand. "The baby is due in a few weeks. I think this will be the last time she appears in public."

"And is it a joyful union?" I asked, trying to make my voice sound normal.

"We all think so. They seem happy in each other's company."

But I was hardly listening. This woman leaving my family table had taken the friendship of my sisters – but more importantly, the love of the man I adored. As I thought of Archibald, I felt a pang of sorrow; he had not even come to greet me before he left. Did our relationship mean nothing to him?

Part 4

Chapter 31

1520

Lorna

I sat by the door of the hut we were staying in, polishing my clarsach and Angus's fiddle. My brother was inside, lying on the pallet we shared last night. He had been terribly hot, so I made him drink two goblets of ale that morning and insisted he go back to sleep. It was so unlike him, but he had been a little peaky since we arrived. I was sure the drenching we all got on the voyage had given him a chill.

That evening there was to be a banquet inside the castle, and I needed him well for it. Hector Mor was to meet Mary Macdonald, his wife-to-be, and the wedding would take place tomorrow. After I'd finished my polishing, I planned to go into the woods and practise my tunes. I would have to find some peace and quiet to do that – here by the castle was full of people and animals and noise.

I looked along the track towards Dunyvaig Castle, where swirling plumes of smoke rose from the tower and flags fluttered in the strong breeze. The sea gate was open, and men were scurrying back and forth from the many boats bobbing out on the water, unloading goods into carts or directly onto horses which passed into the castle. Our hosts Donnie and Ann told us Dunyvaig was an important port for exporting salted beef and cow hides. There were cattle everywhere here, not just for milk, but for their meat. I saw two great beasts being killed the day we arrived, and Donnie explained that they were being prepared for the wedding feast.

I had not yet been inside the castle, but I'd walked to the

entrance the day before and stood gazing up at its strong walls, trying to avoid stepping in cattle dung. I said to Ann afterwards there was somehow a warm, welcoming feel to the whole place, where everyone seemed to greet strangers with a smile. It was wholly unlike Duart Castle, where there was a pervading sense of fear. Even in the daylight, there was something of an eery atmosphere at Duart.

It was difficult to say what was different: both castles were right on the water, this one at the end of a spit of land jutting into the sea around a sheltered bay. And of course Duart was the same, but higher up on the cliffs. Perhaps it's the stories I'd heard about Duart Castle, mainly from my grandmother, about terrible and cruel happenings inside. I'd never forget when she told me about another Lachlan Maclean, an ancestor of Hector's father, having murdered eighteen wedding guests at his widowed mother's wedding and torturing his new stepfather. There had been much blood shed at Duart.

Here though, I knew of no such tales, though of course there must be: every castle has its stories of battles and bloody disputes. Donnie told me all about how important the Macdonalds of Dunyvaig were and even though the Lords of the Isles were based in Finlaggan, at the other end of Islay, they were all kin, all Macdonalds. I rubbed the cloth hard over the back of the fiddle while I remembered what else Donnie had said: that although the Lords of the Isles' power had diminished since the Scottish king insisted the Lordship be forfeited, everyone on the islands believed they'd be restored. "Why would we islanders want to live under the sway of a king who lives on the mainland and who rules over a kingdom that has no interest in us?"

"Lorna, I see you are busy at work, as usual."

I jumped at the voice and looked up to see Hector Mor with two of his men. I laid the fiddle down beside my clarsach and stood tall, so my eyes looked directly up into his. He looked down at my shoulder to where my thick plait sat, defiant in its heaviness.

"Do you braid your hair every morning, Lorna?"

I shrugged. "Sometimes I leave it loose, but if it's windy I can't see a thing, and if I'm playing it gets in the way of the strings."

What an odd conversation to have with a man; though I remembered he had mentioned my hair before. His own hair was unruly and wavy, but at least less lank and greasy than Lachlan Cattenach's.

"How are you finding the people here on Islay, Lorna?"

"They seem like fine people, kind and warm. I like it here."

"Good. And your brother? Has he been practising? Remember I want the Maclean musicians to exceed all expectations tonight and tomorrow at the wedding."

"Angus hasn't been too well, but hopefully he'll be fine later. He's sleeping right now."

Hector Mor raised an eyebrow then turned towards the castle.

Since he was in such a good mood, I thought I could perhaps venture a question about Catherine, who had been on my mind such a lot, especially having been with little Amie on the voyage over here.

"Hector Mor, do you mind if I ask you something?"

He turned back and gazed once more into my eyes. His were dark, almost black, but kind and warm. He leaned forward, as if I was about to ask something secretive.

"Is Catherine – Lady Maclean – back at Duart now with your father? I didn't see her at all those last days before our departure."

He pursed his lips together then, taking his time, began to speak. "Lorna, I know you and her Ladyship spent a lot of time together. Indeed, I presume that is why you're now so...how should I say...forward and self-assured. Catherine was like that too."

"Was? Has she changed?"

"I mean 'is', Lorna, obviously. But the truth is, I don't know where she is. Lachlan Cattanach was dealing with many issues after his near-fatal poisoning and some of these he shared with me, some he did not. I know that he was still trying to find out who the poisoner was."

"But I thought it was Robert Maclean? The man you ran through with your sword?" My heart began to beat fast.

He closed his eyes as if trying to expunge that memory. "So did we all, Lorna, but then my father became less sure. I may come to regret my actions, but I had no choice." He sighed. "I believe – though I don't know for sure – that Catherine and Lachlan Cattanach were discussing what might have happened and if there had been any doubts about the poisoning. Then perhaps she had to leave."

"Leave? And go where?"

Hector Mor shrugged. "Again, I cannot say for a fact, but perhaps she went back to the Campbells in Inveraray."

"What, left Duart for good?"

He leaned in to me and raised his hand. I jerked my head back, but instead of a slap, I felt his fingers rest gently on my hair, which he caressed. "Like you, Lorna, I hope this is not the case. Perhaps it was for her own safety. We will find out when we return to Duart after the wedding." He smiled and his hand went back to rest on the hilt of his sword. He stood up tall and beckoned over his men. "Let us go to the castle. I have much to prepare."

He began to weave his way between cow pats and the frantic procession of people then, just at the next hut, turned to wave, shouting, "See you tonight, Lorna," before bowing towards me as if I were a lady.

I stood watching him, my heart beating madly, not knowing how to react to what he had just said about Catherine; and more importantly, not knowing what to feel about a man fondling my hair with such a delicate touch.

*

Angus was not only hot, he was now sweating heavily. Ann and I spent the afternoon tending to him with wet cloths, mopping his brow. She tried to have him eat some soup, but he refused. He had also stopped drinking more than tiny sips.

"You go along to the castle, Lorna. You are harpist to the Macleans and your role cannot be replaced. You can surely play without the fiddle accompaniment?"

I nodded, lifting my hand from his hot brow.

"I'll stay with him this evening. Now go – I'll send for you if things get any worse."

And so I set off towards the castle; I had no choice. I would play all the pieces I knew Hector Mor loved, those specific to Mull and to the Macleans. I could do this, I thought as I walked along the track, holding my head high.

At the entrance, two guards escorted me to the Great Hall. I marvelled at all the fires blazing; it was far warmer than Duart Castle's Great Hall ever was. I took my place on a stool by the back wall and waited until I was told to play. From here I could see everyone arrive and leave.

Soon I saw Hector Mor enter with a gentleman and lady I'd not seen before; I presumed they were the Lord and Lady of Dunyvaig. He sat beside them at the table and the servants brought them drinks. Then a woman entered with a baby and the nurse from Duart: it was little Amie. The last time I saw her she was crying, and I hoped she was not ill like poor Angus. I peered over: she looked hale and hearty and was smiling and gurgling at everyone. Amie was handed to the lady beside Hector Mor, who I realised now was her foster mother, Lady Dunyvaig. With a pang, I thought of Catherine. This just wasn't right, handing over her child to another family. The lady sat Amie on her lap and played with her for a short while, beaming with pleasure, before returning her to the woman and our nurse. So at least Amie was going to be loved and well cared for here. But Catherine must be missing her so much. Was she truly back at Inveraray with her own family?

I watched the women leave with Amie then turned around when a servant approached and said that Hector Mor wanted me to start playing; his wife-to-be would arrive soon. Perhaps he thought it would be a good portent. I sat up straight, stretched my fingers towards the strings and began to play. I had chosen old melodies I knew he liked and as I finished up the first tune, I felt a hush descend on the room. I hated it when they all looked at me; I had grown used to playing behind the screen, but Hector Mor wanted me to be visible. And so here I was. I kept looking at my strings and my hands, even though I did not need to; I knew the tunes so well. I glanced over to see him nodding and smiling, his dark eyes shining in the candlelight.

After a few songs, Hector Mor stood up and clapped for me to stop playing. Lord Macdonald got to his feet. The door was thrown wide, and a girl entered with two servants behind her. This must be Mary, the bride-to-be. I peered over at her, desperate to see what she looked like, but all I could see was a short, stocky girl enveloped in a billowing cape. She had a round, child-like face surrounded with a thick fur hood. She walked towards her groom and the father introduced her to Hector Mor, whose face remained impassive. He bowed graciously then took her hand to guide her to her place at table beside him. Her expression was a combination of fear and melancholy.

I began to play again and continued all through supper; as the ale and claret flowed, I plucked my strings, while glancing over at them. Though I saw him speaking often, she seemed to say very little. And she never took down the hood to her fur-lined cape. She must have been hot; the hall was stifling from the heat of the fires. How I wished the Great Hall at Duart could ever feel this warm.

I was beginning to worry about Angus. My gift to see things others couldn't see was sometimes a disadvantage and I wanted to dispel the bad feelings deep inside me. I looked over at the table and saw Mary stand up with her two servants, and she left the room without even saying goodbye to her parents nor her husband-to-be. I tried to see Hector Mor's expression but could not; the wedding should be interesting, though that was how marriages were with these sorts of people. I felt myself feeling a little sorry for Hector Mor, but then I shook off that thought; men had everything they wanted in their lives, surely it was Mary I should feel sorry for.

I saw Hector Mor rise from the table and I realised he was coming towards me. He stood beside me as I finished the final melody and leaned down towards me.

"That was grand, Lorna. Thank you. You made the evening far less painful."

I frowned.

"Mary is not a conversationalist." He smirked. "Like you."

I stood up.

"You may go now. And I shall see you tomorrow at the wedding. The Macdonald harpists will also be in attendance, so you will take your lead from them." He turned around and returned to the table while I headed for the door then down the stairs, before running all the way along the track to the little hut, praying all the time that Angus had made a sudden recovery.

Chapter 32

1520

Catherine

I stood on my tiptoes high up on the castle ramparts, looking down from the tower towards the harbour.

"Remember how we used to come up here every market day, Catherine? We would watch the boats and see which of the fisher girls could gut the fish the fastest." Ellen pointed down towards baskets of herring being unloaded from a fishing boat at the quay.

I turned to her and smiled. My sister had become a beauty, with her freckled face and thick, reddish-brown hair. She was soon to be married to a kinsman from Clachan and would travel to the far end of the loch to live with his family. At least her husband-to-be was another Campbell – a known entity, unlike mine.

"Yes, and then I'd run down the stairs and all the way to the harbour, disobeying Mama's orders, to meet a certain boat." I sighed. "D'you remember that too?"

She glanced at me then turned her gaze back down to the pier. "Did you see Archibald at the banquet, Catherine?"

She too had been at that infamous feast to celebrate my return.

I shook my head. "No, remember I didn't arrive till later and he left soon after with our brothers." I bit my lip. "Ellen, I'm so worried about John and Donald – and Archibald. Lachlan Cattanach is a ruthless man, he could..."

"There's nothing he can do to them, Catherine. He is the lone Maclean among many Campbells on the journey back to Mull. All his men are chained up in our dungeons." She grimaced. "Have you ever seen them?"

"No – I wouldn't even know how to get down to them."

"They're like black holes, filthy and festering. And they stink."

"How on earth do you know?"

She grinned. "I wanted to scare Mary one day. She was annoying me – you know how she can spend days on end just whining for no reason. So I had one of the guards let us into the dungeons. There were no prisoners there, but Mary nearly fainted, she was so terrified."

I chuckled. "Poor Mary. Will Mama ever be able to find a husband for her?"

"Unlikely." Ellen shrugged.

She turned to me and beamed. "You will have your little Amie back here very soon, Catherine, you just wait and see."

I let out a long breath. "I just don't know, Ellen. I'm so worried that when they arrive at Duart Castle there will be an ambush and the Macleans will slaughter our dear brothers and…and Archibald." I shook my head.

"He has no means of getting word back to his men as they travel from Inveraray to Mull, so they won't be prepared and John said they would go straight to Amie's room, remove her and the nurse, then come home at once, before the Macleans have time to do anything."

"My other worry is that she's already gone."

"What do you mean?"

"I mean gone, taken to Islay where she's to be fostered." I explained to Ellen about the barbaric practice the Macleans followed, of fostering to secure bonds with another clan or family. Her eyes grew wide as she listened.

"But surely they can't have taken her there already? Isn't she too little? Is she fully weaned?"

I nodded. "That was all being hastened, on Lachlan's orders. And being the greedy wee soul she is, she took to porridge and brose very well. She lapped up solid food like a child of five would."

Tears began to trickle down my cheeks as I thought of her darling, chubby face, her little dimples and the thick, dark curly hair falling over her bright eyes. More and more, I thought she had such a look of the Macleans, though I'd kept hoping her features might resemble Archibald's. Now I feared that was not going to happen.

"Well then, our brothers will just take a boat and sail on to Islay. How far is it from Mull?"

"It's really quite a long way – even further from here I think. But also," I screwed my eyes tight, remembering what Colin had said yesterday, "there's no way a Campbell would be welcome on Islay."

"Why not? Did we not all fight together at Flodden?"

"Yes, but that was seven years ago, and since the dissolution of the Lordship of the Isles, Campbells have supported the Stuart king."

"Yes, but why would we be unable to go to Islay?"

"There would be battles, for sure. The Macdonalds there and all over the islands are convinced the Lordship of the Isles will be restored and since it's based on Islay, they hate the Campbells for supporting King James, even though he's only a boy." I sighed. "It's complicated, but Colin said if Amie is already on Islay, there's nothing we can do." I began to snivel, and Ellen pulled me into her arms.

"Don't be sad, Catherine, it will all work out. Our brothers will find a way, just wait and see."

*

Grandmother and I were walking in the woods at the back of the castle, along the river. Two servants followed close behind, carrying chairs in case she needed to rest. We strolled along the avenues of tall Scots pines. She stopped to look up.

"These trees never cease to delight. Look how high those branches go." She pointed to the top. "Oh, did you see the squirrel on that branch there?"

I peered up and saw a flash of red as a bushy tail sped along a branch.

As we left the shore to walk into the woods, I spotted a sandpiper and grandmother seemed surprised that I knew what type of bird it was.

"I know a lot about the names of birds now, especially seabirds."

"Was it that girl – the harpist – who taught you these things?"

I nodded. "Lorna, yes. And in return I taught her to read and write."

"Excellent. Everyone should be able to read and write, no matter what their station."

"I wondered about writing a letter to Lorna, but I'm sure Lachlan would prevent any communication from me to anyone at Duart."

"Catherine, how were things with your husband before you were taken to that awful place to die? Something surely had happened to provoke such evil in an otherwise good man?"

I took Grandmother's arm once more and we continued walking over the roots towards the burn. I could not possibly tell her about the poisoning; it was too shameful.

"I'm sure he was at one time a good man, but certainly while I was living in that cold, dark castle, I seldom found any warmth or affection. He was always leaving to go somewhere else, anywhere other than to be with me, his wife. His trips away to the Treshnish Islands and Ulva and Islay were many."

"Catherine, you know men have their own things to attend to and these are often away from home. Look at your brother the earl; he is hardly here. It was so fortuitous he was at home when you arrived a few days ago."

I nodded. "I know." We had come to a clearing and I turned to the servants behind us. "Put the chairs here, please. We will take refreshments."

Mama had been furious when she heard I had planned a walk with her mother-in-law – *so unladylike*, she muttered – but I know Grandmother enjoyed the woods just as much as I did. I would not be stuck inside on a beautiful day like today. Mama said she would only permit the promenade if we were accompanied by chairs and drinks – and obviously servants to carry them.

They rushed to help Grandmother into a chair and poured us both a goblet of claret.

"A warming cup would have been more appropriate, but this is better than nothing, Catherine," she said, smiling as she looked around the autumnal scene of fallen russet and golden leaves.

Once the servants had moved to the other side to sit on a tree trunk, I leaned towards her.

"Tell me more about Archibald's wife, Margaret. Is she a kinswoman?"

She lowered the cup from her lips and turned to face me. "Of course she is."

"Where is she from?"

"Inverawe. Her father is Duncan Campbell. I'm sure you will have met her family at some stage."

"But why is she still here at Inveraray? Surely her child is about to be born. Will she have it here at the castle?"

Grandmother sighed. "When they arrived some month or so ago, they were meant to stay for two nights. Then we had those terrible gales – much earlier than usual – and our physician deemed it unwise for her to travel back to either Auchenbreck, where they now live, or even to her family in Inverawe."

"So we have to put her up and have her stay here for several weeks while she is in confinement?"

"Catherine, as you well know, the Campbells pay high regard to the rules of hospitality; that is why Colin allowed your husband to leave unharmed. She will stay here until she is well enough to return to her home, with her husband – and their child."

I sighed.

"He is not yours, Catherine," Grandmother hissed. "He will return from Mull with your brothers and stay with his wife at Inveraray until it is deemed safe for them to leave. And you shall let them be."

It had been a long time since I heard her speak in such tones. It took a lot to rile my grandmother. But on this she was clearly angry. "Is that understood?"

I said nothing while she took my hand in hers. "Sweetheart, soon you will have your own little baby with you, and you can take your time to decide what to do. But until then, they have their lives, you have yours."

She beckoned over the servants. "Let us walk back now, Catherine – there's a sudden bite in the air." She shivered. "Your mama would not be pleased if one of us caught a chill." She got to her feet and I took her arm. We strolled down the path along the river towards the castle, talking of my sisters and their babies.

Then, just when the castle was in sight, I stopped and looked between two hazel trees, gasping as I recognised something. "Do you know what those are called?"

"What, those clumps of tall, straggly leaves?"

"Yes, in the late spring and summer they have a purple flower. It's called Wolfsbane. Or sometimes Monkshood, as the flowers resemble a monk's cowl."

I thought of Archibald and his disguise to come to visit me at Duart. I looked around and thought once more of the woods where we spent so much time during those few days of joy, nine months before Amie was born.

We walked on. "Will Margaret Campbell's baby be born soon then, do you think?"

"Any day now, they say."

"Is she in Isabel's old room?"

"Yes," she said. "Why?"

I shrugged. "No reason," I said, huddling in close to my grandmother on the final steps home.

Chapter 33

1520

Lachlan Cattanach

Dear God, these Campbells were full of themselves. Throughout the entire journey from Inveraray to Connel, people would rush out of their hovels and huts to greet their lords and masters. The two brothers – John and Donald – would nod graciously back to the men and women as if they were gods, not merely the brothers of the Earl of Argyll. Sometimes, they would introduce them to Lachlan, as if he was at all interested, and of course they all bore the surname Campbell. Perhaps the same could be said of his own clan on Mull, but at least the Macleans did not have time for such subservience amongst their people.

All he wanted to do was ride on, through the woods, along the lochs and between the glens, till they got the boat over to Duart. Then they would see who was in charge, then he could plan the next stage. They had positioned him between the two brothers, with their kinsman Archibald Campbell of Auchenbreck at the front and some other kinsmen at the back. The Campbell up front looked different from the others, with his thick yellow mane.

He spent much of the journey wondering how on earth she had done it; how did she make it back to Inveraray? She could not have swum off the rock – how could she possibly have known how to swim? Even fishermen cannot swim. Perhaps she had been rescued by some of these Campbells out in their fishing boats; yes, that must have been how it happened, and of course they would have been delighted to help not only a damsel in distress but one of their own. Though as he mulled over these thoughts, Lachlan could not help but think of another option, which involved his harpist Lorna, whose attitude to him at the pier that day suggested she knew something. Good God, his overly sensitive son Hector Mor might also have been involved.

"Maclean, we will rest here for the night," a voice shouted from behind. "Let us all dismount."

And so his train of thought was interrupted; tomorrow he would return to it.

"When we get to Duart," Donald said as they sat around the campfire later eating bannocks and cheese, "we intend to go straight away to your daughter's room and take her back at once to her mother. We shall not linger."

Lachlan said nothing but glanced up at the trees.

"Then – and only then – shall we release your five kinsmen from our dungeons," said his elder brother.

Still he said nothing, though he wanted to howl with rage at the man's imperious tone, as if the Campbells could tell the Macleans what could and could not be done. Instead, he spread out his plaid behind him and lay his head down, as if to sleep. But he was wide awake, listening to them whisper about their plan to take Amie home as soon as possible. He was trying not to chuckle as he thought how they would react when they realised she was not on Mull, but instead over the sea on Islay.

As their hushed voices gave way to silence and gentle snores, Lachlan looked up at the dark sky, listening to the boughs creaking above his head. And soon a smile played on his lips as he studied the moonlight, watching the branches sway and the twigs dance as the wind got up. Dark clouds began to converge, flitting across the moon. God was surely answering his prayers: this gathering storm was just what he needed to help his plan succeed.

*

The boat was dragged well up the beach to prevent it being blown away by the wind. They managed to get themselves over the Firth of Lorne though the boatman at Connel tried to maintain it was too dangerous to take a boat out, even one the size of his. Lachlan insisted and of course they made it, though the heaving from side to side of the boat had been a little precarious at times, the waves cascading over them as they beat against the wind. All of them were drenched.

Donald Campbell looked very pale when they eventually alighted onto the beach at Duart, then he rushed over to a rock and vomited. Sea sickness must be an awful thing, but it never bothered someone of Lachlan's strong disposition. Really, what were a few surges and swells in the water; it was not as if the boat was going to capsize.

He looked back to see the tormented waters heaving towards the shore and crashing on to the rocks as the deluge continued. His men had arrived to tie up the boat and guide them with lanterns up to the castle through the dark. It felt good to be among kin again.

They headed up over the pebbles and shingle as the gales ripped through the low trees at the top of the beach. Wrapping their damp plaids around them, they staggered into the teeth of the wind. Lachlan thought back to the first time Catherine landed here, in similar weather, soaked to the skin after the autumn storms had arrived early. They had to go on horseback from the beach as she vowed she could not walk, her legs immobile after that "most dreadful boat journey". And now here he was with her brothers, just over two years later. What eventful years they had been.

On entering the castle, he invited his guests up into the Great Hall; for they were now Maclean guests and Lachlan Cattanach Maclean was no longer a Campbell hostage. They started muttering amongst themselves that they had to fetch the baby, but he pointed out that no-one could go anywhere this stormy evening – and did they not want their plaids dried off first? He commanded his servants to bring dry plaids and for drinks to be served.

Grudgingly, they removed their plaids, dripping with sea water, and huddled by the fire. The noise of the wind howling down the chimney above the hearth was as loud as it had ever been. The servants poured them some ale and after he had downed his, Lachlan asked the boy to tell Agnes to prepare supper for them and to look after the boatman in the warmth of the kitchen. The Campbells were all still grim-faced but seemed pleased to have the dry plaids around their shoulders.

John, the elder brother, came towards him.

"Sadly, this is no weather for a little one to be outside. We will stay here until the storm abates. Hopefully that will be tomorrow morning."

Lachlan decided to ignore his haughty tone and play the gracious host. "Of course, you are all welcome here at Duart. Beds will be prepared while we eat."

He gestured to the table, which was being laid with food. As they sat down, he called over one of the maids who was helping bring food up from the kitchen.

"Tell the others to be generous with the ale and the claret," he whispered to her. "Top up their glasses often." The girl nodded but she was distracted. She kept looking over to the table.

"Did you hear me, Elspeth?" He recognised the girl – she used to be Catherine's maid but now presumably helped Agnes in the kitchen.

She was biting her lip and frowning.

Lachlan bent down towards her. "What ails you, lass?"

She turned her face away from the table and he had to lean in to hear her.

"That man, my Lord. The one with the yellow hair. He looks

familiar."

She kept biting her lower lip and it was beginning to annoy him. "Stop doing that; speak clearly," he muttered. "How could he possibly look familiar? He is Archibald Campbell. He has never been here and you have never left the castle – to my knowledge."

Her eyes widened. "Can I speak to you over there?" she said, indicating a nook in the wall. Honestly, he was starving, but he decided to humour the girl and so followed on.

"My Lord, I just realised where I have seen him before. When you were away once, that man was here, but he was dressed as a priest. I remember his face – and on a couple of occasions when his cowl was down, I saw that mane of yellow hair."

"I don't understand," he said, shaking his head. "He is clearly not a priest. He is a Campbell nobleman, from Auchenbreck I believe. When was this and where was I?"

"I think you may have been hunting wolves, my Lord, for when you returned, you had the skins made into the coverings for her Lady's bed."

"Was Hector Mor with me or was he here in the castle?"

"He was away too, but when he arrived back, the priest – that man there – left very soon after."

Lachlan's heart began to race. "Was he here with any of the other men at the table?"

She shook her head. "Just him and his servants."

"Did he spend much time with her Ladyship?"

She looked down. "Yes."

He grabbed her chin. "Alone?" he hissed.

She nodded.

He took a deep breath and removed his hand from her face. "Did they stay inside or venture out?"

"The hems of her gowns were sometimes covered in earth, as if she had been in the woods."

And then something came to mind: something that Hector

Mor had said to Lachlan when he'd returned, jubilant from the wolf hunt, about a familiar looking priest being here from Inveraray Castle. He towered over the girl, fists clenched at his sides. "Do not speak of this to anyone. Do you understand?"

She nodded and began to bite her lip once more. Poor girl, she was terrified of him. "You have done well, Elspeth. Thank you for telling me this." Lachlan smiled. "Now go and top up those men's drinks: be generous, let the ale flow."

Chapter 34

1520

Lachlan Cattanach

He held his candle aloft and groped along the wall as he headed up the stairs to where the Campbells slept. He spoke to one of the men standing guard outside the door, and the guard unlocked it quietly and they both stepped inside. Every one of the Campbells was snoring or wheezing; clearly the abundance of Maclean refreshments had helped them fall asleep immediately. Lachlan lowered the candle over each body and soon came to him, thankfully a little away from the others, by the wall. He beckoned the guard over, putting a finger to his lips. He knelt beside him and placed his dagger at the man's throat.

"Archibald Campbell, we need to talk," he whispered in his ear.

He woke with a start and tried to move his hand to his dagger, but the guard held his arms fast. "Make a noise and your pale white throat will be slit. I fear there will be a lot of blood." He shook his head. "That would be a pity."

He did not move, and Lachlan gestured to the guard to remove his dagger and pull his arms behind his back. Slowly they dragged him to the door.

"Come with me to the Great Hall," he told the guard, and together they hauled him down the stairs.

The fire was out but the smouldering embers guided them to the table.

"Tie him to the chair," Lachlan said, handing him his belt.

While the guard was doing this, he strolled over to the table and poured himself a goblet of ale. He gulped it down then went to sit beside Archibald. He motioned for the guard to wait over by the stairs.

"Archibald Campbell," he said, smiling. "I hear you have been here before?"

The tip of Lachlan's dagger hovered just under his chin.

He shook his head, his eyes wild with fear.

"Think again, please. This is of great importance."

"I've never been here, Maclean. I can assure you."

"Well, that is not what I heard from my servants."

He teased his dagger down, nearer Archibald's throat.

"Why would I have come here?"

"Because I believe you knew my wife and perhaps thought she needed, how shall I put it…spiritual guidance?"

"I never…" Lachlan's dirk was now touching his skin. "Yes, I came once to see if she was all right, her sisters had heard she was lonely."

"And why would they send you? Were you two perhaps childhood sweethearts?"

He shook his head. "I came in my capacity as a kinsman, that was all."

"I see, so then why did you dress as a priest instead of presenting yourself as a cousin?"

"I thought it better for…"

Lachlan leaned towards him, never allowing his blade to leave the man's neck. "I am tired of these lies, Archibald. So let me tell you what happened: you came here, you abused my hospitality, you took advantage of my poor, innocent wife – then you left. Is that not true?"

Archibald tried to shake his head but as he moved, the tip of the blade slit his white skin. Red began to seep onto the edge of the knife.

He remained motionless. "I did come to see Catherine, it's true, but I never imposed upon her."

"So you never went to the woods alone?"

He opened his mouth to speak then shut it.

Keeping the dagger at Archibald's throat where the blood was now trickling down his shirt, Lachlan gulped down the rest of his ale. "This is what we are going to do, Archibald Campbell. You will do exactly as I say. Do you understand?"

"Yes," he mumbled. "But..."

"There are no buts. I overheard you saying to your kinsmen as we travelled from Inveraray that your dear wife – Margaret, is it? – is with child and shall deliver her baby soon." Lachlan smiled. "What joy babies bring."

Archibald's eyes were wide with horror.

"If you do not do as I say, I will send Maclean kinsmen to Inveraray or indeed Auchenbreck and..." He sighed. "Well, although many mothers do of course sadly die in childbirth, it would be a great pity for you to lose your young wife so soon thereafter."

He raised his dagger and placed the blade in front of Archibald's immobile face. "At last you understand me. Now listen very carefully while I tell you precisely what I want you to do."

*

The following morning, the wind had abated a little, perhaps just enough for a boat to cross the firth. Lachlan was in the Great Hall early, awaiting their arrival. As he had anticipated, they were up at dawn and had gone upstairs to the nursery to try to take his little girl. Of course the door was locked and so they trooped downstairs, with no choice but to join him at table.

"Ah, good morning to you all."

"Why is the child's room locked, Maclean?" growled the second brother, Donald. He strode over to the table, scowling. He was the most belligerent of them. His elder brother was more brooding, a deep one, but in his experience, they could often be the most dangerous.

"Do please sit down. Eat, drink! You will be thirsty after your long sleep." He gestured to the chairs around the table.

"Where is my sister's daughter, Maclean?" asked John, whose face was devoid of expression.

"Start eating, please, all of you, and I will explain what has happened."

Reluctantly they all sat, and he looked directly at Archibald Campbell, whose eyes were bloodshot, presumably through lack of sleep. He immediately looked away.

"I discovered some news late last night and did not want to wake you. Hector Mor, my closest kinsman, is on Islay getting married." He decided he would not tell these Campbells he had a son. Instead, he grabbed a hunk of bannock.

"And?" John gave him a steely, cold stare.

"I just found out that he has taken my daughter Amie with him."

Donald leaned across the table. "Why would he do that?"

"As you know, I have influence not only on Mull, but also on Islay – and Tiree, in fact. On these islands – and across swathes of the Scottish Highlands, as you will no doubt know – the people uphold the time-honoured practice of fosterage. We Macleans believe strongly in the benefits of this tradition. We have formed excellent relations with the Macdonalds of Islay. Hector Mor, as I said, is about to marry Mary Macdonald of Dunyvaig and it is there, at Dunyvaig Castle, that my daughter Amie will be fostered."

"But she is still a baby. Is this the normal custom?" Donald growled.

"Children can either be fostered as babies or as children. It was my decision to have Amie fostered once she was weaned."

"So she is on Islay now?"

"I believe so, though I cannot be sure. All I know is that Hector Mor set sail some five or six days ago for Islay and, depending on the winds and the tides, they should certainly have arrived by now. Though if the child needed rest, then they were going to stop at Colonsay or Oronsay for a day or two."

"Then shall we set sail there now?" one of the younger kinsmen asked.

Donald turned and snapped at his cousin, "Campbells are not welcome on Islay, has your father taught you nothing, Iain?"

John held up his hand and everyone around the table looked at him. "It is certainly a pity that you had no idea she was being taken away. Could you not have told us about this possibility before, Maclean?"

"As I said, the tides and winds are the deciding factor when you live on an island as I do. I did not know when they would set sail. I presumed it would tie in with Hector Mor's wedding, which I believed to be next month." He shrugged. "Clearly, I was wrong."

John's usually inscrutable expression changed. His eyes narrowed. "So how do you suggest we get our sister's child back?"

Lachlan raised a finger. "I have been thinking about that, and I think the best plan is that I go over to Islay whenever the weather is favourable and fetch her back, cancel the fosterage agreement with Macdonald, then Hector Mor shall deliver her back to you in Inveraray."

"And how, pray, do we know you will keep your word this time, Maclean?" John was now leaning in towards Lachlan, his mien decidedly menacing.

"The five men now entrapped in your dungeons are, after Hector Mor, my closest kinsmen. Do you honestly think I would leave them there to rot and die?"

John Campbell downed his ale. "You will go to Islay as soon as the weather allows. Give Amie to your kinsman to bring directly to Inveraray and her mother." He raised his hand as Lachlan opened his mouth to speak. "That is a statement, Maclean, not a question. And if we do not see our niece within six weeks, before winter sets in, then your five men in our dungeons shall perish." He raised a finger. "And not a quick death – theirs will be slow

188

and wretched. Is that understood?"

Lachlan nodded and looked at the grim faces around the table. Archibald was hunched over his food, eyes down.

"That seems to me like a perfect solution. And now I will go down to the kitchen and discuss with the boatman the possibility of your journey home today."

"And of your crossing over to Islay."

"Of course," Lachlan said. He bowed as he left them at the table, sure in his conviction that the tides and winds might be favourable enough for the relatively short boat trip over the firth to Connel for the Campbells; but perhaps, sadly, not good enough for himself to sail over the great seas to Islay.

Chapter 35

1520

Lorna

I was peeling an onion to add to the soup when I heard a noise. It wasn't Angus –I'd just checked on him and he was sleeping. Sadly, still not a deep slumber, but rather the tormented sleep of an ill boy. How much more could he sweat out of that thin little body? Ann and Donnie were to be at the castle all day, helping to prepare for the wedding feast there later, so I was staying inside with Angus until Ann returned.

I wiped my hands and went to the door. Hector Mor stood there, two of his men behind him.

"Is everything all right?" I asked. Why would he come here on the morning of his wedding day?

"Yes, I just came to ask how Angus is today. Will he be able to join you to play at the wedding feast?"

I shook my head. "He's sleeping, it's all he seems to do. That and sweat. Every time he awakens, we try to get some drink down him."

"May I see him?"

I could hardly say no, so I stepped aside to let him past and noticed his men approach then stand guard at the door.

I pointed to the pallet in the corner and watched Hector Mor tiptoe over. He knelt and put the back of his hand to Angus's brow.

"Has he eaten anything, Lorna?"

"Not really – we try to get broth down him, but it's not easy."

He turned towards the fire in the middle of the room where the pot was hanging from the swee. "I don't suppose you have any meat or bones to put in the soup?"

I laughed. "What do you think, Hector Mor?"

He grinned. "I thought not. I'll have a cow heel sent along, to put in the soup. My mother used to swear by that if anyone was ill."

"Thank you," I said, looking into his dark brown eyes, which were full of compassion. How could he be so different from his father?

He got to his feet and came towards me. "Will you be able to play tonight with the Macdonald musicians?"

"Do I have any choice?"

"You see, you never used to be this forward, Lorna. Before Catherine arrived at Duart, you would hardly speak at all, rather like my bride-to-be." He sighed.

"She will come out of herself once you are married, surely."

He shook his head. "I don't know, Lorna, I really don't."

"She's only a child, though. How old is she? Fourteen?"

"No, she's sixteen – small for her age, I grant you. But she's of an age to be perfectly capable of conversation, she simply chooses not to communicate... Well, with me anyway."

"Perhaps she's just shy. Give her time."

"Sadly, I have no choice in the matter." He headed towards the door where we could see the broad backs of his men. I was following when he stopped suddenly and turned around. I was right in front of him, and he reached out his hand. I stood stock still while he touched my hair then stroked the side of my face with such tenderness, I was deeply moved. I gazed at him but could say nothing. Even if I had not been choking with emotion, what was there to say?

He turned and went out the door without a word, and I collapsed onto the stool by the fire, where I sat with my head in my hands. After a while I raised my head high, stood up and took a deep breath. This would not do. I had to finish the soup then practise my tunes for the wedding feast.

I was just adding dulse to the pan when another noise at the door made me swivel around. It was one of the servants from the castle, a young girl, carrying a large bundle wrapped in cloth. She proffered it to me, and I thanked her. Unwrapping it, I saw it was a cow's heel. It seemed he really did care.

I took the heel outside to wash it in a basin. The wind was getting up, and I hoped it was not the start of the autumn storms. I had just sat on the low stool outside the door when I heard a commotion from the castle. All morning, there had been crowds of people down at the shore, unloading provisions from the many boats tied up alongside the sea gate. There were also some grand vessels arriving at the port and some ladies and gentlemen disembarking in their finery, presumably guests arriving for the wedding feast. Most of them went directly into the castle, but I looked along the path and saw a procession of horses with riders heading in our direction, away from the water.

As I stared, I realised that it was Hector Mor and his men, trotting towards the woods. Villagers were coming out of their houses to wave at him and he smiled and waved back. He must be on his way to the church for his wedding. I wondered if the bride too would follow. Ann said they would have a short service in the doorway of the church, just the bridal couple and her parents, then they would return for the wedding feast and a castle full of guests. As he approached, I smiled, and he drew in his reins to slow down. "We head for Kildalton church, Lorna." He leant towards me and whispered, "Wish me luck!"

I nodded and waved at him as he headed towards the woods, where the scarlet and yellow leaves were swirling and whirling in the wind.

I had just finished scrubbing the cow's heel when another procession interrupted my thoughts. It was a cart pulled by two horses and inside were two ladies and a gentleman. As it approached, I could see it was Mary and her parents. She wore a dark blue gown trimmed with gold and on top of that was the same fur-edged silvery grey cape she had worn the night before.

And just like last night, the hood was firmly up around her head. I gazed up at their faces and saw that, though her parents smiled at everyone wishing them well, Mary's face remained glum – not quite angry, not quite sad, perhaps just wretched. And off they sped, towards the woods to meet Hector Mor and his men.

*

I sat beside the other musicians with my clarsach on my knee. I had asked them what they were playing and the leader – a lad of perhaps eighteen or nineteen – told me their tunes. His name was Johnnie and when we were practising together, I was impressed by how good he was on the fiddle. But it made me sad Angus was not here too.

Before I had left him with Ann, he was awake and slightly less hot, but he said his head was so sore and he was coughing a lot. Ann would try to get him to drink more of the nourishing broth and I was sure he looked a little better because of it; but that could have been wishful thinking. She promised to send for me if he got worse again and I said I would be back the minute the music was over.

"Don't rush back, Lorna. It's a wedding, you'll be playing late. It will be fine, don't worry."

And so we waited for the last of the guests to arrive and sit down at the tables, which were looking grand, the goblets and platters shining in the flickering candlelight. Compared to Duart, where the candles were always lacking, it all looked so pretty and dare I say, romantic. I hoped Hector Mor would be happy and that Mary could somehow warm to the prospect of marriage to him. I actually smiled as I wondered if she would ever take her fur cape down off her head. Having seen her twice, I had no idea at all what colour her hair was; her mother's was dark brown, but her father's was fair.

There was a sudden hush as the bridal couple arrived and headed towards the table to take their seats. I strained my neck to see how she was looking, but again she had her cape hood up, so not even a stray lock of hair showed, and she was not smiling at all.

"Johnnie, does Mary ever smile?" I whispered to the lad beside me. "Or even speak much?"

He swivelled around, his lank brown hair swinging as he turned towards me and muttered, "Yes, she does. She has..." And then Lord Macdonald gestured over to him to start to play, which he did; and we all joined in. I kept looking over at Mary, who stared straight ahead while Hector beckoned over a servant to pour her wine. She never engaged with him, hardly even acknowledged his presence. She talked to her father on her other side, but I could not see her speak to Hector Mor at all.

We continued to play throughout the evening, all sorts of tunes, though we'd been told not to play laments; this was a celebration, there must be nothing melancholy tonight. And it certainly was true that there was great merriment amongst the guests as the claret flowed, but still Mary sat, glum and hooded like a priest.

We had just finished a lively pibroch when a servant approached. "They say you're to go to the table. His Lordship wants to thank you."

"All of us?" Johnnie asked. There were five of us playing.

"He said just you two," gesturing to me and Johnnie.

We laid down our instruments and headed to the table. We stood in front of Lord and Lady Macdonald, both rosy-cheeked and merry with wine.

"Johnnie, well done. And to our gifted Maclean harpist. You've brought such cheer to this happy gathering," Lord Macdonald said. His wife nudged him and pointed to two goblets in front of him.

"Ah, yes, take a cup with us, both of you," and we lifted our drinks and bowed our thanks. I sipped mine, for I had never liked claret, but since I was thirsty after all that playing, I drank it easily.

I was just thinking that not everyone sitting beside Lord Macdonald was looking as happy as he was when I noticed Hector Mor lean over the table towards his father-in-law. He was beaming. "Alexander Donald, haven't they played well? What joy they have brought to this feast."

"That they have, Hector Mor. Our fiddler and your harpist play together as if they have done so for years."

As we turned to look at Hector Mor, I could not help but look at his new wife. The transformation on her face was unbelievable. Her facial expression having hovered between shades of glum to hints of morose, her grey eyes were now twinkling, and her pink lips were parted as she smiled. Dear Lord, what had brought this about?

Hector Mor laid his hand on hers and looked directly at her. He too seemed surprised by the change in her appearance.

"We have enjoyed the music greatly, have we not, Mary?"

Without looking at him, she nodded and continued to smile – a beautiful, full smile that made her look, for the first time, rather lovely.

And as I turned around to go back to my seat, I saw Johnnie's face. He too was beaming, gazing directly at her. I glanced back and realised all at once that the smile on her face was not because of the pleasure the music had brought her and it was certainly not for her husband: it was for Johnnie.

I stumbled back to my seat and picked up my clarsach to play. Johnnie followed and sat down beside me; his expression was inscrutable. "And now you see her smile, Lorna. It is not for everyone, but..."

We were interrupted by a figure running through the door towards us. What was the hurry? And then I realised it was Donnie.

"Lorna, you're to come home at once! Ann says the boy's taken a turn for the worse."

Chapter 36

1520

Catherine

I sat in Grandmother's chamber, sucking the finger I'd just stabbed with the needle. I had never been very good at embroidery, but Mama said I could not sit and read a book while there were other people present. She herself was holding court in the corner, talking to one of her more biddable daughters – Jean – who had come to visit. She had left her two small children and baby twins behind. Thank God – I didn't think I could stand to see my elder sister blissfully happy with not just one but two babies when I had none. It was so unfair: she had married into the Lamont family, already allies of the Campbells, and she did not have to journey over the sea to get here.

I could not help thinking she hadn't aged well. When she laughed, I could see she had lost a couple of teeth and her hair was thinning and dull. Perhaps that is what three pregnancies did for you; well, I did not plan to have as many children as she. Although I had to admit, Mama looked remarkably youthful still, even after twelve pregnancies.

Grandmother nudged me and asked if my finger was all right.

"It's fine, thank you. I was hoping to read instead of having to do needlework, but it was not permitted."

She smiled that knowing smile of hers and we both looked over to Jean, who had turned to us.

"So, Grandmother, what do you think Catherine ought to do now? Mama says that once she has her child back, she must return with her to Mull and make amends with her husband. Do you agree?"

Grandmother sighed. "I think it is still too early to make any plans as to Catherine's future. She has just had to undergo the most awful experience and it will take time to heal. For now, I believe she ought to wait for the safe arrival of her daughter. Later, she can decide her future and also what is best for the little one." She patted my hand. "Besides, your brothers might have their own ideas once they return from Mull."

Ah, my brothers: it's always about the men being the heroes, isn't it? They make all the decisions, then act on them courageously, while we women simply sit around waiting at home, chattels to the end. I opened my mouth to say something to that effect, then thought better of it; Mama would accuse me of being a difficult, cantankerous daughter, unlike my sisters who simply did as she asked. At least Ellen was less acquiescent; I hoped that did not change once she was married.

The door swung open and Mary ran in. She sped over to Jean and embraced her.

"Mary, do stop running. I have told you before. Girls of your age are on the brink of becoming ladies, and ladies do not run. Ever." Mama shook her head as her youngest daughter settled herself down beside her older sister. Poor Mary was of an age where spots dominated her face; she was covered by red blotches and blemishes.

I turned to Grandmother and whispered, "Does Aggie still work in the kitchen?"

"Yes, these are her excellent wheaten bannocks here," she said, taking a bite from a thinly buttered bannock. "Why?"

"I was just wondering if she might be able to make a remedy for Mary's skin?"

She nodded. "Coincidentally, I spoke to Aggie just yesterday about it. She was going to search for something – I've forgotten the name of the plant – the next time she was in the woods."

"I may go with her; I'd like to learn about herbal remedies." I smiled.

The door opened again, and my sister Isabel came in. She too went to embrace Jean then stood in the middle of the room, beaming. She coughed, and once she had our attention, addressed us all as if giving a victory speech. "The physician says that Margaret Campbell is in labour. God willing, there should be a baby born soon at Inveraray."

My sisters all clapped their hands with joy and even Mama nodded with pleasure.

I let out a long breath. So, Archibald's wife was soon to give birth. Would he be back in time to see it as a new-born? Would it be a girl, like my Amie? What colour would that baby's hair be, I wondered. I kept thinking about Lachlan and what wiles he may have used to put my brothers and Archibald in danger. I shook my head as if to remove thoughts of jeopardy and instead stood up as Isabel headed back to the door.

"Isabel, I've not had time to visit your friend Margaret Campbell yet. Is she up to visitors now or is she in pain yet?"

My older sister looked at me as if I was deranged. "Catherine, did that time on the rock affect your brain? Obviously she does not want visitors. She is having labour pains and only the midwife, the maids and I are in attendance. Once she has safely delivered, then of course you – and indeed all the family – can visit to pay our respects." She turned on her heels. "And now I must go."

Off she sped up the stairs, and as I watched her go, I thought, how dare that woman upstairs take my sister away from me? And indeed, how dare she give birth at Inveraray Castle? She is not a truly noble Campbell like our family, she is simply married to an Auchenbreck Campbell. I turned and went to sit beside Grandmother, who was giving me one of her unfathomable looks.

*

"So, Aggie, what's the name of the plant you think might help Mary's skin problems?"

We were walking along the river towards the woods up at the back of the castle. I had deliberately not told Mama I was coming out with Aggie; she would, as usual, have made such a fuss. I had told Ellen though, just in case there was any news I needed to hear about that woman who was still labouring away after two whole days. Much as I hated her, I did not envy her this, remembering the pain of childbirth all too well. And as I thought of it, I sighed. When would my own darling baby be back home with me? The fact my brothers had not yet returned was worrying; had Lachlan done something awful to them?

"It's called St John's Wort, my Lady. It has little yellow flowers that even now in the autumn should still be blooming. I'll need to use some flowers and the leaves then make them into a sort of poultice to lay on Lady Mary's skin. But not for too long, or it can cause a rash; just enough time to draw out the pustules. The poor wee lamb. You never suffered with blemishes at that age did you, my Lady?"

"No, I didn't, Aggie. I've been lucky." I looked around as we came into the woods. The tall Scots pine trees swayed gently in the breeze and the gold and russet leaves swirled around our feet.

"How do you prepare the plants back in the kitchen?"

"Oh, it's not too difficult. You need something to pound them all together then... Well, if you really are interested, my Lady, you can watch me do it?"

I smiled. "I would like that very much, thank you, Aggie."

We strolled on past the clearing where Grandmother and I had stopped for refreshments, then passed some silver birches and oaks.

"Slow down a bit, my Lady. The plants often grow near the oak trees, it must be the type of soil they live in."

We both scoured the ground for the yellow flowers till suddenly she cried, "There, over there, can you see?"

I followed her to spot some bright yellow, open flowers with dark red-brown berries amongst them.

"Are the berries only around in the autumn?"

"Yes, and I won't pick those – they can be poisonous."

"How poisonous?"

She shrugged her shoulders. "Well, if you ate a whole lot of them, you'd die." She laughed. "But you're hardly likely to do that, are you?"

I bent to pick the little flowers and their leaves, trying to avoid touching the berries.

"So what happens if birds eat the berries?"

"I suppose, depending how many they ate, they might die too." She stretched out her hand in front of mine. "Actually, my Lady, you'd better not pick the flowers. If anything happened to you and your mother knew I'd taken you into the woods to pick plants, I'd not come out of it well."

She grabbed the flowers and leaves from my hand and rammed them into her pockets, then pulled up some more before standing up straight, holding the base of her spine. "The trouble with all these plants is, if you've a bad back, it just tends to make it worse."

We both looked towards the flashes of red to our left, where two bushy-tailed squirrels were running up a thick trunk. We both smiled.

"Right," Aggie said. "Let's go down to the river and I'll wash my hands. You'd better do yours too."

We headed down to the river and as we passed some hazel trees, Aggie stopped and pointed towards some shrubs. "Since you're interested in plants, my Lady, do you see that one over there? The tall one with the straggly leaves?"

"Yes," I said, standing stock still.

"Never touch those. They're highly poisonous, especially in the late springtime, when the flowers are just out. Later in the season – now, in fact – they're a bit less deadly."

"But I'm sure you've never used it as a poison, Aggie?" I grinned.

"Now, who would I want dead, my Lady?" She chuckled. "I make remedies that cure people, not make them ill."

"Of course. So when can I watch you make Mary's remedy, Aggie? I'm interested in the process, how you pound the herbs and so on."

She shrugged. "If you really want to, then I'll send for you when I'm doing it. Now, let's wash our hands."

We had just plunged our hands into the cold water when we heard a noise. We both turned to look in the direction of the castle and saw two servants striding towards us.

"What on earth can they want?"

I sighed. "That Campbell woman's probably had her baby," I muttered.

"My Lady," said the stout lad who arrived first. He was panting, out of breath. "Lady Ellen says you're to come back at once. Their Lordships have arrived back from Mull."

As they turned on their heels and I wiped my hands on my gown, I was aware my heart was beating fast. Dear God, please let them all be safe; and please let them have my darling girl with them.

Chapter 37

1520

Lorna

I stayed by my brother's side all night. As he tossed and turned, sweating profusely, I mopped his brow and tried to get him to drink something – anything – but he was unable. He was muttering nonsense, clearly hallucinating, and I did not know what more I could do.

As the gusty winds of the night gave way to a calmer morning with a soft grey light, I noticed a slight change in Angus. His breathing was sometimes rapid then he seemed to stop breathing at all. Ann had come to join me and frowned at the sight of him. She was clearly worried.

"Lorna, the lad's not well at all, I fear." She patted my arm. "Do you want Donnie to go and fetch the priest?"

As I realised the implications of this, I held my brother's hand even tighter. "No. Thanks, Ann, but he is going to pull through – aren't you, Angus?"

I was so tired I could hardly stand, but I forced myself to go and pick up my clarsach, then I sat down on the floor beside his pallet, took a deep breath and began to play. I started with a slow melody, befitting the sombre mood in that cold, gloomy hut, then thought about Angus playing on his fiddle. It was always the fast tunes he loved, the reels that got everyone tapping their feet.

So even though I wasn't used to it, I picked up his fiddle and bow and began to play a reel. Guided by the notes in my head, I continued, a little rusty at first. There were some mistakes and it sounded a little scratchy, but after adjusting the way I was holding the bow, I played on, hoping the melody was not too offbeat. I'd learned the fiddle when I was younger of course; everyone in my house played. But another instrument is always different, and I hadn't played for quite a while; simply because Angus was so good. After a couple of tunes, I felt I was becoming more familiar with it and was able to increase the pace a little. By the third reel, though the tempo was slower than usual, I found I was tapping my foot along with the music myself. I looked down at Angus and noticed he had turned his head a little, perhaps to raise his ear to hear better. Play on, Lorna, play on.

Ann came back into the room and stood still. I turned to look up at her and saw her eyes widen.

"I think he's listening to the music, Lorna. Keep playing." She began to clap her hands softly together, in time to the music.

And so I played on. I have no idea how long I carried on, but at some stage his eyes blinked open, and Ann knelt to get some ale down him. He spat it out, but I whispered to her to try him with some of the cow's heel broth and she ran to get a bowl. Donnie came over to join us, placing his hand on my shoulder reassuringly.

I did not want to stop playing and so watched as my kind hosts raised Angus's head a little then managed to spoon some of the broth into his mouth. As I watched him swallow and prepare to take the next spoonful, I remembered us all gathering at my mother's bed as she lay dying. Her last words to me, whispered as I held her bony hand, were to look after my brother. I was not about to renege on that promise, nor abandon him here on Islay. He would get better, somehow.

He managed almost a half bowl of the broth and the sweating and rambling seemed to have stopped. His breathing also became more regular and when Ann brought me a cup of ale, I stopped to take a sip; I was so thirsty. But then I saw his brows furrow, as if he didn't want me to stop. And so after a quick gulp of ale, I started again and played on and on, faster and faster

– until there was a loud tapping at the door. I turned to see Donnie, bowing then standing aside. It was Hector Mor.

*

"How is the boy this morning?" He strode into the room, a grim expression on his face.

What was he doing here so early the day after his wedding? It didn't seem right.

Ann stepped forward and I could hear her whisper, "We nearly lost him, he was so bad. But he seems to be pulling through. It's a miracle." Ann swept past him, picking up a bucket on the way. She was obviously heading to fetch water. Donnie stood at the door chatting to Hector Mor's men. I could hear him say there were no wolves on Islay; there weren't even any foxes so if they wanted to go hunting, they could be disappointed.

Hector Mor approached, but I carried on playing the fiddle, glancing over at Angus to see if he was still the same. He seemed to be in a peaceful sleep now, more like the day before than last night when he was so agitated, so very ill. Hector Mor stood over me, unmoving for a moment, then lay his hand on Angus' brow.

"He is much cooler now. It looks like the fever's gone. Do you think his body's sweated it all out?"

I nodded and laid down the bow and the fiddle. I kept staring at my brother to check if he wanted me to carry on, but he was now sound asleep, snuffling calmly, and, I hoped, oblivious to the fact I'd stopped playing. My shoulders drooped with exhaustion and relief.

"Why are you here?" I looked up at him through bleary eyes. I must have looked awful after a night without any sleep at all.

"To ask after young Angus. My father would want me to; he is always solicitous towards his harpist's family."

"Oh, I see," I said, getting to my feet. I gestured for him to go towards the fire, away from Angus; I didn't want to disturb his sleep. "So your new wife does not expect you to stay with her the morning after her wedding?"

He opened his mouth to speak then turned away, before looking again directly at me. "Do you need anything else for the boy? Shall I have some beef broth sent down? I don't imagine you will have much time to make it yourself. I'm sure the kitchens at Dunyvaig will have some."

"Thank you, that would be good." I glanced up at his glum face. He did not have the air of a blissfully happy newly-wed.

"We shall be leaving for Duart in a couple of days' time. The winds have already abated and we should be able to travel by then. I shall take the Maclean servants as well as my men." He looked directly at me, his expression tinged with sadness. "I presume you will not be ready to travel back to Mull?"

I shook my head. "Angus has been so ill, it would be foolish." I frowned. "But how will we get home?"

"I have to return in a month or so, to take the wet nurse and Amie's other maids home. They are staying on to help her settle in. Obviously that's providing the weather is suitable, but I could collect you and Angus then, to bring you home."

"Well, that is very kind of you, but..."

"Who knows, my wife may have had enough of us on Mull by then and be ready to return home to her own people."

I didn't know what to say. So I changed the subject. "Hector Mor, is there any way you could get a letter to Catherine for me? I think you probably can find out where she is?"

He sighed. "I shall try my very best."

"Do you really think she is back in Inveraray with her own family?"

"I ..." he started then turned away once more. "I don't know," he muttered. "We can but hope."

He began to walk towards the door, the heavy, trudging walk of a man burdened with sadness. "Hector Mor, could you get me something to write on – and some ink? I learned my letters with Catherine on the sand. But I'm sure I could easily use ink."

He nodded. "I shall send a man over later this morning."

He had such a despondent air.

"Shall I see you before you leave?" I asked.

"Am I not to take your letter to try to dispatch it to Catherine?"

"Of course."

I heard Angus snoring and ran over to him. His skin was a normal colour again, the deathly white pallor had gone.

"Even if he is well enough to get up, I don't think the long voyage is a good idea," I said, returning to Hector Mor.

He nodded, then stretched out his hand towards my face. But Ann came in, lugging her heavy bucket in two hands, the water slopping over the top. Hector Mor bowed graciously to us both then stepped outside into the damp autumn morning.

Chapter 38

1520

Catherine

I ran into the courtyard, panting. Aggie and I had run all the way and she had gone back to the kitchen. I could only see the grooms, come to tend the horses; my brothers must have already gone inside. I swept past the men leading the steeds to the stables, headed for the stairs up to the Great Hall then suddenly slowed down. I pulled my hair up into the ribbon, but not tightly, leaving some ringlets loose around my face. Archibald used to like it like that.

I walked through the door and scanned the room. There was Donald and John and the other family members. I could not see Archibald; and there was certainly no sign of my Amie, but perhaps the servants had taken her away to her room. They all looked exhausted and were slumped around the table, goblets in hands. Donald stood up as I came towards them.

"Catherine, we are back. Will you join us?"

"Where is my child?"

He sighed and John came towards me, hands outstretched. "She wasn't there. She is already on Islay, just as you had feared."

I sighed and sank onto a chair. "Could you not go and get her, sail over from Mull? It's surely nearer than from here. You could surely have travelled there with him?" I could not bear to say his name.

"No Campbells are welcome on Islay, you know that, Catherine. Your husband has said he will go there as soon as the weather is fair enough and collect the little one for you."

"What? You believed him?"

"He will fulfil his promise, Catherine," Donald said.

"Why should he? And how is my darling Amie going to get to Inveraray? Surely you will not allow him to bring her?"

"His closest kinsman, Hector Mor, will bring her."

"Hector Mor?" I drummed my fingers on the table. "Well at least he is more honest than his father."

"His father?"

"Yes, Lachlan Cattanach has a son! I did not need to marry him; he could just have married his mistress on the Treshnish Islands and legitimised Hector Mor as his heir." I raised my hand and a servant came to pour me some claret. As I sipped, I looked over the rim at my brothers.

"He will honour his promise, Catherine. For we hold his kinsmen in our dungeons. They will perish if Maclean does not send the child here, with Hector Mor, within six weeks."

I shook my head. How could my often bellicose brothers be taken in by my husband's so-called promises?

"He will not do this, I know he won't. Dear God, do I have to go to Islay myself?" I was shouting now, I was so angry.

A door opened and Colin entered. He had clearly heard my raised voice and was frowning. "Catherine, there is nothing we can do until your baby is brought back to us. It has all been agreed. Do not worry."

I shook my head.

"We have six weeks, Catherine, then we will make another plan – remember, we have his kinsmen held as hostages down below."

He lifted a letter he had been holding in his hand. "I have been invited to Edinburgh in three weeks' time. The regent wants the Scottish lords and the island lords to gather at the castle to discuss our way forward. The last king abolished the Lords of the Isles back in 1493, but still they continue to meet at their assemblies at Finlaggan on Islay. So the Duke of Albany – as well as Queen Margaret, the king's mother – wants a council to try to forge a truce between us all whereby the island lords can still have control of their lands, but are loyal subjects to our young king when he comes of age."

I did not care about any of this. Why were they now discussing politics and not my child?

"And so?" I remarked.

"Don't be so sulky, Catherine," my brother snapped. Sometimes he could be so pompous.

"Don't you see why the timing is ideal?"

"Of your journey to Edinburgh? No."

"Not only will your husband be there, but so will your daughter's foster father, Macdonald of Dunyvaig."

I gasped. "Of course. And so you can speak directly to him about getting my Amie back."

"Shall I travel with you, Colin?" Donald asked.

"No. I shall take John with me. He is second eldest, this is such an important meeting."

Donald shrugged and was about to speak when Isabel entered, her face a picture of joy.

"The baby has arrived. At last! After three long days and nights in labour, a healthy baby boy is here. God be praised!"

*

Everyone had left the table after supper, but I moved from my seat over to the fire. There was a definite chill in the air. Grandmother came to sit beside me, stretching out her hand to mine.

"I heard from Donald that Amie is on Islay, so won't be back with you for a short while."

I nodded.

"The men are doing their best, Catherine, you know that. You must trust them to bring her back here to you."

I sighed. "They have no idea what kind of man he is."

"We have been over this, time and again. Clan chiefs are noble men; they stand by their promises. You will have your baby with you soon, I am sure of it." She smiled. "Now it is late. Will you not come upstairs to bed?"

"I won't be long, thank you. I am enjoying listening to the crackling of the wood in the fireplace and watching the flickering of the flames. It's so beautiful, soothing." I smiled at her and returned my gaze to the fire.

Grandmother stood and kissed the top of my head. "You always were a romantic girl, my darling Catherine. Sleep well."

I must have fallen asleep for when I awoke, it was not flames I saw, but embers. I shivered and looked around. There was no one here, not even a servant. Dear Lord, it must be very late. Why did no one waken me? I got to my feet, grabbing a candle from the table. I went towards the door and was about to step onto the stairs when I heard a noise. I looked through the gloom to see someone shrouded in a large cape carrying a candle. I stood still, watching the figure descend the stairs, wondering who on earth was coming downstairs in the middle of the night.

As the figure approached, I gasped. I recognised the fine features of the pale face and the beautiful blond hair. It was Archibald. What was he doing? I was about to greet him when I quickly drew backwards into the shadows. I thought back to earlier when, after he had arrived back with my brothers, he had gone straight to sit outside his wife's room, obediently, like a lapdog, while she gave birth.

I had nothing to say to him right now. Had he forgotten our feelings for each other, our passionate and enduring love? There would be a way out of this situation with his wife – and now this new baby of theirs. A baby boy: of course she would bear him a son. She was so perfect in every way, the child had to be male. And so now he had an heir. But I would find a way to change the circumstances we now found ourselves in. I would find a solution; it was just a question of how.

I started to follow him, but stopped. For he seemed to be heading not downstairs to the courtyard but down the smaller back stairs. They were completely dark. Even as he held his candle high, it was pitch black. I had never been down there, but I thought it was the way to the armoury, where they kept the weapons. Why on earth would he go there – and why the stealth?

I took a deep breath. What if he was meeting someone in the weapons room; did he need some of my brothers' arms and did not want them to know? Perhaps he had simply lost his dirk and needed a new one. And though I did not care what he took, I did not want anyone to find us together, alone in the dark at midnight, in case my interfering sister Isabel reported back to his wife. I sighed and headed slowly up the stairs to my room, still wondering what could possibly lure him down in the middle of the night to the depths of the castle where there were only daggers and swords.

Chapter 39

1520
Hector Mor

Hector Mor had just dispatched one of his men to take the letter from Lorna to Catherine at Inveraray Castle when his father arrived in the courtyard. Lachlan Cattenach patted his son on the back.

"So, Hector Mor, how is married life suiting you? I hope Mary enjoyed the little assembly we had last night for her to meet her Maclean kinsmen and women."

Hector Mor shrugged. Who knew what his wife was thinking? Certainly not him. "I'm sure she did. Thank you for inviting them and for such kind words of welcome to her. And for bringing over the Lochbuie Maclean harpists; it won't be long till I get Lorna back here." He sighed; if only Lorna was here now, he might feel a little less unhappy.

"So married life is all you hoped it would be?" His father winked, but Hector Mor ignored him and began to walk towards the stairs to go inside. "I have things to prepare, before our trip to the Treshnish Islands tomorrow."

"You're taking Mary to meet your mother?"

"Well, I can't exactly invite my mother here, can I?"

He could not help snapping at his father. He was not blissfully happy, as Lachlan clearly thought he should be. He could not fathom his new wife. She did speak sometimes, but rarely to him and then it was only polite niceties. He had no idea whether she was simply missing Islay and her family, whether she hated him or whether she was just always this glum.

"She doesn't say much, does she?"

Hector Mor exhaled deeply. He was keen to get rid of Lachlan. He now realised he felt a not inconsiderable contempt for his father, after the way he had treated Catherine. He was still trying to understand how his father could have done what he did. When Hector asked him what had happened to her, he was told she was in fact not dead but very much alive at Inveraray Castle. But he refused to say more and there was certainly no remorse about the awful way he'd tried to abandon her to the tides and waves in the middle of the sea.

"Mary says enough, I think she is just shy. I can't think of any other reason she is like this." Hector Mor was trying to justify to himself why, after five days of being married, she would still not permit him in her room at night. She said a formal good night on the stairs then went swiftly into her room where the maid shut the door firmly behind her.

"You've had relations I presume, Hector?" Lachlan was now frowning.

"What business is it of yours if we have or not?"

Good God, what an interfering, unpleasant man his father had become. Hector Mor took the first stair towards the Great Hall.

Lachlan put a hand on his son's shoulder to pull him back. "Stop. You're behaving like a sulky child. Listen to me; you have your rights. You must do what you, as a husband, want to do." His eyes narrowed. "Remember you are her master. At all times. Don't stand any nonsense; that way only mischief lies. Look how Catherine got away with so much after I was too lenient with her."

Hector shook his head. How could he possibly think that? Thank God Catherine had in fact stood up to his father. It made her the strong woman she was. "I will deal with this in my own way. But thank you for your advice. We shall see you at supper."

"Very well. Oh, and Hector, tell my lovely Marion I shall see her just as soon as I can. That I miss her madly and..."

But Hector Mor was striding up the stairs two at a time. Lachlan Cattanach stood on the bottom step, chuckling.

*

After supper, Mary had left with her maid as usual to go to her room. Lachlan had also left, thank God, so Hector Mor downed a large goblet of claret then headed for the stairs to her room. He knocked at the door and when there was no answer, pushed it open. The maid rushed over and stood in front of him, as if her slight frame could block his way.

"Excuse me," Hector said to her, gesturing for her to stand aside. Since she refused, he walked around her to his wife, who sat at a small table with a looking glass on it. Her eyes were wide with horror. It was the first time he had seen her without her hood up over her head. She wore a little cap over her hair, which he could see was very fine and sparse. It was nothing like Lorna's glorious, thick mane.

"I was hoping we could speak here in your bedroom, Mary? Away from the servants and Lachlan Cattanach." He turned to the maid who was now hovering by her mistress's side. "Leave us," he said, pointing to the door.

Her eyes glanced from Hector to Mary, but when he gestured again, she knew she had no choice.

Once the door was shut, he stretched out his hand. "Mary, will you come over to the bed with me? We need to talk. We are now husband and wife."

Still she sat on the stool, head bowed. He grasped her hand from her knee and smiled. "I think we will be more comfortable on the bed. Come. We shall just talk tonight if that is what you prefer." He nodded. "I am a man of honour."

She pushed both of her hands onto the table, swung her feet around then stood up onto the stone floor. And as she turned to her side, he gasped. Here was the reason she only wore wide, billowing capes; this was why she did not want him close.

"Dear God, who did this to you?" He pointed at the taut, rounded belly protruding from her night shift.

Standing in front of him, head lowered, was not the young girl he had thought he had married, but a woman who was clearly going to have a baby soon.

"How have you kept this secret for so long?" He dropped her hand and she sat back down on the stool, refusing to look at him. He pulled a chair over to sit beside her. "Mary, it's all right. Don't worry, it's not your fault – I'm just shocked. It's such a terrible situation you are in. Your parents presumably don't know and that's why you wear those voluminous clothes?"

She nodded.

"What man would do this to someone so young and innocent?"

And then she took a deep breath and raised her head. Looking directly at him, her grey eyes unblinking, she said. "No man 'did' this to me." She spat out the word. "It is the result of the love between two people."

His jaw dropped. "What are you talking about? Love that results in a child is for marriage only. You know that. Your parents have brought you up well, surely."

She shrugged. "I find that I no longer care. Besides, your mother is not married to your father and..."

He raised his hand. "Mary," he hissed. "What were you hoping would happen when you married into our family? That I would take on a child who is not mine and that everyone would overlook the fact you lay with a man out of wedlock?" He let out a long breath. "What manner of... of woman are you?" The word 'harlot' was on his lips.

"I am a woman who loves a man I would never be allowed to marry." She looked at him, brazen. "My parents would not consider him as his status, though not lowly, is not worthy of their noble plans. And so I had to marry you and now you understand why I have never been unhappier."

He shook his head, there was so much to take in. "So you thought I would not notice? And when you have the baby, you thought I would just presume it was mine, even after, what, only a few weeks of marriage? When is the child due?"

"In about two months' time."

He got to his feet and strode around the room. "So if you are now deeply unhappy, I cannot believe you were happy when you discovered you were with child?" He could not believe what he had just heard.

"I was," she said, head raised in a haughty manner. "Because I love him and he loves me, it's as simple as that."

"But it's not simple, is it?" He was now shouting. "Do you not realise that love is rare in the marriages arranged between families like ours? Love is a bonus. And now your indiscretion, your wanton behaviour, has ruined everything – not only the bond between our families, but your life. Can't you see that?"

He bent down towards her, his face now distorted with fury. "Who is the man?"

She lifted her chin, keeping her mouth shut, clearly determined to say nothing.

"I repeat, who has fathered this child?" He took hold of her shoulder and began to pinch.

She breathed in sharply and tried to shake off his grasp, but he held tight as she stuttered, "If my father knew his name, he would kill him. He would not understand about our love, our..."

"But you expect me, your husband, to just shrug it off and say nothing?" He released his grip but leaned in closer. "You were a stranger to me when we married. You are even more of one now. You obviously did not think beyond the fact you were marrying, at your father's command. My wishes and hopes were never considered." He sat down again.

"I will leave now; I must think very carefully about the future. But until I have come to my decision, you will remain here, in this chamber. We shall not be travelling to the Treshnish Islands

216

tomorrow to meet my mother. She is indeed not married to my father, but she is a true and honest woman. And I fear she might not be happy with the manner in which you have treated your new husband." He smirked. "In fact, I think she would be so angry, she would slap your face." He got to his feet. "And if she did, I would stand by and applaud."

He strode to the door and threw it open. The maid was crouching there, clearly listening to the conversation. "Your mistress will not be going anywhere tomorrow. Once I have formulated my plans, I shall return."

Chapter 40

1520

Catherine

My sisters and I sat at the bedside in the lying-in room. There was an unpleasant aroma in the air, but no one dared mention it. It was a strong, sickly smell of blood, which was rather strange as the bed linen would have been cleaned since Margaret delivered her child. She was trying to speak but was clearly too weak for conversation so lay still, eyes blinking shut. Instead, Isabel was recounting hour by hour the stages of labour this poor woman had to undergo. My sisters were sitting on the edges of their chairs, both enthralled by the gore of it all and amazed by the bravery of the person in the bed.

Tired by all this fawning, I got up and went towards the crib, where the baby was fast asleep. The nurse jumped up and offered me her seat, but I declined. I could see this perfect little creature well enough from standing. He was chubby of cheek and rosy of complexion. He clearly had not suffered during the three long days and nights of labour, only his pale, weak mother had. I glanced over at her, lying in the bed, eyes now firmly shut just as Isabel got to the part when the midwife could see the head.

Well, this baby looked nothing like its mother; rather, he had a definite look of Archibald, though he was completely bald. It was the skin colouring. Sadly, my darling Amie had nothing of Archibald about her; her skin and hair both had the darker colours of a Maclean. I looked over at the nurse, who was now folding tiny clothes by the wardrobe, her back to me, then I stretched out my hand towards the baby. I stroked his warm, fat cheek and thought back to when my own little one was born. I remember

218

feeling elated, even though I was exhausted. Whereas Margaret looked completely worn out; she was as white as the pillow her head lay upon.

I leaned over the baby and pressed my hand down on his little chest to check his breathing. It was regular and strong; he was a survivor, for sure. I pulled the bed clothes further up the crib; it was not as cosy over here as it was by his mother's bed. I tucked the blankets tightly up around his neck to try to make him warm. I had just placed my thumb and forefinger onto his pretty little nose when there was a knock on the door. A maid rushed over to open it and took something in her hand. As she came towards me, I quickly removed my hand from the crib. I could hear the baby snuffle and turn his face away as she handed a letter to me. "This has just come for you, my Lady."

"Thank you," I said, turning the letter over to try to recognise the hand.

I went towards the bed where the unpleasantly cloying odour still hung in the air. I tiptoed past my sisters and stood at the head of the bed where I bent low over Margaret.

"I've got to go now, but I'll be back soon," I whispered. "You are looking well, considering your ordeal; and your baby is beautiful." I meant only part of what I said.

I turned and patted Ellen on the shoulder as I passed. I raised the letter in my hand to show her why I was leaving and headed for the door.

Outside, I sped to the library and began to read. It was from Lorna; her writing was still child-like, but I was able to read it easily. Where could she have got paper and ink from? My heart beat fast as I read on, thinking only that she was so near my darling little girl. She told me about Hector Mor's wedding, how she had played her clarsach with the Macdonald fiddler. She wrote that his bride did not look happy at the celebratory dinners. Well, perhaps like me the poor girl was a pawn in a deal brokered by men to strengthen their families' bonds.

Lorna said she had travelled on the galley with Amie to Islay and she was hale and hearty. The wet nurse was still with her as she was being weaned. And then she saw her again at a dinner at Dunyvaig Castle where her foster mother cuddled her as if she were one of her own. I was not sure I could read on, that sentence made my blood run cold. But I continued to the end, feeling a pang of sadness as she wrote about poor Angus being so very ill – but that thankfully he was now recovering, and soon Hector Mor was going to return to Islay to collect them.

I lay down the letter. I was pleased that at least dear Lorna was near my darling little girl, but that would all change once she and Angus had been taken back to Duart. I raised my head to the ceiling and wondered if there was anything I could ask her to do before she left Islay.

*

I had been up in the woods briefly in the morning chill to clear my head, but hunger made me return inside. I was so warm in my new wolfskin fur coat. It was truly magnificent. My sisters and sisters-in-law were jealous of it; I could tell when they had come to admire it. Colin's wife Jeanne kept running her fingers through the soft, fluffy fur, purring like a cat. I wanted to tell her a wolf is related to dogs and hounds, not cats.

I went over to the table and placed my coat on the chair while everyone else took their seats. I looked around at the other guests; there at the far end I could see Archibald, his head down. I kept staring at him, hoping and willing him to look up soon. We had not spoken at all since I returned here, which was so very odd. A servant was holding the jug of ale at his shoulder and as he turned his head to raise his goblet, his eyes flashed around the table to mine. I smiled at him but his face was impassive; it was as if we had never been in love. What did this mean?

"Catherine, you are being asked whether you want your glass filled." Grandmother had sat down beside me and gestured to the servant at my side. She looked over to where my gaze lay and whispered in my ear. "Archibald's still worried about his wife; she seems unusually weakened after the birth."

I turned and smiled. "I saw her earlier this morning, she will be fine. She had a long labour."

"Let us hope. I just came from there and thought she was terribly pale. I think she has lost an awful lot of blood."

"All women do, surely."

"Not all women have to suffer three days' labour." Grandmother sipped her claret. "Still, the baby is hale and hearty, isn't he?"

"Hmm," I muttered, staring at the bannocks in front of us. I took one and nibbled on it. "Do you remember how the bannocks tasted at Duart? They were always tough and chewy. These ones at Inveraray are so light."

"Yes, I've told you before it's Aggie who makes our morning bannocks." She took one from the ashet in front of her. "How is her remedy for poor Mary's skin going?" She peered around the table, but there was no sign of Mary.

"I think well. She keeps the poultice on for most of the morning so hopefully in a few days her skin will be better."

I looked over the table, deciding what I would eat. There were roasted blackcock and plover and some salted venison and mutton; thank God, there was not a vile-tasting seabird in sight. What did they eat on Islay, I wondered? Hopefully it was more like our dinners here and not those at Duart, though of course like Mull it was an island, so perhaps they had to rely on seabirds too.

I reached out for one of the plovers which had always been a favourite, then raised my head as I saw my brother Colin enter, stony-faced. He leaned down to whisper to Donald, who was sitting to my other side. I could only hear the word "prisoners". I strained to listen and was not able to hear what he said, but Donald's face took on a look of incredulity. "They can't have escaped!" he hissed, while pushing his chair back to stand up. They retreated behind us to talk, now out of earshot.

"Where are the dungeons, Grandmother?"

"Well, I've obviously never been down there but I believe they are directly below the armoury."

"Two floors below the ground floor?"

She shrugged. "Yes, they must be."

"So how could prisoners possibly escape if they're so deep in the bowels of the castle? And presumably they're all locked up and under guard?"

"Have they escaped?" Her eyes grew wide.

"I'm sure that's what Colin and Donald are discussing." I nodded towards my brothers.

"Well, I suppose the guards take shifts, but there would always be someone there, fully armed." She took a sip from her glass. "But the men there will not be a threat to us here; they would be heading immediately back to Mull, surely."

We watched my brothers walk towards the far end of the table. They had just bent down beside Archibald when the door was thrown open and Isabel ran in, wailing.

"Archibald, you must come. Now! Nurse says she's taken a sudden turn. There's so much blood and..."

Mother stood up and reached out to grab her daughter by the hand. She leaned in close to my sister's face. "In this family we do not howl like commoners." My mother's whispers were never quiet. "If there is news, go and give it to Archibald himself, not to every person around our table."

Everyone watched, entranced, as my sister sped over to Archibald and hissed, "Come now! You must come upstairs... She's dying!"

Chapter 41

1520

Hector Mor

The tides were favourable for their arrival on Islay five days later, so the boat from Duart was able to land at Dunyvaig; they did not need to travel by land down the coast from Claggain Bay. Thank God – the journey had been tedious enough with Mary refusing to speak the entire way besides conversing with their kind hosts on Colonsay, where they had to keep up the pretence of being happy newly-weds. She continued to wear that voluminous cape with her fur hood tight around her face. Though as he pulled his plaid around his shoulders, he thought how useful the hooded cape must be against the biting wind that was coming directly from the north.

"Hector Mor," the boatman shouted, "I can't see anyone outside the castle – there's no one there to tie up the boat. Are we not expected?"

"No, we're not." He did not want to send any advance notice of their arrival; what was the point? "Sail round into the bay and I'll wade ashore and drag the boat up there. You can sail her round later to the sea gate and tie her up."

Hector glanced at Mary, who was gazing up at Dunyvaig Castle, her family home, the only home she had ever known. There were tears streaming down her pale cheeks. She had no idea what was about to happen to her. And in a way, nor did he. He had made plans of course, formulated an escape route from this doomed marriage, one her father would feel obliged to agree to. But she had no idea how her father would react and what would happen to her.

He did not know what she was feeling, though he could not help but feel sorry for her, which was strange, considering how angry he had been with her only a few days before. He patted her hand. "It'll be all right, Mary. Your father is a fair man. After his anger fades, he will take care of you; he won't leave you to suffer alone."

She bowed her head, sniffing, then wiped her tears away with a small cloth her servant handed to her. Then she raised her head again and stared directly up at the castle as they sailed past it towards the rocky shoreline. The wind had thankfully died down a little, but it was still bitterly cold. The boat ground to a halt and Hector Mor jumped over the side, waded to the shoreline and pulled the boat through the rocks up to the shallows. A fisherman mending his nets ran to help him secure the boat and as he did so, shouted for help.

Soon a group of men and women gathered on the shore and as everyone on the boat stepped precariously over the side, Hector Mor took each one by the hand. Then, as he guided Mary over the side with two hands, there was a gasp from the crowd that had gathered. They were clearly wondering why Lady Mary was back so soon from her new marital home. She glanced over at them, but instead of lowering her gaze, she lifted her head high. She was proud, you had to give her that.

"Wait here, Mary. We will walk along together to the castle," said Hector Mor, as he helped the last person off the boat.

He gave her his arm and together they walked, every inch the happily married couple. They strolled up the rocky shoreline towards the castle, smiling and greeting the local villagers along the way. At one of the tiny huts they passed, there was a young woman brushing debris out the door with a broom made of gorse twigs. She looked up and stopped her work in mid sweep. She stared, mouth open. She appeared not to believe her eyes: here was Mary Macdonald and Hector Mor Maclean, wed only a couple of weeks before, walking along the path arm in arm. She flicked some loose strands of black hair off her face and called inside. "They're back, Ann. Lady Mary and our Hector Mor. Why could that possibly be?"

*

A couple of hours later, Hector Mor trotted along the track from the castle on a steed borrowed from Lord Macdonald. He needed to be outside, in the fresh cold air away from the muggy, close atmosphere inside Dunyvaig. It had been a painful meeting with his father-in-law. Hector Mor had suggested all the servants leave the Great Hall while just the three of them sat around the fire. Mary had already told her husband she did not want her mother to be present, only her father. She obviously adored him and presumably thought he would be more lenient towards her without his wife's presence.

Mary had sat beside him, fanning herself in the heat from the well-stoked fire, while Hector Mor announced that his wife was already some seven months' pregnant when they were married. Lord Macdonald was so incensed at the suggestion, he grabbed his dirk and leapt towards Hector Mor, the tip of his blade at his throat. Mary had calmly rested her hand on her father's arm and whispered, "It is true, Father. Leave him be, he is not at fault."

There was dismay etched upon Alexander Donald Macdonald's face as he slumped back onto his chair, muttering, "It cannot be, it cannot be." His anguish was made worse when Mary stood up and unbuttoned her cape. The distress soon turned to anger, and he turned upon his daughter, grabbing her hand and muttering, "Who did this? Name him now, Mary!"

Hector Mor was now passing the hut where Lorna and Angus had been staying. He pulled on his horse's reins to halt. Without dismounting, he called inside and soon Ann appeared. "Are you coming in, your Lordship?"

Hector Mor shook his head. "Is Angus better?"

"He is that," she said, turning around. "Come out here, lad, someone's asking for you."

And Angus emerged from the smoky interior, blinking as his eyes adjusted to the bright morning sun. His colour had returned, his cheeks were once again ruddy pink and the cadaverous bags under his eyes had gone.

"You look well, Angus. Will you be ready to sail home tomorrow?"

The boy nodded.

"Where is your sister?"

"She went to practise her clarsach in the woods yonder," said Ann, pointing to the trees at the end of the track.

"Thank you. I will see you tomorrow, Angus. It won't be long till we get you home to Duart." Hector Mor bowed his head then tightened the reins and set off towards the woods.

The horse slowed down as they trotted amidst the hazel and alder trees, and soon he could hear the ethereal sound of the harp. He dismounted and led the horse under the branches and over the twisted tree roots towards the music. Soon he saw her and approached softly, not wanting to interrupt. She was playing a beautiful melody, with sweet, almost tinkling sounds, one he had not heard before; how did she do it? He was mesmerised as usual, and not just by the music.

She placed her hands on the strings to stop playing, then walked towards him.

"What are you doing here?" She was frowning.

"Will you come up on the horse with me and we can go for a ride? We'll head out to Kildalton. I found out more about the cross there that you were interested in." Saying nothing, she handed him up her clarsach then reached up her hand to his. He pulled her onto the horse and seated her in front of him. She took the harp back from him and he tucked one arm around her waist.

They trotted off under the boughs of the trees and onto the same track they had taken after their arrival at Claggain. It had been only a couple of weeks before, but such a lot had happened in that short time. He leaned in close over her hair, breathing in deep as he guided the horse north-east. They travelled the short journey in complete silence; there was so much to say and yet nothing needed to be said.

Chapter 42

1520

Lorna

Sometimes my gift is a burden – an affliction that I could do without. All the time Angus was so very ill, I knew something terrible was about to happen, so I presumed it meant that my brother would soon die. But as I sat with Hector Mor against the wall of Kildalton church looking directly at the cross, I realised I had been wrong. The dreadful thing that was going to happen was not to do with my brother; it was to do with Hector Mor and his wife.

He told me about the baby on its way and how Lord Macdonald had taken it so badly, especially when Mary insisted that she was happy she was about to have a baby out of wedlock. I could not fathom that – what sort of girl would want that? Surely her lover would be killed, and her baby would be taken away from her?

But no, Hector Mor said she had persuaded her father that she could keep the baby provided she tell him the name of the baby's father. She was ready to do that if he promised not to kill him. Her father said he could promise nothing yet and he wanted to discuss with his wife.

I gasped. "Do *you* know who the father is?"

"No. In a way, I feel it's nothing to do with me."

"I think I know," I said, remembering the wedding night and how her face broke into a smile when she was close to Johnnie, the Macdonald fiddler. I told Hector Mor and he shrugged. "Well, at least someone was able to make her smile."

"Do you think they will just let her live at the castle, have the baby and pretend it was yours – that it came along early?"

"I don't know. Whatever happens though, her pregnancy is to be a secret. That way they could conceal the timing, if necessary."

I turned and looked directly into his black, deep-set eyes. "And your marriage?"

"I told Lord Macdonald that I would leave the marriage silently, provided my terms were agreed to."

"Does it not have to be annulled? By the priest?"

"I may not necessarily want that. It could be more useful to remain married for now, for the sake of the two families. But I don't know yet about that."

"And so you hold the power, don't you? You can ask him for anything at all, presumably."

"If he wants to keep my silence, yes."

I was about to ask him more about his "terms", but he got to his feet. "Come over here; I can tell you about the symbols on the cross now."

I followed him to stand at the foot of the cross that was much higher than me – and taller even than Hector Mor. "It was carved over 700 years ago."

I could not believe something could be that old.

"It was here long before the chapel was built. Kildalton means church of the foster child or disciple – do you remember?

"Yes, and so it's perhaps not coincidental that Amie is a foster child nearby. This is the family's church, isn't it?"

"It is."

"What do all the carvings mean?"

"Here's David killing the lion," he said, pointing at the top.

"What's a lion?"

"It's a huge ferocious beast that lives a long way from us."

"More ferocious than a wolf?"

"Much more." He leant further in. "These are colourful birds called peacocks and they are eating grapes, which are a kind of fruit."

"I wonder what they taste like. Sweet, like blaeberries perhaps."

"And here's the Virgin Mary and her baby."

"And those are angels beside her?"

He nodded then walked around to the other side. "Here are more lions – can you see? And down below are snakes."

"How did those people so long ago know how to carve pictures of creatures they'd never seen?"

"How indeed. It's magnificent, isn't it? Carved from local stone too."

"Who told you all this, Hector Mor?"

"Alexander Donald Macdonald, at supper the night before the wedding. I asked him about it, as I remembered how you were interested in the cross."

So he had recalled that I'd spent ages gazing at the cross while they were all taking refreshments.

"Remember we stopped off here on the way down from Claggain Bay, but I dragged you away."

I chuckled. "You did. And you told me I was too opinionated. And that I should be meeker."

There was a flicker of a smile on his lips. "That's true; and you definitely were never quite as forward before you met Catherine, were you?"

"Did she get my letter?"

"I hope so. I had it sent to Inveraray Castle, where she now lives."

"Are you sure of that?"

"I am." He glanced over to the horse, who was happily munching on the grass. My clarsach was strapped onto its back. "I've heard news from Inveraray, from my father and his men."

He went on to tell me about Lachlan Cattanach's journey over to Inveraray with a coffin, which had a she-wolf in it and how, even after the deception was exposed, Catherine's brother the earl had let him go home, but had kept the other Maclean men in their dungeons as hostages until Lachlan Cattanach brought baby Amie back to her mother.

"Amie, of course. So is he coming over here to collect her and deliver her to her mother?"

He shook his head. "There is no need. The prisoners escaped, somehow. They arrived back at Duart the night before we left. So there is no need now to release Amie from this fostering contract."

I felt my shoulders slump. "If only there was a way, then we could..." I did not finish my sentence as Hector Mor was bending his face towards mine and I stood very still, unsure.

Then he kissed me, and we stayed like that for quite a while. And all of a sudden, I felt sure.

*

The men were loading the provisions into the boat as Angus and I stood on the shore, our instruments in our hands. There was no sign of Hector Mor yet, but most of the servants were already here. It was another bitterly cold morning, and we were all jigging about, hopping from one foot to the other. But the sun was bright and there wasn't a cloud in the sky.

I checked the bannocks in my bag were still whole then retied the drawstrings. Ann had insisted we take them for the journey.

"It's a long way," she said as she rammed them in. "Now you'll be sure to come back and visit us on Islay?"

"If I can, for sure," I said, smiling. I had felt nothing but a strange elation since yesterday afternoon, and she must have noticed it. I'm sure I had been smiling ever since, perhaps even in my sleep.

"Or maybe you'd rather stay on Mull now. Keep playing your beautiful tunes, wherever you go, lass." And she gave me a warm hug.

The boatman was gesturing behind us to his helpers, who leapt off the boat and hurried towards a party of women approaching. As I peered at them, I recognised the nurse and the servants from Duart, and they were carrying something. Dear Lord, it was Amie; she was coming with us. Hector Mor must have negotiated the end of the fosterage contract and was returning her to her father at Duart. Well, I suppose living on Mull was better than being fostered somewhere miles away from home.

They got in the boat, the nurse fussing around the wet nurse, who had been so ill on the journey over. Her face was grim; she was clearly dreading it. And then, just outside the castle walls, I saw Hector Mor, and my heart leapt. He shook hands with Lord Macdonald and then turned and headed in our direction. I pulled Angus towards me and told him to get into the boat. I followed, tucking myself in beside the nurse so I could see little Amie. She truly was a bonny wee thing, with her curly dark hair and plump, dimpled cheeks; she was lively too, her bright eyes glancing all around as if eager to find out about the world.

Hector Mor strode down to join us and stepped into the boat. He glanced over at me and I saw a glimmer of a smile. He turned back to look at the castle where the sea gate was now closed.

"Usual route home, your Lordship, stopping at Oronsay and Colonsay on the way?" asked the boatman, now standing at the helm.

"No," was the answer. "Change course. We're not going north. We're heading east."

"But that's not the way home."

"We're not going to Duart quite yet."

"But..."

"We're heading for West Tarbert. The boat'll be hauled a mile or so overland to Loch Fyne in the east."

The boatman spread out his hands. "Why?"

"We're taking the little one home."

"But her home's Duart surely. Mull."

"Mull is where her father is."

Hector Mor stepped over the bags towards the boatman and pointed towards the sun, low on the horizon. "It's time to set sail. We've got a long way to go before it's dark."

Chapter 43

1520
Catherine

Margaret, Archibald's wife, was dead; and I wasn't sure quite how I felt about it. I'd hardly known the woman, so of course did not feel sadness for myself. And Archibald presumably was heartbroken. It all seemed rather cruel, that the child survives and the mother – who has been in agony for three long days and nights – dies. I had just come up to Grandmother's room as she had a nasty head cold and the physician had told her to stay in bed, which of course she hated. But that was where we'd both heard the news.

"I wonder if Archibald will bury her at his estate at Auchenbreck. Or will he take her back to her own family home at Inverawe?"

"What about the child?"

"He has a name now," Grandmother said, blowing her nose. "Did you hear?"

"No." Why would I be interested?

"He is Archibald Dugald Campbell. Dugald is a family name at Auchenbreck, apparently."

I shrugged and went to look out of the tiny window. It was very windy outside and there was a bitter draft coming in through the slit in the wall.

"Do we know any more about how the prisoners escaped?"

"I heard that one of the guards was taken ill and was sleeping instead of being on duty." Grandmother knew everything that went on at the castle before anyone else.

"That's odd. But surely there are always two guards?"

233

"Yes, that's what I had thought, but seemingly not."

"Are they still working here at the castle?"

"I don't know. You can ask Colin more about that," she said, lying back on the pillow.

When she was in bed, she always looked older. Perhaps it was her long silvery-white hair, which was usually tied up behind her head. Her face also seemed more lined these days; but she was still such a beautiful woman.

There was a noise below in the courtyard and I strained my neck to peer down. There were four men coming out of a door carrying a coffin; and then I saw Archibald come down the stairs.

"I'm going downstairs to see what's going on. I'll be back later." I headed over to kiss her on the cheek, but she held up her hand. "Don't come near me. I don't want you becoming ill."

I sped down the stairs and out into the courtyard. I slowed to a sedate pace and went over to Archibald, who looked terrible. He was ghastly pale and red eyed. I had not spoken to him since I returned.

He turned as I spoke his name but did not smile. "Archibald," I said, patting his arm. "I was so sorry to hear about your wife. She will, however, now be at peace." I had been well-groomed in the correct things to say by way of condolence.

"Thank you," he said, scowling. "She had seemed so well, and the doctors thought she would be fine, even after her terrible ordeal. But she had simply lost too much blood." He shook his head. "They couldn't save her."

"I assume you're taking her to Inverawe to be buried in her family plot?"

"No, we are going to Auchenbreck; she will be laid to rest alongside my family. We were her family, after all."

His cold expression surprised me. He could have lost both his wife *and* his baby, but instead he has a perfect little son.

"And will you take the child with you?"

234

"No. Your sister Isabel has kindly said he can remain here for as long as possible. She organised a wet nurse too; I am truly in her debt."

Good old Isabel, she always loved being in the middle of any drama.

"And shall you return here after the burial?"

"I do not yet know. I..."

We both turned to see Colin at our sides. He was looking sombre, as befits the sight of a coffin.

"Archibald, this is not the time, nor the place, but when you return after the burial, can we discuss further the situation surrounding the escaped prisoners? Things just don't add up and I wondered if you had any more insight into how it could have happened."

"I know less about the layout of your castle than you do," he muttered, averting his eyes from my brother.

"Yes, but Donald said there's just a couple of things he heard that..."

"Be careful how you're loading the casket, man!" Archibald shouted at the servant who was helping to hoist the coffin upon the litter between the horses. "I'm sorry, your Lordship, but we must leave. I am keen to get most of the journey done before dark."

Colin nodded. "Of course. We shall see you when you return. And in the meantime, do not worry about your child. He is safe here and will be well looked after in Inveraray Castle."

And as Colin and I watched Archibald mount his horse and trot off after the coffin, I wondered how long it would take for this grief to pass and for him to realise that his first and dearest love was still here, waiting for him. I thought too about the baby and how lucky he was to have my family looking out for him. Unlike my own darling child.

*

Donald was sitting staring into the fire when I came up the stairs and into the Great Hall.

"Come and sit – take a glass, Catherine," he said gesturing to the servant to bring me a glass of claret.

I sat down beside him and took a welcome sip of wine.

"How is Grandmother doing? John said she has been told to rest."

"She's fine, just a bad head cold. She hates having to stay in her room though."

"I can imagine." He turned towards me. "And how are you doing, Catherine? Did you hear Archibald has taken his wife's body back to Auchenbreck for burial?"

I nodded. "Yes. I just spoke to him."

Donald narrowed his eyes. "There's been something odd about him since we were on Mull. I can't put my finger on it, but he's hiding something."

"Really? What could that be, I wonder?" There was no way my brothers would have known – or indeed need to know – about Archibald coming over to Duart to visit. They were always rather strict about the boundaries and sanctity of a marriage; to my knowledge, none of them had ever strayed, and they would obviously never contemplate their wives doing so.

"Colin was wondering," he said, shifting forward towards me, "if he had anything to do with the prisoners escaping."

"What? But why would he do that?" The implications were dire, for it would mean his first love's baby – who he had possibly fathered – would not be returned if there were no hostages. "What could possibly persuade him to do that? He is a Campbell, after all."

"He is indeed. Anyway, say nothing. And besides, we can't do anything until after his wife's funeral."

"Is he due back then?"

Donald shrugged. "He's leaving the baby here so presumably he'll have to collect him."

"Or he could send his people to do that if necessary."

Donald sighed. "That's true." He leant back on his chair and took a deep swig of ale.

"Colin and John leave in a week or so for Edinburgh, provided the weather is fair enough. The regent wants them all to have this meeting before winter sets in."

"And it's at the castle?"

"Yes. And you know your husband will be there too."

"I don't like to call him my husband now. Not after all he has done to me."

"Yes, but in law..."

We were interrupted by Mary running in through the door.

"I couldn't find you, Catherine. Wait till you hear this, both of you!" She stood in front of us both, cheeks ruddy after the exertion of racing upstairs.

I stared at my little sister, marvelling at how her skin had cleared up so well after only a few days of Aggie's herbal remedy. What an asset she was, what a handy servant to have, one who knows and understands the good – and the bad – in the plants around us.

"Ellen and I were up on the tower and we could see a galley sailing in from the south towards the harbour. We went down to ask the servants about it; they'd just been at the market. They're all saying it's not a Campbell boat. Who could it be?"

Donald sighed. He too had to put up with a lot from his siblings, especially from our youngest. "It could be any number of other clans, Mary – the Campbells don't have the monopoly of sailing in Loch Fyne, you know."

"But it's just that we thought we saw some women on board and one of them looked as if she was holding a baby."

I leapt to my feet, knocking over my chair as I raced to the door, my brother and sister following close behind me.

Chapter 44

1520

Lachlan Cattanach

He was standing in St Margaret's Chapel, gazing around in wonder at the size of it. Not because it was vast; rather because it was so small, the same size as his own chapel at Duart. And yet here he was within the walls of the king's own castle at Edinburgh.

"You'd have thought they'd build a bigger place of worship for kings and queens, wouldn't you?"

Big John was staring up at the ornate arches before the altar. "It's magnificent, Lachlan. There's a real feeling of peace in here." They were both whispering, awed by this holy place.

Peace – now that was not a word Lachlan ever imagined would come out of the mouth of his oldest friend. He was the most bellicose of all his men; though, when he thought about it, perhaps also the fairest.

"Yes, apparently it's been a place for the royals to worship since King David's day. And that was a long time ago, even before we islanders were given the charter of Lordship of the Isles."

They were both quiet as they looked towards the altar.

A sound at the tiny door made them both swivel round, hands to their dirks.

"We're to go now up to the Palace Yard, your Lordship." One of Lachlan Cattanach's men who'd been standing guard outside, disturbed the silence of the chapel.

"Come, let's go and see where the Scottish king will dispense his wise counsel."

"He's only eight years old, so I don't imagine that will be

anytime soon," Big John muttered as he followed his master out of the tiny chapel.

As they entered the Palace Yard of Edinburgh Castle, they saw many clan chiefs with their men, each family gathered in their own huddles. Soon, a hush descended as the door under the tower of the Royal Palace opened and a nobleman appeared.

"That's the Duke of Albany," Lachlan Cattanach whispered to his men. "I thought it might be Queen Margaret welcoming us, but clearly she's not invited, even if she's the king's mother."

"Did you not say the young lad's essentially kept a prisoner by the regent?"

Lachlan Cattanach nodded and pointed to the procession of men filing into the palace after the duke. "In we go. Macleans of Duart, stand proud."

"Will they try to take our weapons before we enter the palace, Lachlan?"

Big John's huge hand encompassed the hilt of his dirk.

"You cannot disarm a nobleman, so they would not even try. Come, let's go and see what this regent is about to propose."

Once they were in the Great Hall, Lachlan Cattanach and his men stood watching the other great families from the mainland and the islands of Scotland file in.

Lachlan lowered his head a little when he noticed the Inveraray Campbells arrive, Colin the earl looking every bit as haughty as he had been at Inveraray.

"I can see two of the Campbell brothers there. Maybe there's more but I don't recognise any others." Lachlan Cattanach leaned to all his men to whisper, "Keep away from the Campbells over there. We are here to talk about peace, remember."

*

Lachlan Cattanach and his men sat around a table in an ale house in the Grassmarket. It was the nearest tavern to their lodgings at the West Port.

"Go and fetch some more ale," he shouted over the noise to Big John at the other side. He downed the contents of his goblet and handed it to his friend, who pushed his sturdy body through the throngs of people standing around drinking.

He looked around at the other men and wished he had a table at the wall. He didn't know why, but he felt vulnerable in the middle of this dark, crowded room. It was probably because he wasn't used to a city as big as Edinburgh. Nor was he used to being equals with so many other men; he was accustomed to being the chief of all he surveyed. Here there were so many clan chiefs and other noblemen. He looked around and thought he saw one of the Campbells in a corner. But just as he was peering over in the dim candlelight, Big John set his freshly filled goblet on the table, and he turned back to his men.

"That was an interesting assembly this afternoon."

"Yes," said Billy, "but will any of the others truly want peace, do you think?"

"Albany sounded quite convincing when he said it was the only way to unite Scotland, but..." Lachlan Cattanach shrugged. "Do we really want that?" Like the other island lords, he wanted the Lordship of the Isles to continue, perhaps not in opposition to the Scottish king, but to complement his rule, when he came of age.

And that was the problem: while the king was so young, there was only the regent, who none of the island lords respected, even though he was half French.

A tap on his shoulder made him swivel around. His men's hands moved swiftly to their belts where their daggers were kept.

It was an elderly man with white hair and a pockmarked face; he had never seen him before. "Lachlan Cattanach Maclean, I have been sent to ask if you have a moment to come outside. Lord Macdonald of Dunyvaig is asking for you."

"Alexander Donald? Well, why does he not come inside?"

"There is no room in here." The old man gestured around the dingy room that was packed with men. "And he does not have much time."

This seemed rather strange. Lachlan Cattanach had looked around all the men at the assembly up at the castle earlier and had not spied Alexander Donald Macdonald. But he must surely be here, to represent Islay.

"Why does His Lordship want to see me?"

"It is a matter concerning the fosterage of your child."

Lachlan Cattanach got to his feet. "Is everything all right with my Amie? Did he say?"

"He asked simply that you come to see him and indicated that it is most urgent, for he leaves Edinburgh early in the morning."

Big John got to his feet and pushed his way past the sweaty bodies to stand beside Lachlan.

"He insists you are alone. For the matter is delicate," shouted the man over the noise of the crowds.

Big John grasped his friend's shoulder. "It's a trap, Lachlan. Don't go!"

Lachlan Cattanach shook himself free and turned to him. "If Macdonald needs to see me about my daughter, I have no choice but to go, do you understand?"

He nodded to the old man, who led the way out through the teeming throng towards the door. All the way, Lachlan Cattanach had his hand on his dirk and at the door, he stopped to pull his plaid around him, for a bitter wind was now howling outside.

It was a starless sky, pitch black besides a few candle-lit windows.

"So where is he, man? Where's your master?" Lachlan Cattanach followed him to a dark close, where he stopped.

"You are to wait here. His lodgings are just along there," he said, pointing to the unlit alley.

And that was when a man came out of the shadows and pushed Lachlan Cattanach against a wall. The old man had grabbed his hands and yanked the dagger from his grasp; another emerged from the dark close and held his arms tight behind his back.

"So, Maclean, here we are in Edinburgh. The last time we met was at Duart Castle, where you tricked us into leaving before we had managed to get your daughter back to her mother." It was one of the Campbells. He peered into the gloom to see which one. Good God, it was John, the quiet brother; they are always the ones to watch.

"Where is Alexander Donald Macdonald?"

"I have no idea, Maclean. As you well know, Campbells and Macdonalds are not friends."

"But I thought there was a message about my daughter?"

"Did you now?" John Campbell tutted as he stared close at Lachlan Cattanach. His face, usually so inscrutable, was a picture of hatred. Even in the semi-darkness, Lachlan could see his brother-in-law's eyes flash with anger.

"Where is your brother the earl?" Surely Colin would want to keep his brother-in-law safe.

"He is already in his bed. I shall join him at our lodgings shortly."

"Does he...does he know you are here?"

"My elder brother is not my keeper, Maclean," he said, raising his hand, which Lachlan now saw held a blade. It glinted in the faint candlelight from a window above.

"Campbell, I don't know what your intentions are, but let us speak man to man, nobleman to nobleman..."

"You were no nobleman when you tied my sister to a rock. You were no nobleman when you sent one of your men to release our prisoners. You were then – as you are now – a common traitor, for you did not keep your promise to us to bring our niece to Catherine."

"I can do it now, Campbell," Lachlan Cattanach stuttered. "I shall go and find where Macdonald of Dunyvaig is lodging and annul the foster contract. Your sister can have Amie all to herself. I shall do this right..."

"You shall do nothing more, Maclean."

He smiled a ghastly, gruesome smile and with one deft movement plunged his dagger into Lachlan Cattanach's heart. He slumped to the ground, yelping like his beloved hound the day his wife had tried to poison him. She failed in killing him then; but now, her brother succeeded.

Chapter 45

1520

Catherine

I tore down the steps into the courtyard then out past the guards. I crossed over the path outside the castle and ran towards the harbour where I could see Ellen standing amongst some fishermen looking south over the loch. I stopped to catch my breath and Donald and Mary came up behind me, also puffing.

"How did Ellen get past the guards?" Mary muttered. "I was only allowed because I was with Donald."

"She's older than you," Donald said, as the three of us strode over towards Ellen.

"Is that the galley out there?" I pointed to a boat coming towards us. "There's a lot of people on it." I put my hand above my eyes to try to block the sun as I peered towards them. I recognised no one yet, but it was still too far away.

"Is it the person in the stern of the boat you thought was carrying a baby?"

Ellen nodded. "Yes, look, you can see, she has a bundle in her arms, but it's moving." My sister put her arm around my waist. "It could be your little girl, Catherine."

My heart was racing. "But who would be bringing her to me? I can't see Lachlan there." I screwed up my eyes again and gasped. "Oh, but that man's his son, Hector Mor. He must have been sent from Islay to bring her to me."

"You see, I knew it would all work out," said Ellen, kissing my cheek.

"And that looks like Lorna, our harpist. Remember I told you about her? She became my friend while I was living at Duart."

244

"Is she the one you taught to read and write, Catherine?"

"Yes." I let out another gasp. "That's the Duart nurse, the one holding the baby. It must be Amie," I said, my fists now clenched by my sides.

Hector Mor moved to the bow of the boat and threw the rope over to a man on the pier, who tied it up. Then, once the vessel was alongside, he leapt onto the jetty. I moved forward, my brother and sisters by my side, and waited till he turned around.

When he did, he smiled at me, and I could not help but notice once again how his rugged looks were so like his father's, but Hector Mor's were thankfully less coarse.

"Catherine," he said, tilting his head in greeting. "We have a precious load on board." He turned and beckoned for the nurse to come forward. She handed the bundle to Lorna, who was now standing at the bow. She transferred it with great care to Hector Mor and I rushed towards him.

I looked down and there was my girl, her dimpled cheeks plump and rosy as she drooled and chuckled just like I remembered. I stretched out my hands, took her in my arms and clasped her tight. I inhaled the delicious smell of her beautiful curls then held her out at arm's length to look at her properly. She was gazing around at all the people staring at her, everyone beaming at the joy only a baby can bring. And I wept.

*

I spent most of the day by her side. Mama kept saying that I must let her rest, but even when she did, I stayed beside her, holding her soft, warm hand while she snuffled softly. I wanted to take her to see Grandmother, but as I stood at the door to her room, holding Amie aloft, she beamed and held up her hand. "Dearest girl, you have your baby back." She was sounding a little hoarser than earlier. "I am so pleased for you. I shall be down at supper today or tomorrow hopefully and can embrace you both then. But now I do not want you to catch this cold."

She blew me a kiss and I shut the door quietly, then went to introduce Amie to all my family; everyone except Colin and John, who were not yet back from the assembly at Edinburgh Castle. Mama said she was so looking forward to hearing what the ladies were wearing in the city; I somehow doubted my brothers would be taking any notice of the gowns.

Later in the day, Lorna came to sit with me in the nursery. She told me about her time on Islay, how ill poor Angus had been and how Hector Mor had come back with his young wife after only a few days of marriage and that she would remain on Islay. When I asked what had happened, she lowered her gaze.

"I think that's probably for Hector Mor to say." There was a flicker of a smile on her lips. "But we are good friends now, Catherine."

"Who? You and Hector Mor?"

She nodded, blushing. "Very good friends."

I grabbed her hand. "Lorna, this is wonderful news. Oh, and thank you for your letter, it cheered me up so much. You have no idea how difficult these past few weeks have been."

I raised my finger to my lips as I realised Amie had fallen asleep in my arms and I laid her down gently in the crib. Nurse insisted on tucking her in and whispering that I could now leave her, that she would send for me when she awoke. I nodded agreement and went over to the other cradle in the room, the one belonging to Archibald's baby. "Is he doing well?"

"Yes, my Lady. He continues to be hale and hearty, despite the fact he has lost his mother."

"He still has a father," I muttered while guiding Lorna down to the Great Hall, where we joined Hector Mor and my brother Donald, who were drinking ale together.

I noticed the change of expression on Hector Mor's face when we entered; he looked at Lorna with such fondness.

"We shall have a celebratory feast tonight, Catherine," Donald said. "You have your daughter back, and we want to thank these kind people who brought her all the way from Islay. Maclean here was telling me how arduous the journey has been."

"Not really, it was just at Tarbert where we had to haul the boat overland to get to the Loch Fyne side. Apart from that, it wasn't too bad, was it, Lorna?"

She shook her head and smiled at him.

"Thankfully it only rained once."

"Lorna, I have just had a thought," I said, turning towards her. "Would you play for us tonight at the banquet? Our Inveraray harpists are talented of course, but no one can play the clarsach like you."

"Of course. I shall go and practise now if that's all right? And I'm going to check where Angus is; he was drinking milk in the kitchen when I last saw him."

I nodded and sat down as Donald guided Lorna out.

"Hector Mor, I will never be able to thank you enough. I know Lachlan said to my brothers that he would fetch Amie from Islay, but I do wonder if he ever actually meant it."

Hector Mor shrugged. "I'm not sure I can forgive my father for what he did to you, Catherine." He leant in towards me. "Though you were perhaps not totally without fault, were you?"

Dear Lord, of course he knew about the poisoning. "I had to do something, I was frantic; I could see no other way of keeping Amie." I looked directly at him. "And I am so sorry you had to kill that poor, innocent man. I can never forgive myself for that."

He sighed. "And nor can I, Catherine. I shall ensure Robert's family are well taken care of, but that will never bring him back."

There was a flurry of people at the door. Colin rushed in, John behind him. "We have just heard the news about your daughter, Catherine. That is wonderful." They both came over to embrace me.

"But we bring other news that is not so joyful," Colin said, sitting down. His expression was bleak.

"This is Hector Mor," I said, gesturing to him. "He is Lachlan Cattanach's son. He is the one who rescued Amie and brought her to Islay."

"We are in your debt. Thank you. But I'm afraid the bad news also affects you."

John was now standing with his back to us, warming his hands at the fire. Colin looked from Hector Mor to me. "While we were in Edinburgh, an appalling murder took place."

Colin continued. "Lachlan Cattanach is dead."

Chapter 46

1521

Catherine

I have never suffered such grief. When my father died it was awful, but he died a hero on the battlefield, so somehow it was different. As I walked back along the river towards the chapel, I looked up and saw a bird above me. It had orange-red legs and was soaring high. It was a redshank, like the one I saw when I was on the rock. I watched it fly down to the water then rise high above the loch. This is the bird that sings to the souls of those departing into the next world: how apt that it should fly above us today.

I sighed and wiped my tears as I saw people entering the small chapel beside the castle. Mama said clansmen and women would come to pay their respects and that the whole family must be gracious and hospitable. But I just wanted to sob. Even playing with my adorable Amie that morning had not helped alleviate the feeling of despair.

I joined the mourners at the entrance and walked in, finding my place at the front beside the rest of my family. As the coffin was brought in, we all stood and turned around and I saw Archibald creeping in at the back. I gasped and hissed to Ellen, "What is he doing here?"

"Remember his grandfather was Grandmother's brother. Presumably he is representing the Auchenbreck Campbells." I stared at him, but he was looking straight ahead at the casket. He had sent for his son a couple of months ago; thank God, that baby had been with us long enough. He had clearly felt he could not come to Inveraray himself; my brothers were still a little

249

wary of him after all that had happened six months before.

We were all silent as the funeral service began for my wonderful grandmother, who had been taken so suddenly by the ague. I could not come to terms with it. Yes, death was everywhere, but I had believed she was invincible. When Mama said that it was her time, I wanted to slap her face. But instead I rushed to cuddle my darling Amie, feeling solace in the snugness of her perfect little body and the warmth of her dear little kisses.

The service was not long, and I tried to keep myself composed throughout. I thought of how she had kept me strong, her steadfast and enduring presence had helped me through so much; how I would miss her. But I did not weep, rather I celebrated her life, with all the others in the chapel. And I thanked God that I had her for so long beside me as guide and mentor.

After the service, I saw Mama stop on her way out and speak to Archibald, presumably inviting him for refreshments inside. Perhaps because of my overwhelming grief, I could not determine what I felt for my first and only love; was the passion still there?

*

I was speaking to several of the guests in the Great Hall afterwards when I spotted Archibald in a nook. He was alone, and I realised he was only here under duress. I sidled over to him with a glass.

"Thank you for coming today, Archibald. It would have meant a lot to Grandmother."

He bowed. "It was my duty to be here. Our families go back a long way, Catherine."

"And is that the only reason you are here?" I smiled and sipped my claret, gazing directly at him over the top of my glass. I had almost forgotten just how beautiful his deep-set blue eyes were.

"I obviously also wanted to thank your sister Isabel for taking such good care of my son."

"It was hardly as if she was up all night feeding and tending to him herself, Archibald." Really, did he think my sister did anything without a host of servants?

"But she arranged everything for him, which helped so much when I was grieving."

He sighed.

Dear God, did I have to mention *her*? Well, I would not; I refused to utter his wife's name. The funeral today showed that life is for living, as my grandmother did to the full. We must all move on.

"And how are you these days, Archibald, now perhaps the grief is not as raw?" I spat out the last word. I was reciting phrases I knew I ought to say, but really, he had known her for such a short time. Whereas he and I had known each other for years and years.

"I have come to terms with it all. And I have my son." He smiled. "And what about you, Catherine? How are you liking living back at Inveraray?"

"I like it very much." I took another sip of wine. "There were so few happy days when I was living on Mull."

I sighed.

"But there were perhaps joyful moments when you had a priestly visitation?"

He smiled.

So he had in fact remembered those blissful days with fondness too. "Yes, indeed." I paused as a thought occurred. "And then nine months later my darling Amie was born." I gazed at him, unflinching.

His expression changed, his eyes opening wide. "I hadn't realised it was nine months later."

I shrugged. I knew perfectly well Amie was not his daughter, she now looked even more of a Maclean, with her dark hair and olive complexion. But I was in no rush to disabuse him of the notion for now.

He frowned. "But why did you not tell me, Catherine?"

I tossed back my hair. "Remember I was a married woman, Archibald." I lowered my gaze, "And now, sadly, I am a widow."

He shook his head. "I had not even contemplated that..."

"Archibald," I interrupted, "would you like to come with me for a stroll? We can perhaps talk more freely outside. Or just walk together. There is a nice path up into the woods from the back of the castle."

He smiled and nodded his agreement.

I raised my finger. "Wait for me at the top of the stairs to the courtyard. I must quickly fetch my coat." I raced up to my bedchamber to fetch my wolfskin coat and tidy my hair quickly at the glass. Then I opened my drawer to collect my gloves and headed downstairs. Grabbing a carafe of wine and a goblet from a servant, I rushed to meet him and we slipped out, unseen, down the stairs to the courtyard.

Once we were on our way to the woods, I took him by the hand and turned to look at him. It was nearly six months since he had left that day with his wife's coffin. His spirits were surely raised since I first spoke to him today – perhaps my presence was all he needed to make him glad. Indeed, his look was familiar, it reminded me of when we used to go into the woods at Duart, for our passionate trysts.

Over the gnarled tree trunks we went, and under branches where new growth had begun. We said very little; nothing was required yet, just our bodies stepping together in harmony. But when we got to the clearing where Grandmother and I had come often before, I stood up against a tree and smiled. He came towards me, beaming. I had him in my power. He took my hand in his and leaned towards me; and I knew I wanted only one thing.

But I slipped out of his grasp and walked to the other side of the clearing. "Let us have a glass of wine first to celebrate our reunion, Archibald."

And as I sat down, balancing on a tree trunk, I pointed down the hill to some beautiful purple flowers.

"Those are my favourite woodland flowers, Archibald. Please could you go and pick some for me while I pour our wine?" I pointed down to the straggly bush with the tall purple flowers.

"Of course, Catherine. I've never seen them before – they are beautiful," he said as he strode into the tangle of bushes and trees. Once he reached the plant, he began to pick. "Are these enough?" he shouted to me, showing me the stems he had gathered into his arms.

"Yes, thank you. Now come, let us enjoy our wine together."

He put the flowers by my feet, gazing up at me. I smiled and lifted the goblet then handed it to him.

"You first," I said, watching as he quaffed it all down. I continued to gaze up at him.

And as I sat watching him, smiling, I saw his face change. It was as if there was a numbness around his jaw; he tried to move it but could not. And as I stared at this transformation in him, I thought of how I'd only recently realised he had been the one to release the Maclean hostages in our dungeons that night I saw him late on the stairs. He was the one who prevented me getting my Amie back sooner from Islay; he betrayed my brothers, his kinsmen, and broke his promises to the Campbells of Inveraray.

His biggest betrayal, of course, had been to me, by marrying another. A sudden sweat enveloped his pale face, and he shuddered as if in pain.

"Catherine," he muttered through a distorted, frozen jaw, "I feel terrible, I feel..."

I got to my feet, picking up the carafe, but taking care to avoid stepping near the purple flowers. I walked away, down the hill, not turning around, even when I heard a guttural cry and the sound of him collapsing onto the damp earth. Night was falling, and as I pulled my beautiful wolfskin coat up around my neck, a chilly, late spring breeze came whistling through the branches.

Soon only the birds of prey would be seen amidst the trees at moonlight as they feasted on whatever was there, in the woods.

I lifted my gloves and hurled them deep into the bushes then returned to the castle and my beloved Grandmother's wake where, at the door, a servant relieved me of the carafe, offering to pour me a glass of claret. I accepted, downing it quickly then asking for another. Then I walked to the stairs and headed up to see my darling Amie. I opened the door to the nursery, tip-toed over to her crib and stroked the warm, dimpled cheek. Smiling down on her angelic face, I knew at last that my future was with her and her alone.

THE END

Author's Notes

The story of Lachlan Cattanach Maclean putting his wife on Lady's Rock to die in the early sixteenth century is shrouded in mystery and intrigue. The Lady's Rock that you pass on the ferry from Oban to Mull, south-east of Duart Castle and south-west of Lismore, is probably not the place the attempted murder happened. It now has a black and red navigation beacon on it but – crucially for the story to ring true – it is only covered completely with water during equinoctial spring tides. However, if it was that rock she was put on, she most certainly would have perished from hypothermia or simply starvation, if not from drowning under the waters of a high tide.

There is another rock – Liath Sgeir – which is due east of Duart Castle, and it is situated west of the southern tip of Lismore. In Thomas Hannan's book *The Beautiful Isle of Mull* (1926), he cites "Lady's Rock (formerly Lersker)" – clearly a phonetic rendering of Liath Sgeir. And this rock, just off Lismore, though not completely covered at high tide, could also be the rock in question.

But whichever rock it was, there is also some confusion over who exactly was Lachlan Cattanach's wife: most accounts state she was Catherine Campbell, but some insist her name was Elizabeth or Janet Campbell.

This is what we know about Catherine, who I elected to be our heroine, and the other main characters in the book.

Catherine Campbell: she was born, probably the ninth of twelve children, to Lady Elizabeth Stewart of Lennox and Archibald Campbell, the second Earl of Argyll. The Earls of Argyll lived at Inveraray; the tenth Earl of Argyll, Archibald Campbell, became the first Duke of Argyll in 1701. Her approximate birth date is 1486 and she first married Lachlan Cattanach

256

Maclean. Then, after his death, she married Archibald Campbell of Auchenbreck. Some records say she died in 1567 or even 1578, when she would have been a very old woman, especially for those times.

Lachlan Cattanach Maclean, her first husband, born after 1465, was the eleventh Chief of Clan Maclean. He assumed the role of Laird of Duart after his father Lachlan – like Catherine's father – was killed at the battle of Flodden in 1513. He is alleged to have had many mistresses and one of them, Hector Mor's mother, was Marion Maclean of the Treshnish Islands. Lachlan Cattanach was murdered by Catherine Campbell's brother, Sir John Campbell of Cawdor, to avenge the attempted drowning of his sister. The killing took place in Edinburgh in 1523.

It was one of Lachlan's descendants (not ancestors, as I write in the book), Chief Lachlan Mor, who in 1588, on the day of his mother's second marriage, learned that the bridegroom intended to ally with the Macdonalds. (By then the Macleans and Macdonalds were enemies.) As a consequence, Lachlan killed eighteen of the wedding guests and imprisoned and tortured the bridegroom.

Hector Mor Maclean, who was described as "good, kind and brave", married Mary Macdonald of Islay, whose father was Alexander Macdonald of Dunyvaig. They had nine children. He died around 1568.

There were a couple of interesting aspects of Scottish history that influenced the narrative, namely the Lordship of the Isles and the practice of Celtic fosterage.

Lords of the Isles

Circa 1367, Lachlan Lubanach Maclean married Mary Macdonald, daughter of the Lord of the Isles. In the marriage dowry, he gained extensive land in Mull, including Duart Castle. From then on, links were established between the Macleans of Mull and the Macdonalds of Islay. The first wife of John, first Lord of the Isles (before his marriage to Mary's mother Margaret Stewart, daughter of future King Robert II) was Amie MacRuari; they married in 1337. After her marriage was "set aside", she is credited with building a church in Benbecula and restoring Teampull na Trionaid in North Uist.

The Lordship of the Isles ended officially in the late fifteenth century, but the hopes of restoring it and the glory of Finlaggan did not. The title Lord of the Isles was annexed to the Crown in 1542 and is now one of the titles of Prince William as heir to the throne of the United Kingdom.

Finlaggan on Islay now has a wonderful visitor centre where you can see the small islands in the loch – Eilean Mor, with its palace complex including chapel, houses and graveyard, and Eilean na Comhairle, which housed the council chamber where the assemblies took place. These would have been attended by the Bishop of the Isles and the Abbot of Iona, as well as nobles and clan chiefs from the islands and west coast, including Maclean of Duart, Maclean of Lochbuie, MacNeill of Barra and Macleod of Lewis.

Celtic Fosterage

In medieval Highlands and Islands, there was a practice among clans of fostering children to create new or strengthen existing alliances between the noble families. It was a means of maintaining cohesion in society at the time. Though the child was usually about seven or eight when this took place, it was not uncommon for it to happen to babies. Though it was usually boys, girls were also fostered. For both, cattle and horses would have been given as means to pay for his or her upbringing. A boy would have learned the arts of a nobleman including riding and swordsmanship, while girls would have learned the skills of a noblewoman, including poetry and music.

The fosterage lasted usually around seven years when the child was returned to his or her own family: girls usually at the age of about twelve, boys fourteen. But having been with the foster family during such a crucial stage in his or her development, close bonds were usually maintained between foster parent and child.

The Gaelic word for foster child is dalta and I was keen to use this in the narrative, since Kildaltan (also spelt Cill Daltan) church on Islay means church of the foster child and is only four miles away from Dunyvaig Castle, where Hector Mor's wife was from. The Celtic cross at Kildalton dates from the late eighth century and is similar to crosses created about the same time on the island of Iona. It is one of the finest Celtic crosses in Scotland.

Joanna Baillie

This Scottish poet and dramatist, born in 1762, wrote many plays, but it was her 1810 play 'The Family Legend: A Tragedy', that provided me with some inspiration. The play was not only dedicated to Sir Water Scott; he also wrote the prologue which include the lines:

'Yourselves shall judge – whoever has raised the sail
By Mull's dark coast, has heard this evening's tale.
The plaided boatman, resting on his oar,
Points to the fatal rock amid the roar
Of whitening waves and tells whate'er tonight
Our humble stage shall offer to your sight'...

I read with fascination the scenes in the play of the return to Inveraray of Lady Maclean after having been rescued by fishermen from the "fatal rock". They were most certainly full of Gothic melodrama, especially when Lachlan Cattanach suddenly realised that the veiled figure who was guest of honour at dinner was his wife, whom he presumed was dead; but that made them even more gripping.

*

The interpretations of the story of the Campbell noblewoman who had been put on a rock in the middle of the sea by her husband, Maclean of Duart, are many. Some suggest it was purely legend as no one could have survived the ordeal, but I lifted the basic tenet and wove a story around it. I took the tale on a voyage from Mull to Islay and back to Inveraray, all stunning locations in the west of Scotland.

And as I wrote, I realised once again how different and how hard times were then: cold castles, inordinately long and arduous journeys to travel anywhere, roasted seabirds regularly on the dinner table. But I also understood that even five centuries later, feelings and emotions have changed little. The urge to survive is still as strong; and the unconditional, irrefutable love a mother has for her child will never change.

Acknowledgements

Charlène Busalli
Eleanor Campbell, Duchess of Argyll
Alison Diamond, archivist, Inveraray Castle
Shuna Dickens, clarsach player
Dr Anna Groundwater, National Museums Scotland
Shona MacIntyre
Allan Maclean of Dochgarroch,
Donald S Murray
Robert Philip
Dr ES Thomson
Cathy Tingle
Jean Whittaker
Ellie Johnson, proofreader

Many thanks to Isabelle Plews for reading and re-reading *Lady's Rock* – and for enthusiasm and encouragement.

To Anne Dow for commenting sagely, thank you.

And as ever, thank you, Jenny Brown, for wise counsel and good cheer.

Also by Sue Lawrence

Sue Lawrence's 'Scotland's Leading Ladies' trio of novels, of which *Lady's Rock* is the third, highlights the lack of agency and choices for women in Scotland's past – even for those from wealthy and powerful families. In these novels, the voices of three real women, their stories long lost, are heard at last.

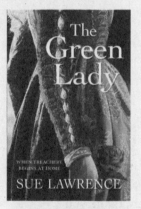

A gripping tale of court intrigue, secrets, treachery and murder, based on the true lives of Lilias Drummond, Alexander Seton – 1st Earl of Dunfermline and Lord Chancellor of Scotland – and his aunt Marie Seton, one of the "Four Marys" who were ladies-in-waiting to Mary, Queen of Scots.

"Compelling."
—*Historical Novels Review*

A thrilling historical novel based on the extraordinary true story of Lady Grange, who in 1732 was kidnapped on the orders of her powerful husband, who faked her death and secretly exiled her to a remote island beyond the Scottish Outer Hebrides.

"The wronged lady finally has her say."—*The Times*